Midnight Witness

PARKER'S LANDING

BOOK TWO

ASHLEY A QUINN

TCA PUBLISHING

Midnight Witness

Copyright © 2025 by Ashley A Quinn

Cover art by Christine Riley

ISBN: 978-1-959943-45-7

Printed in the United States of America

CHAPTER 1

Mina

Blood whooshed in my ears, my heart thundering against my ribs.

This was it.

Inhaling a deep breath, I tried—and failed—to steady my hand as I lifted a silver key to insert it into the back door lock of what would be the expansion to my little coffeeshop, The Cozy Cup. After months of planning and waiting, it was finally mine.

No thanks to the ridiculous Miranda Benning. Someone needed to take her real estate license away. I don't know how she sold any properties. She was a sneaky, underhanded, lying witch. Thank goodness for Claire, my best friend and realtor. She'd read through every iteration of the contract to make sure Miranda didn't try to slip in a clause somewhere that wasn't agreed upon. It only happened once, early in the process, but it was enough to keep us on our toes.

But it was over, and I didn't have to deal with her anymore. I wouldn't have at all if it weren't for the fact that I *needed* this building. Since it was already attached to my coffeeshop, it was perfect for my expansion plans. I could stay open for most of the renovation and not have to move all my equipment to another location.

The key scraped the doorknob as I inserted it. With a quick twist, the lock clicked, and I opened the door.

Mustiness and the smell of years of dirt hit me as I stepped inside.

Wrinkling my nose, I shut the door, then wandered deeper into the back room. I felt along the wall for the switches I remembered seeing when I toured the building, flipping them on when I found them.

Bright, fluorescent light flooded the space, giving the dingy interior no place to hide.

My shoulders slumped at the sight that greeted me. Mr. Shuman hadn't emptied the building's contents like he said he would.

At least, not back here, anyway.

Old paintings and rusted signs lined one wall. I hoped there were no more in the front of the store or in the basement. This place had been an antique store before Shuman retired late last year and decided to sell.

My gaze moved over the rest of the space. It really wasn't too cluttered. Other than the paintings and signs, there was only a dusty desk in one corner. But it was covered in suspicious little brown pellets and bits of paper.

Great. A mouse problem.

I heaved a sigh. First thing on the list after I met with the contractor today was to hire an exterminator and make sure there weren't any four-legged friends currently in residence. Or six-legged ones, for that matter. The health inspector would not like that, and it would have to be rectified before any work occurred. Once we knocked down the wall to connect the two spaces, anything over here was fair game for the coffeeshop.

Walking through the back room, I headed for the swinging

door that led to the main store, flipping light switches on as I passed through.

A bit of weight lifted off my shoulders when I saw that most of the displays were empty. I would have preferred for everything to be gone, but hauling out display cases and a few paintings was much better than removing all the small antiques and furniture that had been here just a few months ago.

But still, item two on the agenda was to get a dumpster and to have a small sidewalk sale with all this stuff. While the display cases were in decent shape, I couldn't use them. It might have actually been better if he'd left the furniture. At least some of that had been tables and chairs.

I wandered closer to the art leaning against the wall as one particular piece caught my eye. It fit the nature theme I wanted to put in the café. I'd have to leaf through all the prints and canvases Shuman left behind and see what I could use.

The soft creak of the back door's hinges, then the thud of a heavy boot hitting the pine floor of the back room, brought my head up. It sounded like the contractor had arrived.

Changing direction, I headed for the rear of the store to greet Les Decker, the local contractor I'd hired for the renovations. He'd done the coffeeshop renovations when I opened five years ago, so when I decided to expand, he was one of the first people I called.

But it was not Les who stepped through the swinging door.

My eyebrows drew together, and my step faltered as I stared warily at the tall, fit, and rather handsome man holding a storage clipboard and a pen.

"May I help you?" I clutched the building key in my fist, turning it so it stuck out like a poker. I was not above stabbing him if he tried anything funny. I would give zero fudgesicles about marring his pretty face.

A wide smile brightened his face, and a touch of amusement entered his eyes under the swath of wavy, golden brown hair hanging down on his forehead. He raised a hand. "I'm Luke Decker, Les's son. You can put the claws away." He tipped a finger toward my hand and the key clutched between my knuckles.

Heat suffused my cheeks. I knew they were probably growing red, and I hoped my makeup could hide that fact.

I let my fingers relax and straightened my spine, bringing me to my full five-foot-three height. "This might be Parker's Landing, but I'm still a woman alone. Excuse me for defending myself."

Some of the amusement faded from his expression. His head bobbed once. "My apologies. Let's start again." He held out a hand. "I'm Luke. It's nice to meet you."

Blowing out a soft huff, I stepped forward to take his hand. "Mina Kensington. You too."

His warm palm enveloped mine. Strong, calloused fingers gripped my hand. When he let go after a quick shake, those roughened digits slid over my skin like delicious sandpaper.

Spicy tingles raced up my arm.

A curious gleam in his gray eyes had me wondering if he felt it too.

Mentally, I rolled my eyes at myself. *Yeah, right.* He probably just noticed my awkwardness.

Clearing my throat, I shifted and clasped my hands, letting the cool metal of the building key bite into my palm. "So, how come you're here and not your dad? I was expecting him, and he didn't say anything about sending someone in his place."

Fine lines appeared on Luke's face, making me question just how old he was. Initially, I pegged him for his early to mid-twenties, but those lines said differently. So did the sage maturity now written on his expression.

"Dad, um…" Luke paused and cleared his throat. "He had a heart attack the other day."

"Oh my goodness!" Any wariness I still felt over this stranger's appearance evaporated, and a different sort of wariness took hold. A pit formed in my stomach, and I sent up a silent prayer that Les Decker was still alive. "I'm so sorry to hear that. Is he doing all right?"

"Yes. He's been transferred to the cardiac rehab side of things at the medical center. Hopefully, he'll be home in a week or two. It wasn't a mild heart attack, but it wasn't as bad as it could have been, either."

The tension in my shoulders abated. "Good. I'm glad to hear that."

"Me too. It was…" Luke shifted on his feet and took a deep breath. "It was scary."

"I bet." I could only imagine how he felt. My parents were both in great health and living out their dream on the family homestead near Hoonah.

"In any case, he was adamant the business didn't shut down during his recovery. Somehow, I let him convince me to add project manager to my duties at the company."

"What were your original duties?"

"I'm an architect."

My eyebrows shot up. "How old are you?" Because now that he wasn't frowning and the lines disappeared around his eyes, he once again looked like he was barely old enough for the ink to be dry on his university degree.

"Twenty-six."

And just like that, I felt old. At thirty-two, I knew the age gap wasn't huge, but somehow, it felt significant—like I had lived a lifetime in the six extra years I'd been on the planet.

"But don't worry, Ms. Kensington. I've had my general contractor's license since I was eighteen. I grew up helping my dad on jobs. He had a hammer in my hand before I could walk."

The image that provoked brought a smile to my face. I could see Les doing that. He was extremely serious about his work, and it showed in the finished product.

"Well, that's good. So, are you up to speed on what I'm looking for?" Les and I talked about it, but he'd yet to see the building. Today was supposed to be about coming up with a feasible plan for my ideas.

"Mostly. How about you walk me through the space and show me what you want? I'll take some measurements and get started on the plans."

"Sounds good." I glanced around, deciding where to start.

CHAPTER 2

Luke

When Dad asked me to meet Mina Kensington today to go over her café plans, he failed to mention how devastatingly beautiful she was. Client or not, I was still a man. One with a weakness for curvy brunettes. Mina's glossy, dark-brown hair hung in waves around her shoulders, framing her heart-shaped face and aquamarine blue eyes.

Hiding just beneath the tips of her hair, rounded, soft curves strained the fabric of her white t-shirt, which bore the coffeeshop's logo. I'd actually never been to The Cozy Cup. While I was from Parker's Landing, my life and office were in Juneau now, and when she first opened, I was away at college in Seattle. When I came to Parker's Landing, I either went to Dad's office or to my parents' house.

My gaze quickly traveled the length of her body, taking in the nip at her waist and the fullness to her hips, which were on display thanks to her tight jeans.

The woman was a total knockout.

I looked away as I felt my body react. While Dad didn't have a policy against dating clients, it wasn't exactly profes-sional. Maybe once we were done with her café, I'd ask her out, but for now, I needed to keep my hands to myself and my mind on her building—not her body.

She led me deeper into the space toward the long wall that separated us from her coffeeshop next door.

"I want to knock down as much of this wall as possible. I know it's load-bearing, so whatever we have to do to make it work is fine. I can live with columns. Nearly this entire side will be café seating space. We need to reconfigure the kitchen at the coffeeshop and incorporate the back-room area of this building to make a larger prep space."

"What about that?" I pointed to the staircase coming down in one corner that led to the second floor. "Do you want to leave it or move it?"

"I think it depends on what you can do under it and on the second floor." She changed direction, walking over to the old oak baluster, patinaed dark with age. "Above the coffeeshop is just storage. A lot of the walls have plaster chipped off, and the floors are so worn there's no gloss left on the wood. I just store extra supplies up there. Here, the second floor has been better maintained, but I'm not sure what to do with it. I don't really want to put seating up there. For one, I don't think I'll have the business to support that much table space. This is Parker's Landing, after all, not Juneau. And two, it would put a larger workload on my servers to have to carry trays up and down the stairs, not to mention make it more dangerous."

Staring at the stairs, I chewed on the inside of my bottom lip, contemplating uses for the space. "You could try to find a tenant to rent the upstairs, either for a business or as an apartment. We can convert it to either. A shop would cost less, especially if you have an agreement with the tenant to let them and their customers use your bathrooms."

"Okay. That's sort of along the lines of what I was thinking. If we can just clean up the upstairs for both sides, and maybe add some shelving, I'll look into renters. I can put a small giftshop up there and sell branded merchandise and other kitchen-type things myself as well."

"That's not a problem. I looked up the plans for this building and for the coffeeshop before I came. We shouldn't have to do much more than knock down walls and support the roof. All your plumbing on both sides is on the interior wall between the back rooms and the main store areas." A corner of my mouth kicked up. "Gotta love Alaska's cold. Keeps things off the outer walls."

"Usually," she said with an answering smile.

We wandered around the vacant space, including the upstairs, for several minutes. I took some notes, like adding an extra dumpster for the junk the previous owner left. There were also some cracks in the walls I wanted to investigate. In an old building, usually they were due to age, but we could get some earthquakes here, so there could be issues with the foundation.

As we passed through the door to the back room, I eyed the wall separating the space, noting some discoloration. It looked like there might be some water damage.

My eyes tracked toward the ceiling. It was clear, but that didn't mean water hadn't run down the wall cavity.

I added a note to my list to check the roof.

"So, how soon do you think you can start?"

Looking up, I was struck again by Mina's beauty. Her alpine blue eyes shone like twin beacons.

She raised a hand to tuck a strand of hair behind her ear, the movement quite graceful.

She asked you a question, Decker.

Clearing my throat as my subconscious mind admonished me, I glanced around the space. "I can get a crew in here for demo Monday. I don't need permits to knock anything down, except the wall between the buildings. A lot of the cosmetic stuff—refinishing the floors, replacing drywall, paint—can all be done without much fuss. As for connecting the spaces, I'll have the plans drawn up this week"—I paused, remembering all the other projects on my plate now—"or early next week. Once you look them over and approve them, I'll submit permits. But there will be plenty to keep the crews busy until we get approval for knocking down the common wall."

The corners of her eyes crinkled as she bestowed a bright smile on me. "Great. That actually works out well. I want to go through the stuff Mr. Shuman left behind. I can do that the rest of this week and clear some of this out." A small furrow formed between her eyebrows as she glanced at the art lining the one wall.

"Would you like me to drop off a dumpster before Monday?"

The furrow disappeared. "That would be amazing. I was wondering where I could find one on short notice."

"I have one at the yard. I'll bring it over this evening and put it out back. Does that work?"

She nodded. "That's perfect, thank you."

"Not a problem. I actually already had it on my list." I turned my notepad around so she could see where I'd written, "Dumpster for junk."

Mina chuckled. "That's what a lot of it is too." She sighed. "He said he would clean it out." She shook her head. "It's not as full as it was when I looked at the place before putting in an offer, but his definition of cleaning it out and mine are wildly different."

I agreed. The space should be empty of anything not bolted down. "Don't worry about it, though. Anything you don't get through, my crew and I will pitch."

"Can you guys remove the old shelving units and displays out there?" She gestured to the main store.

"Of course." It truly wouldn't be an issue. We could roll a lot of it right out the door and into a dumpster. The rest we could smash up and carry out in pieces. In fact, I hoped most of it was too wide to fit through the door. Demolition days were great stress relievers, and God knew I needed some of that in my life.

"Perfect." Mina's sunny smile made another return.

Seeing that more often would ease some stress as well. She had a gorgeous smile. It lit up her entire face.

Once again, I reminded myself to keep my mind on the task at hand. "I just need to take some measurements, then I can get out of your hair."

She swept an arm out. "Have at it. I need to head next door. Can you lock the back door when you're done?"

"Sure. I'll follow you outside right now, though. I need to grab a few things from my truck."

"Oh, okay." Spinning on her heel, she headed for the back door.

My gaze strayed to her curved rear. Those jeans should be illegal.

Focus, Decker.

Right. Squaring my shoulders, I looked away from Mina Kensington's tempting curves and followed her out the door.

CHAPTER 3
Mina

"**M**an, you were right. There is still a lot of stuff here."

I glanced back at my friend Claire's words as we stepped over the threshold into the back room of my new building. We were here to sort through all the items Mr. Shuman left behind. "Wait until you see out front. He left most of the displays."

Claire's nose wrinkled. "That's just rude."

I shrugged, tossing my keys onto the small card table I set up earlier, so we'd have a place to set things. "Maybe he thought I could use some of it. None of them are in terrible shape." I put my tote bag down next to my keys.

"I guess that could be true." Claire set her bag down beside mine. "It still would have been nice if he asked first, though."

"What can you do? The displays really aren't that big of a deal. Luke said his team would take care of them. It's more this stuff that's the hassle." I gestured to the art leaning against the walls.

Glancing around, Claire nodded. Her dogs, Betty and Pebbles, strained the ends of their leashes, sniffing anything they could.

I eyed them, amused. The new puppy, Betty, was adorable. She was little more than a black ball of fluff. A ball of fluff that liked to annoy her small Yorkie friend.

As I watched. Betty gave up sniffing the floor and hopped over to Pebbles, tackling her. The little dog did a quick roll and sprang to her feet, barking.

"Pebbles, that's enough." Claire gave her dog's leash a soft tug, then looked up at me. "Maybe I should have just crated Betty after all."

"Nonsense." I waved a hand. It didn't bother me at all that she brought them. I completely understood why. No one wanted to keep a dog confined to a crate any longer than necessary. Her boyfriend, Ozzie, got called in for a burglary investigation, so no one was home to keep an eye on the little stinker. "They'll be fine. Let them off their leads. I'm sure there are plenty of new smells to keep them occupied for a while. And it's not like it's a problem if Betty tinkles on the floor. It's all getting replaced. She's just impatient to be let loose." I walked over to the pile of paintings and photo prints leaning against the far wall and grabbed one in a large frame, pulling it over to block off the stairs to the basement. The last thing we needed was either dog going down there and finding heaven only knew what. I hadn't even been down there yet. Honestly, I was a bit afraid to go down and take a look. When I toured the building, there had been some boxes and furniture down there, but I didn't know if Mr. Shuman had removed it all. My fear was that everything that had been upstairs was now downstairs. I'd never seen a dumpster or a moving truck here to remove the items from the store. There could be piles and piles of more junk downstairs, and I just didn't even want to think about that.

Claire unclipped the dogs' leads, and they immediately ran in opposite directions, noses glued to the ground.

"Where do you want to start?" Claire asked, setting the leads on the table by my keys.

"Let's flip through this stuff, then we can tackle the main room." I tipped my head toward the front of the store before eyeing the basement stairs. "We can end with the dungeon."

A wry smile sprang to life on Claire's pretty face. "Sounds like a plan. You take that wall." She pointed to the one I'd dragged the picture away from to block the stairs.

"So, tell me about this contractor," Claire said, moving toward the other wall. "I thought you hired Les Decker, but you said the guy's name is Luke?"

"I did. Luke is his son. Les had a heart attack."

"What?" Claire gasped. "Oh my goodness! Is he all right?"

"He's doing okay, from the way his son talked, but he's been sidelined for the foreseeable future. Luke's taken over the business until his dad can return."

"Wow. That's quite the task. He's young, isn't he? Early twenties, if memory serves me correctly."

"Mid-twenties. He said he's twenty-six. I guess he's the company architect. Now he's also the main project manager."

"Do you think he's up for the job?"

I waved my head back and forth, continuing to flip through the prints lined up against the wall. "He seemed to know what he was talking about. I guess we'll find out."

Letting go of the last frame, I stepped back. "None of these fit the vibe I'm going for."

"Yeah, I'm feeling the same thing over here." Claire flipped through the last few pictures, then turned away from the wall.

"Let's head out front." I grabbed a sheet from my tote that I brought to put on the floor. Anything I planned to keep would go on it.

Claire called the dogs, and we headed up front.

Unfolding the sheet, I let it fan out and settle on the floor in an empty corner.

"You know, you were right. These are in pretty good shape."

I looked up from straightening the sheet's edges to see Claire walking through the displays.

"You could put a notice on the windows and talk to the other shopkeepers tomorrow. Let them know they can come by and grab any of them they want." She looked at me. "It would save some dumpster space."

"True. But then I'd either have to leave the coffeeshop to let people in or pay someone to sit here for several hours."

"I could probably do it. I have an open house from two to four, but I could hang out here from say, ten until noon?"

"You're sure?"

"Yes."

"I mean, if you want to do that, I won't say no." Sending her a quick smile, I headed for a bank of art. "Whatever doesn't get taken, I can have Luke's crew put out on Monday and hold a sidewalk sale. I'll just put my staff on a rotation to man it."

"That works. It's really not a problem for me to sit here tomorrow. It just feels like a waste to—Betty! Pebbles! Oh my goodness."

At Claire's exclamation, I glanced over. The dogs each had a corner of the sheet I just laid down in their mouths and were backing up, pulling it across the floor.

Laughing, I moved to help Claire wrestle it away from them.

Pebbles dodged Claire's outstretched hands, quickly circling around to grab a different corner. Betty stumbled when Pebbles let go, falling sideways.

I laughed harder. "Who knew Pebbles would be the difficult one?"

Claire's laughter joined mine. "Me. She's always been the problem child. It's how Ozzie and I first met, remember?"

"True." I wish I'd seen my friend running down the sidewalk in her fuzzy, hot-pink slippers after her little dog and stumbling into the hunk of man that was Oscar Quartermaine. But I'd heard all about it after the fact. It amused me how little regard she had for him in the beginning. Now he was living in her house, and I wouldn't be surprised to hear wedding bells ring soon.

"Oh, come here, you little turd." Claire reached for Pebbles again, but once more the dog scampered away.

Straightening, Claire sighed and propped her hands on her hips. "Perhaps the sheet was a bad idea."

Chuckling, I nodded. "It's fine. Let them have it. We can just pile everything right there. I can cover it up with the sheet before we leave or move it onto it tomorrow."

With a huff, Claire gave her dog one last glare and moved toward a stash of knick-knacks in one of the display cases.

The front room took us longer to go through, but we still made quick work of it. I found a few art prints and a flowerpot I wanted to keep. Not even enough to be worthy of spreading the sheet out again. It would all fit in my car. So, we toted it to the back room and left it near the door. I would take it all home with me tonight.

"You ready to tackle this basement?" I tipped my head toward the stairs, still leery of what awaited.

She swept an arm out. "Lead the way."

Mouth twisting, I moved the picture frame out of the way, then bent down and scooped up Betty. I figured both dogs would want to follow us, and I didn't want the puppy to fall down the stairs.

Claire picked up Pebbles, and we made our way down the concrete steps.

A lone light bulb flickered to life when I flipped the switch. The dusty, sixty-watt bulb barely illuminated the first fifteen feet.

But that was enough.

"Wow," Claire muttered.

Wow was right.

The basement was full of furniture and boxes, some of them open with random items peeking over the top.

My shoulders slumped. "Well, now I know where most of the stuff upstairs went." This had not looked like this when I toured the building.

"I guess let's each grab a box and start taking stuff upstairs. It all has to go, right?" Claire moved forward toward a box with glassware peeking out the top alongside a statue of a bear.

I sighed. "Yeah, eventually." With so much chaos and the enormity of how much stuff was down here hitting me, my legs refused to propel me forward, my body frozen in a state of decision paralysis. I simply didn't know where to start. "Maybe we should leave it for Luke's team. They can clear it all out."

Claire paused, her hands on the box. "We should at least look through things down here and see if there's anything you want to keep."

I cast a skeptical look at her. "I doubt there's much I want to keep."

She shrugged. "Maybe so, but let's look. At the very least, it keeps me from going home to an empty house."

Sympathy for my friend finally set my feet in motion. "Oh, all right." I crossed to the stack of boxes opposite Claire's and opened the flap.

"So, has Ozzie been working a lot of long hours?" I shot a quick glance at Claire to gauge her reaction. She kept her eyes on the box and its contents.

"Some. No more than usual. It's just the end of the week, you know? I was looking forward to unwinding with him after we were done here, then he got called in. Now I have no idea when he'll be home."

"You said it was a burglary investigation, right?"

She nodded.

"Well, then, it shouldn't take too long, should it? I mean,

it's not like a murder." Thank goodness. We'd had enough of those around here for a long time.

"True. I guess it depends on how good the leads are and if he catches the perpetrator." She waved a hand. "Ignore me. I'm being melancholic. It's just been a long week, and I'm tired thanks to a certain fluffball." She turned her head to eye her black lab puppy, who currently had her nose stuffed in a crevice between the shelving units lining the wall to my left.

I smiled. "You're the one who bought the dog."

Claire huffed a short sigh, then chuckled. "I know."

Over the next couple of hours, we worked our way through the pile of boxes and furniture, taking a few pieces upstairs that I intended to keep. Claire found a few things for her home and office as well. By the time we reached the back of the basement, I was happy she convinced me to go through things. I was also happy we were done.

"I need ice cream," I muttered, rubbing the small of my back.

"Hey, that sounds good." Claire glanced at her watch. "And the parlor's still open. Let's go." Bending over, she scooped Pebbles off the floor.

Laughing, I followed suit and picked up a dusty Betty. The little dog squirmed in my arms, then looked up and licked my chin. "You want some ice cream too? I bet we can convince your new mama to get you some."

Claire glanced back at me as she put a foot on the bottom step. "Like she needs sugar."

I shrugged. "Make it a small and ask for two cups. You can split it between her and Pebbles."

As if agreeing, Pebbles barked.

"See?" I chuckled. "She says, 'Yeah, Mom. I want ice cream.'"

"Fine," Claire sighed.

CHAPTER 4

Luke

The soft thuds of car doors closing echoed around me as I got out of my truck and met my crew outside the old antique store beside The Cozy Cup. Taking a sip from my steaming travel mug filled with coffee so strong it could strip the ancient varnish off the banister inside, I nodded to my foreman, Kado Strayer. "Morning."

"Hey, bossman." Kado gave a quick smile of greeting, then turned and took a demo fork from the back of his truck. "You ready to knock down a few walls?"

I chuckled. "We have to cart out a bunch of junk first." Saturday, Mina called and left a message, saying that the old owner shoved all his inventory downstairs rather than getting rid of it. She wanted it all gone.

I had a plan for it all, though. Since what was downstairs didn't impact demolition, it could stay for now. Once we started cleaning up the debris, I'd send some of the crew down with a couple of hand trucks and have them cart it all up.

Heading toward the door, I shifted the tablet in my hand under my arm, then took the key from my pocket as Kado and the others filed in behind me. "Not all of it goes in the dumpster." Inserting the key, I twisted the knob and let us inside, flipping on the lights.

Mina also emailed me a list of the items upstairs she wanted to set out front for sale. And to make it extra easy on us, she marked them with blue sticky notes.

A man had to love a woman who was that organized. It made this process so much easier.

"Anything marked with a blue sticky note goes out front. The owner said she's having a sidewalk sale." I took a quick glance around the back room. It was completely empty except for a small card table by the door. That had a small sign on it that said to leave it there.

"Got it." Kado waved his demo fork. "Let's go, guys."

I set my coffee on the table, then went back out to my truck to get a can of spray paint. While the guys toted the displays and other junk out, I planned to mark the areas that needed demoing.

Finding what I wanted in the bed box on my truck, I went back inside, bypassing the back room except for the small counter and shelving unit fixed to the wall by the stairs.

Out in the main store, I woke up my tablet and pulled up the building plans, and started marking walls with bright green paint.

"Are we taking out the floors too?" Kado called.

I glanced over. "Yes." Mina wanted the same floor throughout. The Cozy Cup floors were going, too, once we broke through the connecting wall.

Kado gave me a thumbs up and immediately dragged a heavy shelving unit across the floor, no doubt leaving scratches in the wood.

I rolled my eyes, a sardonic tilt lifting one side of my mouth. At least he asked first.

Marking the walls didn't take me long. Not many were staying. So, once I finished and returned the paint to my truck, I grabbed a sledgehammer, some eye protection, and my gloves and set to work.

The cabinets on the one wall in the back room were the first to go. In minutes, they lay in splintered pieces on the floor. The long counter and cabinet unit needed to be removed as well, but I decided to leave it for later. It wasn't in the way, and we could use it to put things on for now.

Using my foot, I nudged the biggest pieces of the ruined cabinets to the side so the guys could carry things through to the dumpster out back.

With that done, I found a screwdriver and popped the hinges out on the swinging doors that separated the back room from the front of the store. The doors would eventually be replaced with something that fit the café's theme. Right now, they were just in the way.

Hefting the old ones onto my shoulder, I took them out and tossed them in the dumpster, the wood making a satis-fying thwack-thump as it hit the hard steel.

Dirt and wood crunched under my boots as I walked back inside. Snagging my sledgehammer, I walked unimpeded through the doorway and turned right as I lifted my dust mask from around my neck and covered my face. This wall had water damage, and I wanted to see where it was coming from.

My first swing cracked the plaster and sent a cloud of dust rising. Small bits of wall broke off, dropping to the floor with a soft skitter.

I hit it again, moving over slightly. The first time, I hit the stud behind the plaster.

This time, my hammer went through. I yanked down, pulling more wall with the hammerhead as I pulled it out.

"That looks like fun. Can I try?"

I paused, hammer raised for another hit, at the sound of the feminine voice coming from behind me. Lowering the hammer, I glanced over my shoulder to see Mina. "Hey. Good morning."

She smiled, sending that same jolt of awareness through my body that she did last week.

I willed my body not to react.

This job would last an eternity if I couldn't get that feeling under control.

"Can I try?" She nodded toward the wall.

"You want to demo?" I glanced at the hole I made.

"Yes. Not the whole place, obviously." She fluttered a hand at the cavernous space. "But I'd like to do a little."

Lifting a shoulder, I took off my safety glasses and held them out. "Sure. I don't have an extra mask on me. I could probably find one if you want, though."

"This is fine." She sent me a sheepish smile. "I ducked out during a lull in the rush to see the progress. Then I saw you smashing the wall." She shrugged. "It looked like fun." Taking the glasses, she slipped them onto her face.

I grinned behind my mask, making the corners of my eyes crinkle. "It is. Best part of construction. Do you want my gloves?" I held up a hand.

"No. They won't fit and will probably just make it harder for me to hold the hammer."

"Good point." Passing her the sledgehammer, I stepped back, then swept a hand toward the wall. "Have at it."

Mina shuffled forward and raised the twelve-pound sledge. I crossed my arms, curious if she'd actually be able to swing it with enough power to break through the plaster.

But I shouldn't have doubted her. The woman took a baseball player's batting stance and swung for the fence. A hole appeared beside the one I'd been working on.

"Nice hit."

She tossed me a saucy smile. "Thanks. I like baseball." Winding up, she took another swing, widening her hole. After a couple more whacks, she had a sizeable opening.

Stepping closer, she peered inside.

"You see any water damage in there?" I asked, moving in behind her.

"Um… there's some plastic." A furrow wrinkled her brow.

"Plastic?" I dug in my pocket for my phone and flipped on the flashlight. "There shouldn't be any plastic in the wall."

One slight shoulder bobbed. "That's what I see. Shine your light in there." She pointed at the hole.

I did as she asked, but from my vantage point, I couldn't see anything.

With a hum, she stepped back a bit and jabbed at the plaster with the hammer, breaking it away to widen the hole.

Now I could see the edge of yellowed plastic.

"Maybe it's insulation?" Mina said.

"It's weird insulation, if so. These old buildings, they typically used newspaper or sawdust. It's more likely there was a leak, and rather than fixing it, they put the plastic in to keep it from ruining the walls and floor. Do you see any water collected?" I angled the light a little higher so she could peer inside.

Mina leaned in. Raising a hand, she grasped the edge of the plastic, shifting it.

Her scream caught me off guard.

So did her lurch backward. Her back hit my chest, and she stepped on my foot as she scrambled away from the wall.

I shot a hand out to steady her as she stumbled off the steel-toe of my boot. "Why are you screaming?" Did she see a dead mouse or something?

With eyes so wide I could see white all the way around her brilliant blue irises, she pointed at the wall with a trembling finger. "Eyes. Empty. A-a-a…" Her voice trailed off.

"Eyes? What? Is there a dead animal in there?" That wouldn't surprise me. If water could get in, so could vermin.

A mirthless laugh slid free of her mouth, and she shook her head.

I waited a moment for her to explain, but she didn't. Her breathing increased as she muttered, "Oh my God," under her breath over and over.

Concerned now, I made sure she was steady on her feet before I released her and moved to the hole. Shining my light inside, I shifted the plastic.

My stomach did a flip, threatening to eject my breakfast.

Jerking my hand back, I straightened. "Holy shit!"

Peeking out from the plastic, the black voids of a human skull's sightless eyes stared back.

CHAPTER 5

Mina

This was *not* happening.

I clutched the paper coffee cup between my fingers and stared out at the street from a table in my coffeeshop, watching the police rope off the area in front of my newly purchased building.

Why was there a skeleton in the wall?

Better yet, who would do such a thing?

Was Mr. Shuman a murderer?

If so, why would he sell me the building? He knew my plans for the space.

Mostly.

I leaned forward and absentmindedly chewed on a fingernail. He knew I wanted to knock down the wall between the spaces, but I never told him I planned to knock down any part of the wall separating the employee area from the main storefront.

But still, he had to know that anyone who bought the place would want to conduct renovations. Even if they didn't move that wall, it needed repaired. The water damage was obvious.

An inelegant snort escaped me. *Water damage…* More like body damage.

I shuddered, thinking about that body decaying in there. How did no one smell it?

Lifting my coffee, I took a sip. Maybe they did and thought it was just a dead animal. That happened all the time.

The front door opened, and Claire's boyfriend and resident detective, Ozzie Quartermaine, stepped inside.

My gaze roved over his tall, powerful figure, and a bit of calm settled over me. Ozzie would figure it out.

But it was the man coming in behind him that I wanted to have wrap his arms around me and reassure me that this would all blow over soon.

I locked eyes with Luke.

A spark of attraction zipped through me, but I batted it away. Now was not the time to lust after my contractor—or anyone, for that matter.

The two men walked up to my table. Ozzie dragged a chair over from another, while Luke took the seat across from me. I wished he were beside me. While Ozzie's presence reassured me he'd get to the bottom of this, Luke's was the one that offered sympathy and comfort. I just wanted to lean on those broad, muscular shoulders.

My eyelids slid shut, and I looked away. What was *wrong* with me?

Admonishing myself to get my mind out of the gutter, I looked at Ozzie.

"How're you doing, Mina?"

"Still shellshocked. I don't suppose there was any ID on the body?"

He shook his head.

My mouth twisted. "Didn't think so."

"Not that we've seen yet, anyway. Forensics just got here. They'll remove the remains from the wall, and we'll know more then." Ozzie shifted, leaning forward. "Tell me what happened. How did you find the body?"

"We were just knocking down the wall." I traced the rim of the lid on my coffee. "I came over in time just to see the start of demo and saw Luke busting up the wall. I asked if I could take a few swings. We found the plastic soon after."

"Did you touch anything?" Ozzie looked between us.

"Just the edge of the plastic," Luke answered. "I had gloves on."

"I didn't." My hand twitched on my cup.

"That's okay," Ozzie said. "We're taking prints from everyone who was there, so we can exclude you from what we find. Mina, do you know where Mr. Shuman is?"

I shook my head. "No idea. Talk to Miranda Bennett. She might know since she had to get the real estate contracts to him. He's not in town, I know that much."

His nose wrinkled, and I knew he was not looking forward to that. Likely, he'd heard enough of Claire's horror stories about her colleague to know it wouldn't be an easy task to get information out of the woman. I didn't envy him the challenge.

"Okay." Ozzie turned his head toward Luke. "What made you start with that wall? Just random choice?"

"Actually, no. I noticed the water damage when I walked through with Mina last week. I decided to start there today so I could see if there was an active leak somewhere and to determine if we needed to fix any of the supports behind the plaster."

Ozzie nodded. "Did you notice anything else out of the ordinary about the wall?"

"No. Well, maybe. The location of the water damage. It was low, but there were no pipes there. I mean, I get now why that's the case. It's not water damage, it's… seepage." Luke frowned. "But yeah, I guess that struck me as odd. My original thought was possibly there was a roof leak."

"Do we have any idea who this could be?" I asked. "I mean, someone's been missing for many, many years. That should tell us something, right?"

"It does, but I haven't had a chance to go through missing persons cases yet. The chief might have an idea, but we haven't talked since I got the call. Let us get the body out and maybe get a timeline established. That will give us a better idea of who it could be. And how they ended up in your wall."

The bell over the door jingled again as a frazzled-looking Claire hurried through.

"Mina!" She skirted a table and a set of chairs to envelop me in a quick hug. "Are you okay?"

I squeezed her back. "I'm fine. Just a little freaked out."

Claire stepped back and grabbed another chair, pulling it close to Ozzie.

"Babe, I'm conducting an interview."

"Oh." She paused halfway into her seat. "Sorry. Do you want me to get some coffee and come back?"

He sighed, a small smile tilting his mouth, softening his stern features. "No. I think we're done."

She shot a mock glare at him and lightly slapped his chest. "Don't toy with me, Oscar Allen. This is a serious time. Don't you remember how traumatized I was when I found Mrs. Hammond?"

The levity left his face. "You're right." He looked at me. "I'm sorry, Mina."

"Don't worry about it." I offered him a small smile. "I appreciate you trying to make me smile."

"So, what do we know?" Claire asked, diving in.

Oscar gave her a quick rundown, which wasn't much.

She frowned at him. "What are you still doing sitting here? Go find out who's in the wall."

He chuckled. "Slow down, babe. Forensics has to get the

body out of the wall first. I don't even know if it's a man or a woman."

Claire whipped out her phone.

"What are you doing?" Ozzie asked.

"Your job. I'm looking up missing persons from this area."

He groaned. "Will you let me do this my way?"

"No. My way is faster."

Luke chuckled and met my gaze. I understood his amusement. Claire could be a wrecking ball.

"How long do you think that body's been in there?" Claire asked, staring at her phone.

"I don't know." Ozzie pinched the bridge of his nose. "That's why we need to wait for forensics to get it out of the wall."

She let out a soft grunt. "We'll just do a general search for missing persons." Her fingers flew over the phone keyboard. She paused as the search results came up, then lifted one eyebrow. "That's a lot more people than I thought it would be." She tipped the phone toward Ozzie.

He plucked it from her hand and scrolled. "Yeah." Running his palm over his jaw, he read a few of the article descriptions, then handed it back. "We just need to wait on forensics. I can't narrow it down until I get at least the gender. An approximate time of death would be even better."

Claire huffed and laid the phone face down before resting her chin in her hand. "Fine."

Ozzie put a hand on her back and rubbed small circles. "I'll get to the bottom of it. You just have to give me a chance."

"What else can we do to help?" Luke asked.

"Not much, honestly," Ozzie said to him, then turned to me. "And I'm afraid work will have to stop on the café until we get all we can from the building."

I grimaced but knew he was right. "I figured. You should

know, the basement is full of junk. I don't know if any of it is important."

"Claire told me about it. We'll probably haul it all out and to a secure facility for processing." He rolled his neck. "The chief is going to love this."

"I'll bring you all the things I took from the building. It's not much. Some art, a couple of decorative knick-knacks, and some planters." I scooted away from the table. "In fact, some of it's here."

"We have that stuff at home, too, don't forget," Claire said, waving a finger at him.

Luke stood. "I'll help you gather things."

I glanced up, surprised at the gesture. "Oh. Thank you."

A lopsided smile appeared on his face, bringing out a dimple. "You're welcome."

CHAPTER 6

Luke

I wasn't totally sure what possessed me to offer to help Mina gather stuff. There was a certain element of needing to move around involved. Sitting idle while my mind spun in a million directions about who was in the wall and why wasn't working. I've always been the type who puzzled things out better while I did something mundane. Moving a few things fit that bill. I also knew I would probably end up taking a run later.

Not that any of it would help. I hadn't the slightest clue who we'd uncovered.

But, at the very least, it would help me sort out my feelings about the situation.

"There really isn't much." Mina glanced over her shoulder at me as she flipped on the light in the coffeeshop's storage room. "Just that." She gestured to the artwork propped against the wall.

"I'll take one, you take the other."

"I have that box, there, too." She pointed to a small box on a shelf beside the art. "It's just some stuff I thought might fit the new café's theme."

I moved past her to pick up both paintings. "You take the box. I have these."

"Are you sure?"

"Yes. They're not heavy."

Her brows winged upward, but she didn't argue.

I bit back a smile. To her, they probably were a bit on the heavy side. And awkward. She was tiny.

Though not too tiny. The woman had curves that didn't quit.

Clearing my throat softly, I hefted the artwork. "So, how are you doing? You still look a little shellshocked."

She snorted. "I am. There's a skeleton in my wall. I highly doubt that person crawled in there by themselves and died." She shuddered and tucked the box against her middle. "It just creeps me out to think that I sat at the same table—laughed with—a man who is a potential murderer. And if it wasn't him, then a murderer could still walk amongst us. It's just..." She trailed off and shuddered again, more violently, as a look of disgust crossed her face.

I understood that. I would certainly give some extra scrutiny to the people I passed in town until the police had a better handle on the situation. "How long did Mr. Shuman own the building?" It had been an antique store my entire childhood, so I figured it was at least a few decades.

"Thirty years, at least. I don't know who owned it before that." A small frown creased her forehead. "Do you think that person's been in there longer than that?"

Leaving the storage room, I thought about the body's condition. It was dry and didn't smell, except for an old and musty scent. "It's possible. I don't know how fast people in walls decay. Do you remember a time when the store was closed unexpectedly? Or when people complained of a smell inside?"

"No. But I haven't lived here my entire life. Claire and I

are from the Hoonah area. You'd know better than I would. Aren't you from here?"

"Yes, but I didn't exactly pay much attention to what went on in town. If I wasn't chasing a girl, I was off in the woods hunting or building a dirt bike track." I was a bit of a hellion in my youth. My poor parents were both happy and sad to see me go off to college. And scared, because I was on my own without supervision. Thankfully, I calmed down. I still liked a good adrenaline rush, though.

"I'm going to have to do some digging later," Mina mused.

I lifted an eyebrow. "You should probably leave that up to the cops."

"Pfft." She scrunched her nose. "Even if I wanted to, Claire won't let me. It'll drive Ozzie crazy, but it won't stop her. And even if it weren't my building, I wouldn't want her digging around alone. I'm not saying we'll go out and pound the pavement or anything, but we'll probably cozy up at her house tonight with some hot chocolate and her laptop and do some strategic internet searches."

My gaze traveled through the coffeeshop's front windows to the flashing lights on top of the cop cars blocking off part of the street. Curiosity pulled at my mind, and I glanced at Mina. "You want company?"

She cast a quick glance back at me as we walked. "Digging up information?"

"Yeah. I might not have paid much attention to the comings and goings around town, but I know most of the people. I might recognize names you and Claire won't."

"I suppose that's true. Okay. Let's talk to Claire—after Ozzie leaves." A quick smile flashed across her pretty face, making her eyes twinkle. "And we'll set up a time to get together later."

"Sounds like a plan." Maybe I'd get a few answers to my swirling thoughts, after all.

My mouth flattened as an alternative thought occurred. It was quite possible I would just end up with more questions.

But, ultimately, it didn't matter. I wanted to stay in the loop. It wasn't my shop, but it was my job site, and I'd been there to uncover the remains.

CHAPTER 7

Mina

"Careful. You might give away you like this guy."

A flush colored my cheeks as I let the curtain flutter back into place over the front window, where I'd been watching for Luke. Doing my best to will the red out of my cheeks, I turned to give Claire my best glare. "I do not. I'm just eager to start researching our dead person."

Claire hummed, the grin on her face telling me she didn't believe a word coming out of my mouth. "Sure you are."

I huffed, not ready to admit she might be right. "You're impossible."

She chuckled. "No. I'm just right."

My eye roll was epic and made her laugh. "Please explain how you think you're right." I didn't like Luke Decker. Not like that. I mean, he was handsome, sure. But he was my contractor and practically a baby.

"The entire time we were in the coffeeshop, you kept casting furtive glances his way. I don't think he noticed, because he was watching the street, but I did. Whether you did it consciously or not, you kept studying him."

I did? "I don't know what you're talking about. Maybe I

was just trying to figure out what he could know about our little town and its people."

Claire raised an eyebrow and crossed her arms.

I pressed my lips together and stared her down. There wasn't a chance I would admit to liking the man. Because I didn't.

So what if he looked good in a pair of jeans and a t-shirt?

And had hair a girl dreamed of running her fingers through?

My jaw worked, and I put a lid on that train of thought. That was enough of that.

The thud of a car door closing broke our stare-down. Claire's face broke into a wide smile. "I guess we're about to test the theory that you can't keep your eyes off him." She walked around me to answer the door.

A low growl escaped my throat. She could be so frustrating sometimes.

Pebbles, Claire's Yorkie, barked when she noticed her mistress heading for the door. That brought Betty's head up from her nap on the dog bed by the fireplace. I chuckled as the puppy flopped like a fish in her attempt to get up from the plush pad.

"Grab her, would you?" Claire pointed at Pebbles.

"Yep." I scooped the Yorkie off the floor. She vibrated in my arms as she barked. "Oh, hush. He's nice."

Betty made a break for the door, but I was faster than the little fluffball. As she ran past my feet, I put a hand down on her back. With a quick shimmy of my fingers, I wrapped them around her plump belly and lifted her off the floor.

Immediately, she licked my chin. "Oh, mmm. Thank you, Betty." My nose wrinkled as dog slobber coated the lower right side of my face.

Claire laughed and pulled the door open.

The smile froze on my face at the sight of Luke standing there with a hand raised, poised to knock.

Once more, I wondered how it was legal for a man to look so good in a pair of jeans. The worn denim looked buttery soft and clung to trim hips and muscular thighs. I knew if he turned around, I'd get a glimpse of a firm tush.

"Well, hi." A crooked smile appeared on his face, and he lowered his hand. "I take it you saw me coming?"

Claire nodded. "Come in, please."

Luke stepped inside. His flint-colored eyes roved over the space, taking a quick inventory.

"Thanks for coming." Claire shut the door. "Having a local's insight for this search will be quite useful."

"I'm ready to get started."

Betty squirmed in my grasp and yipped, wanting to greet the newcomer.

The polite smile on Luke's face grew into something more affable and genuine. "Oh, you're cute." He strode closer, reaching out to pet the puppy. Betty instantly went floppy as he scratched her ears.

Pebbles whined and sniffed him, wanting attention as well. Under my arm, her little tail wagged fiercely.

"So are you." He switched his attention to the Yorkie. "I like your bow." With one finger, he nudged the hot-pink bow holding Pebbles' bangs out of her face.

"Are they yours?" His gray eyes met mine.

"Mine?" I blinked, attempting to make my brain work. It had been too busy watching him fawn over a couple of cute animals. Could he be more adorable?

One golden brown eyebrow quirked, and I realized I was staring.

Heat climbed my neck. "Um, no. They're Claire's. I'm just playing gatekeeper. I have a cat."

He tipped his head, still scratching Pebbles by her ears. "That fits."

It was my turn to raise an eyebrow. "What do you mean?"

"Coffeeshop owner. Now the owner of a potentially

haunted former antique store." He shrugged. "People like that own cats, don't they?"

I couldn't help but laugh. "I guess so. Never thought about it, really. But thank you for planting the idea there's now a ghost in my building." The paranormal wasn't really my "thing," but I didn't discount the idea there could be an astral plane lurking between here and the afterlife. I just hoped that if that person's spirit was indeed loitering in the store, it was friendly.

"Sorry." Luke offered me a sheepish smile.

"It's fine." Needing to regain my equilibrium, and to put some space between us because he smelled delectable, I took a step back and set the dogs on the floor. "Let's get down to business, shall we? So I know what to call this ghost when he or she makes their presence known."

Claire rolled her eyes. "You're so melodramatic."

"And you aren't?"

She chuckled, glancing over her shoulder as she led us to the dining area. "Touché."

"So, has Detective Quartermaine shared any information with you since this morning?" Luke pulled out a chair but didn't sit, instead, waiting on Claire and me to get settled.

Cute, and a gentleman?

Another tally mark went on the "Pros" side of the score-card in my mind. Before long, that side would outweigh the two "Cons" I had: his age and our professional relationship.

"No." Claire's expression soured. "He was rather tight-lipped." She picked up Pebbles and settled her on her lap. Betty, not to be outdone, put her feet up on Luke's thigh and barked.

Grinning, he picked her up, only to have her put her gigantic paws on his chest and attack his face with puppy kisses. He didn't seem to mind, though, as he gently pushed her down.

"Do we have anything to go on?" I asked, doing my best to keep my gaze on Claire. Watching Luke with Betty did funny things to my insides.

"Well, I did overhear one of the forensic techs say they think it's a woman." Claire opened her laptop. "So, I guess we can start there with missing persons."

"What about a time of death? Did you overhear anything about how long the woman's been there?" Luke asked.

"No. I don't know how old they think she was, either." She held up a finger. "I do know they're sending her body off to a forensic anthropologist for analysis. Hopefully, they'll get something from that, but it'll probably take some time."

His mouth pulled. "A lot of time. Those people don't work too fast, do they?"

She shrugged. "I have no idea." A devilish smile crossed her face. "But we're going to move things along with the help of our friend, the internet." Stretching her fingers, she opened her web browser.

"What are you searching first?" I leaned to the side so I could see the screen better.

"Missing persons in Alaska." She talked as she typed and quickly had a page of results. "This looks good." She clicked on a link for the Alaska Department of Public Safety. When she scrolled down, a list of names appeared alongside columns for their sex, race, case number, the date they went missing, and the investigating agency.

"Click that." Luke pointed at the screen. "Let's see how far back the list goes."

Claire clicked on the date tab, reversing the order of names.

He let out a low whistle. "Nineteen fifty-two. That's a lot of names."

"Yeah." I blew out a breath, my shoulders deflating as a bit of hopelessness set in. "Without more to go on, I don't know how we'll narrow it down. I mean, there's also the possibility the woman isn't even from Alaska. What if she was reported missing in the lower forty-eight? Or in Canada?" I slumped back in my chair and crossed my arms. So much for helping the search along.

"Let's at least narrow it down to women and see how many people we get." Claire's hands moved over the keyboard again.

Since there was no way to search by gender alone, she set the number of results to one hundred, then clicked on the tab to sort by male and female.

"Looks like just shy of two hundred." She glanced up.

"That's still a lot."

"Yeah, but there are over a dozen, from the looks of it, that were reported in the Juneau area." Luke gestured to the screen, which showed the investigating agency.

Claire stood, walking over to her tote bag, which sat on a barstool at the island, and removed a legal pad and a pen. "Let's write down those names, then search them. Maybe one of them will pop up in a news article with local ties."

I sat up, feeling some hope returning. But only a little. It was such a long shot. Sitting around doing nothing, though, wasn't an option. We needed to find the woman's identity so I could get my renovation back on track. Logically, I knew Ozzie was all over this case. Not just because of my relationship to his girlfriend, Claire, but because that's just the type of person he was. He wanted answers as much as I did and wouldn't rest until he got them.

But more eyes were always better.

I took the notepad and pen from Claire. "All right, start reading."

Settling back into her seat, Claire scrolled, and we soon had a list of seventeen names.

"How long does it take a body to fully skeletonize?" Luke asked.

A quick frown formed on my face, and I shot him a look. "Why?"

"I was just thinking that we might be able to take some of the more recent names off the list. The body didn't have any flesh left on it, remember?"

"Oh. Right." I glanced at the notepad in front of me, then at Claire. "Can you—"

"Already on it," she said, reading my mind. With a few taps on the keyboard, she'd run another search on decay.

"Hmm..." She leaned forward and propped her chin on her hand. "This says it varies widely. A few weeks to a few years, depending on conditions. But..." she scrolled, "I would say in controlled conditions, like in the wall, we could knock a year or so off the list."

My nose wrinkled. "That's not as much as I was hoping for."

"Me, either," Claire replied.

I glanced at the list. Only one name fit the bill. I crossed her off.

"I would say cross off any within five years," Luke said.

With a curious frown, I looked his way. "Why?"

"The state of the wall. The paint wasn't pristine where it was patched, and there was dust everywhere that didn't look like it had been disturbed recently. All the fluid from the body had dried up too. That all takes time." He lifted a shoulder. "I've been through a lot of buildings for renovations. Whoever she is, I would wager she's been in that wall for at least five years. Plus, The Cozy Cup has been in business about that long." He turned to me. "You or one of your regulars would have noticed the store being closed to let the place air out as she decayed."

"Unless it happened after he closed the store down," I said. "That was a year or so ago."

Luke tipped his head. "I still think it's likely been longer than a year, just based on the way the wall looks."

Claire nodded once. "Good enough for me." She looked my way. "So, how many does that take off our list, then, Mina?" She nodded toward the notepad.

I ran a finger down the sheet. "Four more."

"Now we're down to a dozen. That's manageable." Claire opened a new browser window. "Give me the first name."

One by one, we went through the list, but no one came up in any local news, except for the articles about their disappearances.

Clicking the pen, I tossed it down on the table. "Well, that was a waste of time."

"Not really," Luke said.

Tossing a glare his way at his optimism, I crossed my arms. "How was it not a waste of time? We learned nothing about any of them."

"That's not true. We learned none of them has a criminal record. They would have shown up in those police blotter articles the newspaper always puts out, but literally the only news articles we found were about their disappearances."

"So, they were upstanding citizens." Claire sat up. "That's strange." Her brows knit together. "You'd think some of them would have a least a DUI or a drug arrest." She opened a new tab. "Mina, read me the names you crossed off."

My glare softened and my frown turned confused. "What for?"

"Let's see if they have records too."

Still frowning, I read her the first name. "What are you thinking?"

"That I spend too much time with my detective boyfriend," she muttered.

"No, you don't," Luke said. "Because I think we're thinking the same thing."

I waved a hand. "Then can you enlighten me? Because I'm not the true crime enthusiast of the bunch. What are you getting at?"

Claire and Luke shared a look before Luke turned to me, one side of that sculpted mouth tilted up.

"Serial killer."

CHAPTER 8

Luke

I t wasn't hard to read the disbelief on Mina's pretty face. She went from a curious and slightly exasperated frown to rounded eyes and a gaping mouth in a split second.

"What? That's insane. We're talking a sixty-year span. Even if the guy was, like, twenty, when he started killing, he'd be eighty now."

"So maybe only some of them are attributable to a serial killer." Claire shrugged.

Mina pressed her lips together and cocked an eyebrow. "Then the rest with no criminal record are just what? Coincidence?"

She nodded. "Yes."

When Mina rolled her eyes, I held up a hand. "It's plausible."

"But not very likely."

"It's still worth thinking about."

"Mina, give me another name," Claire interrupted. "That new one has a drug conviction."

"I still think you two are chasing ghosts, but whatever." She read off another name.

One after the other, all but two of the new names revealed a criminal past.

"Now, that's weird." Mina turned suspicious eyes on me. "How did you know where to cut it off?"

It was my turn to give her the incredulous look. "Are you suggesting I'm the killer? You remember how old I am, right?"

"Maybe you're a killer reincarnate."

"Then that would mean the killings would have stopped when I was born, and they clearly didn't." I pointed to her list, which contained several names of women who'd gone missing after I was born.

Claire waved a quick hand. "We're getting off track here. The serial killer angle is just one theory. For some of the older disappearances, we'll need to check records. Stuff like that may not have been reported in the news way back then. It's still worth turning the list over to Ozzie. He can get much more detail about these women and their lives than we can."

"So, what did we really learn, then?" Mina uncrossed her arms long enough to gesture at the list.

A soft frown flitted over Claire's face as she thought about that.

I had an answer, however. "We learned that if the missing woman is from this area, she's on that list." I jabbed a finger into the notepad.

"We also have a list we can cross-check against news articles and police records," Claire argued. "We can take that to the library and look for information in old newspapers stored on microfiche."

"I can look in Juneau as well," I added. "The bigger papers might have more info."

Mina let out a soft groan and sat forward, propping her elbows on the table and putting her face in her hands.

The urge to run a reassuring hand down her back blasted

me out of nowhere. How had this woman gotten under my skin so quickly?

I dug my fingers into Betty's fur, helping to control the urge to touch the dark-haired beauty beside me.

"I really hope some search we do turns up something useful. Or that Ozzie gets a lead from her body. The sooner the renovations get back on track, the better."

Claire reached over and laid a hand on Mina's arm. "Have some faith. It'll all get figured out."

Mina offered her a soft smile. "Yeah."

While I admired Claire's optimism and had tried to project my own to buoy Mina's spirits, I had my doubts. There was very little left of the body. Just bones and the tattered scraps of her clothing. I hadn't noticed anything else in the wall with her.

But I also hadn't looked that closely. Not much turned my stomach. I grew up in the Alaskan wilderness, where it wasn't an uncommon occurrence to come across a half-rotted animal carcass in the woods or to see a large predator ripping into a meal.

Those sightless eyes, though…

I suppressed a shudder.

All I could hope was that the three of us and Ozzie could work a miracle and figure out how a body ended up in the wall of the old antique store.

Claire's phone buzzed from her tote bag. She put Pebbles on the floor and got up to dig it out. Her nose scrunched as she looked at the screen. "It's Ozzie."

Mina chuckled. "You're in trouble."

"Probably." She answered it. "Hi, honey." As she listened, she rolled her lips in, her eyes dancing with mirth. "I'm at home," she said after a moment.

I glanced at Mina, who watched her friend with amusement. I liked their relationship. They were very much at ease with one another. Claire seemed to have the same happy, carefree attitude with her boyfriend, if the continued smile on her face was any indication.

Finally, she sighed, then glanced at Mina with a quick, exasperated eye roll, still amused. "Yes, she's here." Another short pause, then, "Fine." After one last, quick pause, she said, "Love you too," then hung up.

"He figured out what you're up to, didn't he?" Mina said.

Claire nodded, stuffing her phone back in her bag. "Yep. He told me to keep my nose out of it, then that he's on his way home with dinner, and if I wanted to eat it, I needed to kick you out." She grinned, softening her words, then snorted. "He ought to know better than to think that I won't get involved. But I'll let him think he's won for now."

Mina chuckled. "You're terrible. Be nice to the man. He loves you."

The wattage on Claire's smile turned up. "I know. And I will be. I'll promise not to do anything dangerous. I learned that lesson the last time." Her amusement dimmed softly, and I couldn't help but wonder what she was talking about.

"Anyway, we should probably end our little investigative session for now." She walked over to the table and shut her laptop.

I knew that was the cue to leave, but I was still reluctant to get up.

My gaze dropped to Betty, who was curled up in my lap, half-asleep.

I scooped the dog into my arms and stood. "I'm tempted to distract you and make a run for it. She's sweet." Despite my words, I passed the sleepy puppy to her owner.

"Then you'd end up with Ozzie at your door. He's as much in love with her as you are."

Understandable. The little fluffball had me seriously considering getting a dog. I wasn't sure how I'd work out letting a puppy outside to potty during the day, but I could probably make something work. Maybe I could just bring it with me on jobsites. Lots of people had work dogs.

The sound of paper tearing snapped me out of my thoughts. Mina had ripped the page containing the list of names off the notepad.

"I'll just take this with me." A secretive smile flitted over Mina's face. "He can't accuse you of meddling if there's no evidence."

Claire laughed. "He still will, but he won't be able to prove it. Can you email me that list?"

"Sure." Mina pushed away from the table and got up.

Together, the three of us crossed to the front door. Claire had her hands full of dogs, so I opened the door, letting Mina pass through first. With a smile, I turned to Claire. "Thank you for including me in your fact-finding mission."

"Of course. You're as much a part of this as Mina. It affects you both."

True. I gave a short nod. "Still, I appreciate it."

"You're welcome."

Mina tugged on my sleeve. "Come on. Just because she kicked us out doesn't mean I'm ready to give up searching yet." She waved the sheet of yellow paper. "The Juneau library is open until eight."

For a split second, I debated telling her no.

It wasn't that I didn't want to.

I did.

But I wanted more so to spend time with her than to solve the mystery, and that was a disaster waiting to happen. She was my client. Dad's first rule of business had always been not to mix business with pleasure. None of his workers were allowed to date our clients, and when it came to doing business with friends, he drafted detailed contracts and made sure the other party understood the terms.

Despite that, though, I couldn't stop the words that came out of my mouth: "Okay, sounds good."

When she turned that wide smile on me that made her blue eyes shine, I knew I was in trouble, and that Dad's rule was toast.

CHAPTER 9

Mina

I had lost my ever-loving mind.

What was I thinking, inviting Luke to research with me? I could have easily waved goodbye as we left Claire's and gone to the library by myself.

But no. Here I was, in my car, following him along Glacier Highway into Juneau.

The twenty-five-minute drive was entirely too long. I had too much time to think. To second guess myself and to wonder about the man in the pickup truck, leading the way.

Things like, so what if he was six years younger? We were both adults. And he was kind. How often did I meet a handsome—unattached—man who wasn't full of himself?

Never.

Because I lived in the boonies, where the most action I saw on a regular basis was in the summer months when Garrett Wier came down off the mountain to do his grocery shopping, but also decided his clothes needed a better clean than what he could do at his off-grid cabin and stripped down to nothing but a pair of cut-off jean shorts as he walked around town, while every other stitch he owned was in a washer at the laundromat. He inevitably ended up at my coffeeshop for his monthly coffee splurge. I never had the heart to tell him to cover up. I might not want to see his wrinkly, old-man chest, but he was harmless and one of the kindest souls I'd ever met.

So, where else could I meet a single man who I wouldn't mind seeing bare-chested *and* didn't disgust me with his attitude?

I might as well be on Mars.

With a huff, I ran a hand through my hair. Maybe I could try one of those online dating sites. Juneau wasn't that far away, so if I set my search distance to include it, I might find a decent guy.

There's one right in front of you.

My lips pursed as my inner self voiced her opinion. Apparently, *she* didn't care about the age gap or the fact that we were in a pseudo employer/employee situation.

Just give him a chance.

I rolled my eyes. She wasn't giving up, which made me think.

Was I wrong to push him to the side because of those things? Maybe not for the employment situation. It was never a good idea to get involved with someone you worked with. But was the age difference really that big of a deal?

I mean, he didn't seem all that immature.

My mind wandered to how I was at that age. Immaturity had long since flown the coop when I was twenty-six. A year later, I was a business owner.

Perhaps Luke was similar. He had a good job, and so far, there had been no talk of partying.

A quick chuckle escaped. Listen to me—apparently, mid-twenties equated frat boy in my mind.

An image of a man I rarely thought about floated through my mind.

Corbin Battle.

My jaw worked.

Oh, yeah. There was the reason I had that idea of men in their twenties.

That jerk had played me, led me on, then dumped me when I wanted to get serious. All because he was more interested in chasing all the tail he could than in building a solid relationship.

A bona fide womanizer, whom I'd fallen for hard.

Not all men in their twenties are just out for a quick lay, my inner self cautioned.

Chewing on my lip, I glanced out the side window for a moment. Rationally, I knew that.

But emotionally?

Maybe younger men weren't the only ones who were immature.

I let out a low, soft grunt, not liking the hard truths his presence in my life had brought out.

They were long overdue to be dealt with, though.

See? I could hear the eyebrow raise in that one word.

I couldn't help but chuckle at myself. I knew my subconscious mind was right. It was the part of the human mind always on the ball.

Lips pressed tightly together, I vowed to listen to her a little more often.

Because there was one thing for certain: I didn't want to end up alone. Watching Claire with Ozzie, lately, had made me face that fear head-on. And if Luke was the man meant to keep me from aging by myself, I didn't want to turn him away because of a past hurt.

"Be open-minded," I muttered as we pulled into the library parking lot. "Just let things happen as they're supposed to."

Peptalk over, I turned into a space beside Luke's truck and shut off the engine.

Climbing out, I met him in front of the vehicles, and we went inside.

"Reference is this way." He gestured toward a desk off to the side.

"Do you know how to use a microfiche machine?" I murmured as we approached the desk. "Because I haven't used one since grade school."

He tossed a quick grin at me. "I've never used one. But that's what the librarians are for."

"How have you never used one? You work for a construction company. Don't you have to… I don't know… search databases and such?"

"Yes, but usually just property and permitting records. That's all digital."

We stopped in front of the desk, where a middle-aged gentleman sat. His thin, mousy brown hair was a bit mussed, and thick gray glasses sat on the bridge of his nose.

He greeted us with a kind smile. "Hello. How can I help you folks?"

"We'd like to look at some of your microfiche newspapers," Luke said.

"All right." The man pushed away from the desk. "Have you searched the catalogue yet?"

"No. We weren't sure where to start."

"Come this way." The man motioned us to follow him and led us to a computer along one wall. "All our microfiche is catalogued in various ways on here." He tipped a finger toward the monitor. "Do you know what newspaper and what edition you're looking for?"

Luke and I shared a look.

I lifted a shoulder. "Sort of? We have a list of names and dates." I reached into my purse and removed the folded-up sheet of paper.

"That's more than what some people come with." The man held up a hand. "May I?"

I handed him the list. "Please."

Taking it, he unfolded it and sat down. "I'll get you

started, so you know how to use the database." He typed the first name into the search bar.

A list of results popped up. Withdrawing a pen from his shirt pocket, he wrote down the catalogue number for the first couple of listings, where the name appeared exact. "We can search by date as well, if you want?"

I glanced at Luke, and by some silent communication, we both agreed not to do that. He shook his head, and I turned to the librarian.

"For that name, I think we're good," I said.

The man nodded. "All right." Leaving the paper on the desk, he got up. "I will leave you to it. When you finish your search, bring me the catalogue numbers and I'll fetch the microfiche rolls for you. I will also tell you I don't think you'll get through all the rolls tonight before we close. That's a lot of names."

After we thanked the man, he wandered back to his desk.

Luke motioned for me to take a seat, then crouched beside me. "You search; I'll write." A small crease formed between his brows. "Although I need a pen."

Smiling, I passed him my purse. "There's one in here."

With slightly wide eyes, he took the bag. "You want me to dig through your purse?"

A half-smile tipped my mouth, and I turned toward the computer screen. "There isn't anything in it that's embarrassing." I traded bags like my underwear, so any purse I carried usually only held the essentials.

He opened it and peered inside. "Still. I know several women who guard their bags like Cerberus guards the gates of Hades."

I sent him a quick look, surprised at the reference, then chuckled. "Maybe if you got into it without permission, I'd get a little grouchy."

"Understandable." He reached in and pulled out a pen. With a quick click, he was ready. "Hit me."

I typed in the next name on the list. Within seconds, we had several entries. I read off the catalogue numbers for Luke to write down.

After checking two more names, I paused. "Do we want to get reference numbers for all of the names, or should we stop here for now?"

Luke looked at the paper, cocking his head. He clucked his tongue, then met my gaze. "We could stop. See what pans out in what we have."

I nodded once and pushed back from the desk. "Let's go find that librarian."

That turned out to be the easiest thing about the next fifteen minutes. Who knew microfiche could be so uncooperative?

I heaved a sigh as the microfiche tried to unspool itself again from the machine. "I don't remember it being this hard." I cast a quick look up at Luke, who hovered next to me.

"You want me to try?"

Thoroughly done with fighting the film, I stood up before he could change his mind. "Have at it." I swept a hand toward my vacated chair.

Grinning, he sat down. Lacing his fingers, he stretched out his arms and turned his hands, cracking his knuckles. "I think you just weren't paying attention. It didn't look that difficult."

"Mmm, sure." I crossed my arms and waited for the inevitable chaos.

On his first try, the film slipped right off the reel, flapping noisily.

A soft chuckle escaped my lips.

He shot a wry look at me and tried again.

This time, it tried to slide off again, but he stopped the machine more quickly than before, then manually wound the beginning of the reel until it was no longer loose. When he pushed the button to make the spools automatically spin, it stayed on and advanced the reel.

The grin he tossed me was nothing short of smug.

"That's not the way he showed us how to do it," I argued.

Luke lifted one broad shoulder. "But it worked. Now, what's the first date?" He turned the paper on the desk so he could read it.

I huffed. Show off.

"Grab a chair and sit, so you can read this too." He motioned to the unoccupied rolling chair at the next microfiche station.

Doing as he said, I scooted close.

A second later, I eased away a fraction. He smelled yummy.

The distance didn't help much, but I was soon able to push his deliciousness to the back of my mind as he found the first article. It was about the woman's disappearance.

We both skimmed it, but there was no mention of Parker's Landing or any of its residents.

He moved ahead, and we read the updates, but those, too, were devoid of any clues that would lead us back to town.

For each of the subsequent names, we found more of the same. Nothing that tied any of them to Parker's Landing or Mr. Shuman.

"Well, that was a bust," I said as we left the library.

"No. We can cross all those names off the list."

I raised a finger. "Ozzie would tell you no one is off the list until *proven* otherwise."

Luke's mouth tipped up on one side. "Okay, we can knock those names down, then. Pin them as highly unlikely to be the woman in your wall. You have to admit, it's better than where we started." He stopped in front of his truck.

"I guess so." I gripped the strap of my bag hanging off my shoulder. "Sorry. I'm just upset we didn't find a smoking gun. One thing you'll learn about me is I'm not the most patient person. And after all I went through to get that building, having to wait even longer is driving me insane."

"I get it. And I'll have a crew on standby, so we can get in there as soon as Detective Quartermaine gives you the all-clear."

"I appreciate that." I would be badgering Ozzie every day about releasing the scene. He'd probably get sick of me, but I didn't care. The café renovations needed to happen sooner rather than later. If it wasn't open, it wasn't making money, which meant the mortgage on that part of the business was coming out of my coffeeshop profits and my savings.

"Try not to stress, okay?"

Warm fingers briefly touched my crossed arms, glitching my brain. It took me a moment to register that he was still talking.

"… tomorrow night?"

I blinked. "Sorry. I spaced out." I waved my fingers. "Thinking. Can you repeat that?"

That same look he gave me last week when he showed up in place of his dad entered his storm-gray eyes. The one that said he felt the spark too.

Like the last time, he ignored it. "I asked if you want to come back tomorrow night and look at more names on our list."

"Oh. Um…" I ran through my calendar in my head. There wasn't anything special going on, so I nodded. "Sure. Maybe a little earlier, so we can get through more names, though."

"I can do that. How about we grab dinner first, then come here?"

The glitch from earlier returned and shifted into a full-on meltdown. My mouth worked, but nothing came out.

He chuckled. "We don't have to."

"No!" I shot a hand out, then reeled it back in and cleared my throat.

Dial it back a notch, Mina, sheesh.

I wanted to roll my eyes at myself, but didn't want Luke to think it was aimed at him. His request took me by surprise, as did my response to him backpedaling. Apparently, I was more eager to see where things could go between us than I thought.

Inhaling, I tried again. "Dinner sounds fine. I can be in Juneau by five-thirty."

A slow smile broke over his chiseled features. Those stormy eyes warmed as his grin grew. "Okay. How about we meet here? I'm pretty familiar with the city, but I don't know about you."

"That's fine. I don't come here much." I knew where the big box stores were, but that was about it. I avoided Juneau. Cities weren't my thing. "Just don't pick anything fancy for dinner. I'm coming from the coffeeshop and will likely still be in my usual work uniform of jeans and a t-shirt."

"That works. I'll be coming from work too." He took a step back toward the driver's door of his truck. "So, I guess I'll see you tomorrow, then."

I backed toward my car. "Yep. Tomorrow." With a quick flip of my hand, I spun on my heel just as the eye roll finally released. I couldn't hold it back this time. I sounded like a teenager with her first crush, not a thirty-two-year-old woman who'd been on her fair share of dates.

But none of the men from my past made my insides liquify the way one lopsided smile and a heated look from Luke Decker did.

"Be careful driving home."

His voice carried over the hood of his truck.

The gooeyness going on in my belly intensified. Forget his looks. It was the genuine niceness that truly did me in. I wanted to wrap myself around him and let him hold up my liquifying bones. It was his fault, after all.

I also wouldn't be opposed to him making the liquefaction

worse, but in much more delicious ways than with just his smile and his words.

Down girl. You barely know him, I reminded myself.

I cast a quick glance over as I reached the driver's door. The sun highlighted the blond in his hair, giving him a bit of a halo effect.

Somehow, I doubted the thoughts running through his mind were angelic. His eyes blazed with the same heat burning in my belly.

Barely trusting my voice not to crack, I replied, "I will." My thumb found the button on my door handle to unlock my car. With a quick click, the locks popped, and I climbed inside before he could say or do anything else to turn more of me into a gooey pile of horny woman.

CHAPTER 10
Mina

"Ow!" I shook my hand at the burn of scalding-hot coffee dripping over the web of my thumb. "Damn," I muttered under my breath. Drawing in a hiss of air, I wiped it off with a damp towel, then grabbed a lid and snapped it on the cup. My mother would yell at me to run my hand under cold water, but my skin had long since developed a callous against minor burns.

Adding a sleeve to the cup, I turned and set it on the counter in front of the receipt to which it belonged. Reading the name, I called it out. "Toren."

A mountain of a man walked up, scooping the cup into a hand so big it nearly swallowed it whole. Inky dark eyes stared down at me from beneath thick, black eyebrows and a swath of wavy raven-colored hair.

I kept my expression neutral as I studied him for a quick second. He was new around here. I would remember a man who looked like him. Not just for his height. He was quite handsome as well.

A tourist, maybe? It was that time of year. One I had hoped to capitalize on with the café, but Miranda Benning and her shenanigans set me back too far.

Not that it would have mattered after finding the woman in the wall.

A tight-lipped smile toyed with the man's mouth. He gave a curt nod. "Thanks."

"You're welcome. Have a nice day." I offered him a sunny smile.

Raising his cup in acknowledgment, he turned and walked away. The bell over the door dinged as he left.

Claire darted inside right after he stepped out. She ignored the stranger and got in line.

I caught her eye and waved. She lifted a hand.

The queue of people in front of her moved quickly, thanks to my efficient staff, and Claire quickly placed her order, then made her way down to the end of the counter.

"Hi." I shot a quick grin over my shoulder as I squirted two pumps of toasted marshmallow flavoring into a cup.

"Hey. So, how did your sleuthing with Luke go last night? Find anything interesting?"

Her question was one-hundred-percent innocent, but that didn't stop the blush from coloring my cheeks as I remembered what happened when Luke and I parted ways last night.

I turned my face away before she could see. "It was fine." I picked up the two shots of espresso I'd just brewed and dumped them in the cup with the flavoring before reaching into the fridge beneath the counter for the milk. "We didn't really discover anything. Just likely crossed some names off the list. But we only got through a handful before the library closed. We're going back tonight." I poured about eight ounces of milk into a small, stainless-steel pitcher, then set it on the espresso machine and stuck the steamer wand into the milk.

"That's a bummer." Claire's mouth pulled down.

"Yeah." Snagging a small coffee cup off the stack, I poured house brew into it for the next order while I waited on the milk to steam for the latte. This time, I managed not to burn myself.

After shutting off the steamer, I snapped a lid on the coffee, then called the name on the order. "Karen."

An older woman materialized from behind Claire. This woman, I recognized. I didn't really know her, but I'd seen her around town enough to know she was a local.

She took the coffee and was gone before I could wish her a good day.

"So, did Ozzie tell you anything?" I asked, forgetting about the woman.

Claire tipped her head side-to-side. "Sort of. He didn't want to, but I badgered him to give me something. He confirmed it's a woman. He also said the clothing on the body looked like it was from the eighties, and that they think she was stabbed. I guess there were slits in her clothes that looked like knife wounds."

I grimaced. Hopefully, the woman hadn't suffered much from those wounds. I could only pray it had been quick.

My mind went to the list of names we'd created as I wondered who it could be. "What about her clothing makes them think it was a woman from the eighties?"

"She had on a shirt with shoulder pads and stirrup pants."

Interesting. "That could be the early-nineties too," I said.

"That's what I told him. He gave me a look like I'd lost my mind, so I pulled up an image of an actress from 1991 and showed it to him. She had on both." A cheshire grin split her face. "Then I told him it was a good thing he confided in me."

I laughed, glancing back as I made a cappuccino. "I bet he loved that."

Claire chuckled. "I got an eye roll, then he changed the subject. I couldn't get any more out of him about the woman after that."

"Well, that's something. It gives Luke and me a place to focus our search tonight."

A sly look crossed my best friend's face. "Is that the only reason you're going back tonight?" Claire raised a hand and pointed a finger at me, swirling it. "I saw that blush."

Like it had a mind of its own, the fire returned to my face. "We're researching." I ducked my head, but I doubted I was quick enough if her renewed laugh was anything to go by.

Who are you fooling? You know it's more than that.

A soft huff passed my lips as my mind reminded me of the flaming pile of hormonal woman Luke reduced me to last night with that cockeyed smile.

"No one would fault you if you were doing more than just researching. He's quite yummy. And he seems nice."

"He is." I glanced up as I reached for a lid. "And fine, you caught me. We're having dinner before we research." Resolving not to be a chicken, I met Claire's suddenly wide-eyed stare.

A slow smile spread over my friend's face. "I knew it." She let out a little squeal and clapped her hands. "When you're ready for a double date, you'll have to let me know."

Despite the turmoil in my brain over my feelings about the whole Luke situation, one corner of my mouth lifted at her enthusiasm. "We haven't even had our first date yet, so it might be a while." I set the cappuccino on the counter and called the name on the receipt, then picked up the next order. It was Claire's.

Automatically, I reached for a paper cup, then paused as I read the order. With an eyebrow quirked, I looked at her. "Iced coffee?" She almost always ordered a hot latte.

"It's hot outside." She waved a hand toward the window, then gestured to her sleeveless dress. "The AC in my temporary office is terrible. Until this heatwave breaks, it's iced coffee and water for me at work."

My nose wrinkled, but I didn't argue. Moving toward the espresso machine, I set the cup down and reached for a portafilter to fill it full of grounds. "How long until your office is rebuilt?" The fire that Grace Alonso set in her attempt to destroy evidence had completely destroyed Claire's real estate office.

"With the rate insurance is moving? Probably next year. I just hope the heat works better than the air-conditioning, or it's going to be a long winter."

A short chuckle slid past my lips. "That's no lie. We'll have to find you some portable heaters if that's the case."

"For sure, because I refuse to freeze."

I didn't blame her. I loved Alaska, but the cold sucked. It was home, though, so I knew I'd never leave for warmer pastures.

Finishing Claire's coffee, I handed it to her.

"Thanks. I better run. Call me later and let me know how your evening goes?" She waggled her eyebrows, grinning.

"It's just dinner. I'm sure it will be typical."

Claire hummed. "Maybe. But I still want to hear how it went and whether you think a relationship with him could work. I also want to know if you two find out anything about our Jane Doe."

Now that I could understand. I nodded. "I'll let you know what we uncover." And that was all I was promising because I wasn't sure what I was even willing to admit to myself about how I felt about Luke.

A sly grin spread over Claire's face as she backed away from the counter. "Don't think I didn't notice the dodge." She tipped a finger at me. "I expect a full report later."

I just stared back, unwilling to commit.

Raising one eyebrow, she waved the finger, then turned, heading for the door. "Have fun."

Chuckling, I shooed her away. "I will. Go swelter." She was relentless.

On a laugh, Claire left.

CHAPTER 11

Luke

Only the steady beat of my fingers drumming the steering wheel filled the silence in my truck cab as I waited on Mina.

I wasn't sure what possessed me to ask her out yesterday. All day, I'd been on edge about this "date." We hadn't called it that, but from the lust burning in her eyes last night that she tried to conceal, and the answering need still coursing through my veins, that's exactly what it was. A date.

Maybe it was the ambiguity around our evening plans that had me walking a tightrope.

Or it could just be the woman.

Mina had the potential to be more than just someone to go out with and have some fun in the bedroom. She was older, for one thing. I knew that didn't always mean a woman wanted a relationship, but she didn't strike me as the bed-hopping type.

And to be honest, I didn't want a woman like that. I wasn't a dumb college student anymore and hadn't been for several years. I had a career—a good one—and I was ready for more. It was too soon to tell if Mina could be the woman who would be by my side when we were old and gray, but I could definitely see her in that role.

Time would tell.

Soon enough, Mina pulled into the library parking lot and a space across from my truck. When her door cracked open and one slender leg emerged, bare from mid-thigh down thanks to her shorts, my heart rate kicked up, thumping in my chest. She wasn't a tall woman, but she had long, shapely legs.

Suddenly, I wanted to see her in a short skirt and a killer pair of heels.

Shoving the vision of her strutting around in black stilettos from my mind, I got out of my truck.

Catching sight of me, Mina smiled and waved.

I lifted a hand. "Hey."

"I hope you haven't been waiting long. It took me longer to get away than I planned."

"You're fine. I've only been here about five minutes."

"Good. So, where are we going to eat? I'm starving."

"How does pizza sound?"

Her chin bobbed once. "I like pizza."

I tipped my head toward my truck. "Hop in, then. There's a great place not too far from here. They sell it by the slice, so we won't have to wait long."

"You don't have to tell me twice." She hurried around me toward the car. "I haven't eaten since lunch, and that was just a sandwich."

"You were that busy?" I asked as we got in the truck.

"Yeah. It's tourist season." She buckled up.

I did the same and started the engine, then pulled out of the space I'd backed into. She wasn't wrong about that. Even here in Juneau, there were more people than usual. It was great for the businesses that relied on tourist revenue, but it would be nice when things weren't quite so crowded again.

"But I don't want to talk about crazy tourists." She waved a hand before settling it into her lap. "I have news."

"Oh?" Chancing a quick glance her way, I quirked an eyebrow.

"Claire stopped in for coffee this morning. She quizzed Ozzie last night and wrangled some more information out of him. Apparently, the woman was wearing a shirt with shoulder pads and stirrup pants. That narrows our search to women who went missing in the eighties and early nineties."

"That's a manageable list." That cut the number of names down to just a handful.

"I know. Although I'm not sure why we're still looking. Ozzie undoubtedly has the same information." She bit the corner of her lip and glanced out the window.

"I'm sure he does, but maybe we can help him narrow it down some. I know with a murder investigation, it'll be all hands on deck, but the department is still small. It can't hurt to have a couple extra sets of eyes." I turned the corner.

"True. I'm not sure that's the way he'll see it, though." A soft, impish smile lit her face. "Claire will get him on our side, I'm sure."

I chuckled, making another turn. "I bet she will." Mina's café reno wasn't my first run-in with Claire Holmes. Because our jobs were related, we'd met before. The woman was tenacious. I could imagine how that would serve her to get what she wanted from her boyfriend.

It didn't hurt that Claire was a beautiful woman. Detective Quartermaine didn't stand a chance with her combination of beauty and brains.

I spared a quick glance at the woman beside me.

Claire's friend was a lot like her in that department. An enticing blend of beauty and intellect. One I found quite captivating.

Returning my attention to the road, I saw the sign for the pizza place up ahead and maneuvered my truck into a parking space on the street. After cutting the engine, I hopped out, meeting Mina on the sidewalk in front of the shop.

"We're not even inside and my mouth is already watering." She tossed me a quick smile and headed for the door.

"It tastes as good as it smells too." Holding the door for her, I followed her inside, and we got in line.

The queue in front of us was short. In minutes, we each had a giant slice of pizza and a drink. I spotted a table near the window and headed for it.

"This place is cute." Mina set her drink on the table, then sank into the black metal chair. "How did you find it?"

"My dad, actually. He brought me here one day when I was a teenager. It was summer, so I was on one of the construction crews as a grunt. We came here for lunch." I sat down across from her, picking up my pizza slice. "I'm here a lot. The pizza is good and it's a quick meal."

"It certainly smells good." She picked up her pizza, folding it in half to take a bite.

I about swallowed my tongue as her pretty pink lips wrapped around the end of the slice. Something hot and needy unfurled in my belly as her eyelids fluttered closed and she let out a soft moan of pleasure.

Sweet Jesus. Dinner was a bad idea.

Forcing my eyes elsewhere, I took a bite of my own slice. How was eating pizza erotic? Was I that hard up for sex that watching Mina eat about set me off?

"So, how is your dad? You said he's been transferred to cardiac rehab, right?"

Her words put a bit of a damper on my libido. "Right. He's doing as well as expected, I suppose. Chugging along with therapy and not happy about being laid up. My poor mom has her hands full keeping him from going stir-crazy."

Mina chuckled softly. "I bet. For a man who's used to being on the go and on job sites all day, it's probably torture.

My own dad would be watching the clock, waiting for them to spring him."

I smiled. "Yeah. My mom's spending as much time with him as she can, so he's not too bored, but it's not the same as going out and living his daily life. I don't think he's quite wrapped his head around the fact it'll never be the same again, either. He's going to have to give up some control of the business and let me do more."

"Are you ready for that?" she asked, lifting her pizza slice to take another bite.

I twitched a shoulder in a small shrug. "I guess. It was always sort of the plan for me to run the business. But I figured I'd have more time to learn it all before that happened." I had also planned to hire a project manager so I could continue the architectural side of things. Depending on when Dad came back, I might do that sooner rather than later. Trying to do both was already almost more than I could handle alone. In reality, I shouldn't even be out with Mina this evening. Or last evening, for that matter. I had too much work to do.

The late nights were worth it, though, to get to know her and to dig into the mystery at her café.

"I would offer to help, but there's a reason I hired your dad to do my renovation." A sardonic tilt lifted one side of her mouth.

An answering one drew up the right side of my face. "I appreciate the sentiment, but I'll be fine. Some of the crew have picked up a bit of the slack. We're managing."

"Good." Turning her pizza slice, she bit off a corner of the crust.

"So, do you have any siblings?" she continued, several moments later.

My head bobbed. "I have a younger sister. She's just graduated from the University of Anchorage with a business degree. She's been doing some catering and trying to set up her own party planning business."

"Seriously? That's amazing. If you bring me some of her business cards, I'll set them out at the coffeeshop. You'd be surprised by the number of people I get looking for someone to cater or plan events."

I smiled. "I'll do that. She's always looking for ways to drum up business." Polishing off the last of my pizza, I wiped the grease from my fingers and face. In just a couple more bites, Mina finished.

Grabbing my drink, I pushed away from the table. "Ready?"

She nodded and stood.

After disposing of our trash, we headed out to the truck and in minutes, were back at the library.

Cool air blasted us in the face as we stepped inside.

My gaze roved over the cavernous space. There were more people here today than yesterday, but it was earlier too.

Heading for the reference desk, the same librarian from last evening sat at the computer. He glanced up as we approached and smiled. "Back again?"

With a polite smile, I nodded. "And with a shorter list."

"That's good, I hope?"

"It is," Mina replied.

"Good. When you're ready for me to fetch the microfiche, just let me know."

"Thank you," I said, then gave Mina a nudge toward the catalogue computer.

Grabbing an extra chair, I pulled it over and sat at an angle. Mina sank into the rolling chair in front of the monitor and opened her handbag, taking out the list of names and a pen before handing them to me.

"All right"—she cracked her knuckles—"let's do this." Fingers poised over the keyboard, she typed in the first name.

We worked through the list, and I wrote down the reference numbers. There seemed to be more articles on these women, perhaps because the cases were newer.

"That's the last thing I see for this one." Mina glanced over, having scrolled through the search results for the final name on our list.

"Sounds good. Hang out here. I'll be right back." Getting up, I headed over to the reference librarian and gave him the list.

Taking the paper, he glanced at it. "Let's go one name at a time, yeah? So I don't overwhelm you with microfiche rolls."

"That works."

"Great." The man pushed away from the desk. "Give me just a couple minutes. I'll bring them to you." He nodded toward the microfiche readers.

"Okay, thank you." Backing up, I turned and caught Mina's attention and tipped my head toward the readers.

She got up and headed that way, picking up the extra chair and bringing it with her.

An older gentleman shuffled in front of her, not paying any attention to his surroundings. She paused, waiting for him, then continued, reaching the readers at the same time I did.

"It's busy in here," she commented, setting the chair down.

"Yeah. I think this place is a designated cooling shelter." Once more, I glanced around the library. Many people were just sitting around in groups on their phones, although there were also plenty who had books open.

"This time of year is when I wish it were worth it to have a pool up here."

I chuckled. "There are plenty of natural streams and lakes you can take a dip in."

She shuddered. "Been there, done that. That's a folly of youth. Even in the summer, the water is cold."

"Nah, it's refreshing." One side of my mouth tilted as I turned my head to look at her.

She laughed, sitting down in the extra chair, leaving the one in front of the machine for me. "Sure. If you say so. I'll stick to tropical waters, though."

An image of Mina in a bikini popped into my head. Those full breasts pushing against her t-shirt would fill a swim top quite nicely. And the bottoms would show off the swell of her hips to perfection.

Swallowing hard, I worked to banish the picture before my body reacted. I sank into the chair beside her and crossed one leg over my knee, leaning forward while we waited on the librarian. "The beach does sound nice. What do you think? Key West?"

She wrinkled her nose. "No. Too touristy. I'd rather go someplace like Aruba or the U.S. Virgin Islands."

"How are those less touristy?"

"They're probably not, but they're bigger, so fewer people per square mile. Key West is crowded."

"Have you been there?" She talked like she knew from experience.

"Yes. Many years ago. It was a family vacation. We had fun, but there were definitely a lot of people around. When I go to the beach now, I don't want to fight for towel space with twelve families, each with three to five kids. I just want to read my book in peace."

"What would you read?"

She lifted a shoulder. "Probably some romance. I like my sappy books." A smile slid over her face. "Let me guess. You like action novels?"

"Sci-fi. And westerns."

Before either of us could ask more questions, the librarian returned with a stack of microfiche rolls. After thanking the man, I took the top one off the stack and threaded it through the reader.

"What reference number am I looking for? And what's the woman's name again?"

Mina picked up the paper the librarian left with the rolls. "The first name on the list is Kathy Burl." She glanced at the number on the roll I'd loaded, then read the reference point.

I spun the dial, and the fiche whirred through the machine. In moments, we were huddled together, reading the news article on the screen.

The scent of coffee and vanilla tickled my nose, along with a heady mix of something unique to Mina. It set off a firestorm in my blood, and it was all I could do not to lean in and bury my nose in her hair.

Clearing my throat, I checked the paper in her hands and moved on to the next news article as I scooted my chair slightly to the side, under the guise of getting a better view of the screen.

We worked our way through the reference numbers for the first name on the list, then returned the fiche when nothing of note came up. The librarian brought us the rolls for the second name. Again, nothing popped up as unusual or indicated that the woman had a connection to the antique store, Walter Shuman, or Parker's Landing.

Microfiche slapped against the roll as I rewound it. Removing the roll from the machine, I reached for the first roll for the third name on the list, Moira Duluth. The librarian had been watching us and was proactive this time, taking the rolls we'd looked through and bringing us the next ones.

Having gotten the hang of loading the fiche and finding the reference points, I quickly found the first article, and we skimmed it.

Mina lifted a hand and pointed at the screen. "I know that name."

I looked at where she pointed. "Rich Stevenson?" Quickly, I read the paragraph. It said Mr. Stevenson was Moira's boyfriend. The article quoted him about the last time he saw her.

"Yes." Mina let her hand fall back to her lap. She pulled the corner of her bottom lip between her teeth, glancing away in thought.

"Is it someone who lives in town?" I didn't recognize the name, but if it wasn't an old neighbor or someone related to a person I went to school with, I probably wouldn't. Not unless I saw him. I was better with faces than names.

Her eyebrows drew together. "Maybe." She wrote the name on the sheet with the missing persons. "I need to think about it."

"We can look him up, too, if you want."

"Maybe," she said again. "It might come to me."

Giving her another quick glance—she still had that damn lip between her teeth—I moved on to the next reference number.

"This says she was a clerk for the title office in Juneau," I said, reading the article. "She disappeared after work one night. Her parents said she never came home."

"She was still living at home?" Mina leaned closer again.

"I guess so. That wasn't that unusual for that period, though, right?"

Mina lifted a shoulder. "Not really, no. A lot of Alaskan families still live in multi-generational households. If she wasn't married, I could see her living at home at that age. Does it say where they lived?"

"Umm…" I skimmed the article. "Not specifically, but since she worked in Juneau, I would assume they lived in the city or close by."

"What else does it say about her?"

"Nothing, really. Just the basics." I ran my eyes over the article again, but there really wasn't much.

"Does it say if the police had any suspects or leads?"

I skimmed toward the end, where it talked about the

investigation. "The camera footage from the store caught her car leaving, but nothing else."

Mina tipped her head. "Did they ever find her car?"

"That's a good question. This article doesn't mention it, but it's from just a couple days after her disappearance." I glanced at the notebook page with the reference numbers. "Let's look." Spinning the dial, I advanced the microfiche to the next article. Together, we skimmed it, but it didn't mention her car. Neither did the next several articles.

A chime sounded overhead as I put the last roll of microfiche into the machine, then an automated voice came over the speaker. "The library is closing in fifteen minutes, thank you."

With a frown, I hurriedly advanced the film. "Let's hope we can get through this last one," I muttered.

"I wish we had more time," Mina said. "I'd like to look into family and friends for these women. Maybe look up Rich Stevenson. I still haven't remembered why I know that name."

"We can go back to my place, if you want, and use my laptop to do some internet searches."

Mina tipped her head, thinking. "Possibly. I can't stay too long, though. Five a.m. comes early."

One side of my mouth tilted up. "That it does." When she smiled back and my heart thumped, I turned away so I could focus. Her pretty lips and twinkling blue eyes were too damn distracting. Scrolling forward, I found the first article.

We made quick work of reading it and the next few short ones in the paper over the subsequent days, but any new information petered out as the case grew cold.

"They never did find her car," Mina said as I removed the roll from the machine.

"No. But that's not all that surprising. There's so much wilderness around here that no one ever visits, hers probably isn't the only vehicle that's been ditched and never found." Gathering the rolls, I stood. "You ready?"

"Yep." Scooting back her chair, she got up before returning it to where we found it earlier, then met me at the reference desk, and we walked out.

"So, do you want to come back to my house for research?" I glanced at our vehicles, then at her. I wasn't sure it was the best idea, considering the way I wanted to reach for her every time I looked at her pretty face, but I couldn't help but hope she would say yes. Forget the sexual attraction; I just wanted to spend more time in her presence.

"Um…" Her voice trailed off, and she turned her gaze toward the road, a small wrinkle forming between her eyebrows. "Sure. But like I said, I can't stay long. Maybe we can come up with a few points to dig into separately when we have time? You know, split the workload?"

I nodded. "Sounds good. Do you want to just follow me?"

"Yes." As soon as the word left her mouth, she took a step toward the curb.

I followed. "I'll go slow so I don't lose you."

A wide smile split her face. "Text me your address. Just in case."

"Will do." Crossing the lot, I got into my truck, sending her a quick text as I started the engine. After buckling up and checking to make sure she was ready to go, I pulled onto the street.

Nerves strummed in my gut, twisting my insides. Which, honestly, boggled my mind. Women never made me nervous. I knew I was handsome and charming. My ego was relatively healthy—but not overblown.

But it felt like the stakes were higher with Mina. I didn't want to misstep and ruin any chance I had with her.

Shifting in my seat, I resolved to be on my best behavior. No crazy, overt innuendo or flirting. But not so little she didn't think I was interested. Somehow, I had to find the balance.

I glanced in my rearview mirror, seeing her car behind me. My blood heated once more, knowing she was following me home.

Blowing out a breath, I tamped down the need.

Balance, I reminded myself.

CHAPTER 12
Mina

When we left the library, following Luke home so we could continue our search felt like a great idea. I wanted to know more about the women we'd identified. We were on to something. I could feel it.

But now, as I stepped out of my car and looked up at the two-story gray house with its black shutters and porch railings, I couldn't help but think about what else might happen once we were inside. All evening, I'd been exceedingly conscious of his magnetic male presence sitting so close while we combed through thirty-year-old articles. The public setting had helped keep my inner hussy at bay, but we'd be alone now.

I was in some serious trouble.

Resisting him in public wasn't terribly difficult. I just reminded myself there were others present.

But alone? In his house? Where there was a bed just feet away? This was a fully caffeinated latte after dinner bad idea with a side of extra syrup.

Could I stop myself from following him up the steps to the front door?

Not on my life.

Keys jingled as he unlocked the door and let us inside.

"You can set your bag there if you want." He tossed his keys onto an entry table, then pointed at it.

I took the folded-up notes from my purse, then set my bag next to his keys. He led me down the short hallway, past a bathroom and a study, to an open-plan room that spanned the rear of the house.

My eyes roamed over the space, taking in the built-in bookshelves flanking a wall-mounted television, a gray couch and chair sitting opposite. To my left, a modern kitchen took up a third of the long room. The soft gray cabinets added a warm touch to the off-white walls and thin-veined, white quartz counters. Under my feet, blonde wood stretched, dotted with rugs in varying shades of gray and cream.

In front of me was a six-person oak dining table. Beyond it, a sliding glass door led to a deck that overlooked a back-yard rimmed by pine trees. Through the boughs, I could just make out the neighbors' houses.

The effect was an interior space that was soothing and inviting, not cold, like one would first think with the lack of color inside.

"Have a seat." Luke gestured to the sofa. "Do you want something to drink?"

"Water?"

With a nod, he moved into the kitchen, filling two glasses from the filtered water tap at his kitchen sink.

I sank onto one corner of the couch, then immediately regretted that decision when I realized I would be trapped between the arm and Luke's body. He'd have to sit close so we could both see the laptop screen.

Pulling my bottom lip between my teeth, I worried the corner as I debated whether to get up and move to the table.

"Let's sit over here," Luke said.

I glanced back to see him standing next to the table.

"We'll have more room to spread out."

Grateful I wouldn't look like a fool bounding out of my seat thirty seconds after I sat in it because I decided I didn't want to be so close to his enthralling presence, I hopped up and came around the couch to take a seat on one side of the table. Luke set the glasses down but didn't pull out a chair to sit.

"I'm going to grab my laptop. Hang on." In a flash, he disappeared down the short hallway and into the study. When he reappeared moments later, he had a silver MacBook in his hands.

Taking a seat at the end of the table beside me, he opened it. "So, what do you want to look up first?"

Those long-lashed gray eyes lifted to meet mine. For a moment, I got lost in their depths. He had such pretty eyes. Like the turbulent ocean in the winter when one of the big low-pressure systems was about to roll in and dump a bunch of snow on us.

A dark gold eyebrow rose over one eye.

I blinked and cleared my throat, glancing down at my notes. "Um…" Inhaling a breath through my nose, I forced my mind back onto the task at hand and read over the things I'd jotted on the page earlier. "Why don't we look up Rich Stevenson? See if, maybe, I can figure out why I know that name?"

Luke nodded once. "Okay."

His fingers dashed over the keyboard, then he flicked them over the trackpad. "I'm not sure what we're looking for." He turned the computer so I could see the screen.

I scooted closer and leaned in, looking at the pictures that populated the top of the search results. "There." I pointed at an image of a man in his fifties. "I knew I recognized the name. He's a local handyman. I've never used his services, but I've seen him around town. Do you know him?" It would make sense if he did, since they might run in the same business circles.

Luke squinted at the screen. "I don't, but I'll ask my dad. I haven't run too many projects in Parker's Landing. Mostly, I worked on the crew before college, but I don't remember anyone named Rich on them. Since then, I spend most of my time in an office, drawing up plans. Dad might know more."

Staring at Rich Stevenson's picture, my mind spun out in several directions. We had a direct connection between Moira Duluth and Parker's Landing now. With someone who knew construction…

The implications of that hit, and I reached out, tugging the laptop closer so I could type.

"What?" Luke asked. "What did you remember?"

"Nothing. I just had a thought. Rich would know how to cut open and repair a wall. I want to know if there's a connection between him and Walter Shuman." I typed both names into the search box.

Results popped up, and I scrolled.

But nothing in the list connected the two men.

My shoulders slumped. "Damn. I was hoping there'd be a smoking gun."

"I think if it were that easy, the cops would have found it a long time ago."

"Maybe. But they didn't know Moira was in Mr. Shuman's wall."

Luke tipped his head. "True."

Mouth pressed tight, I stared at the laptop screen and tapped my fingernails on the table. Was it Rich Stevenson who was responsible for Moira's death? Or Walter Shuman? Or both? If it was Rich, how did she end up in the wall at the antique store? He had to know Mr. Shuman, somehow.

One thing was certain: it was Moira Duluth's body we found. The other women didn't have any ties to Parker's Landing. Rich Stevenson's role as Moira Duluth's boyfriend at the time of her disappearance gave her a direct connection to the town.

I leaned sideways, taking my phone from the back pocket of my jeans.

"Who are you calling?"

"Ozzie." I found his number in my contacts and touched his name.

"Put it on speaker," Luke said.

Tapping the icon, I put the phone on the table as it rang.

"Hey, Mina." Ozzie's deep voice came over the line. "I gave Claire a full report on what I found out today, which wasn't all that much. I'm sure she'll tell you about it in the morning when she stops in for coffee."

"That's great," I said. "But it's not why I'm calling. Luke and I discovered something."

"Oh?" Intrigue with a healthy dose of skepticism tinged Ozzie's voice.

"So, you know that list of names we came up with from the missing persons database?"

He expelled a breath, clearly exasperated. "You mean the list I told Claire to forget? That I was working on it and to let me handle things? That list?"

I rolled my eyes, a smirk tipping one side of my mouth as I glanced at Luke. "Yeah. That one. It's a good thing we didn't listen to you. We narrowed it down based on the style of clothing on the body. I think we might know who she is."

"Because of her clothes?" His voice was full of skepticism now.

"No." I sighed. Why did men have to be so dense sometimes? "We went to the library and looked up the articles on their disappearances. One woman stuck out to me because of her boyfriend. He's quoted in one of the articles. His name is Rich Stevenson. I recognized the name, but couldn't place it, so we searched it. Once I saw his picture, it clicked. He's a local handyman."

A short pause came over the line. "Really?" The intrigue and interest were back in his tone, the skepticism gone now.

I chuckled. "Yes."

"That's good work, Mina. I retract my earlier statement about the list. Maybe I should tell Chief Riggs to hire you as my partner."

Snorting softly, I glanced at Luke with a grin. "I'll stick to slinging coffee, but I'll happily take any consulting fees the department wants to send me."

Ozzie laughed. "I'll keep that in mind, but I wouldn't hold out hope."

"Oh, don't worry, I won't." I knew the finances for most law enforcement departments were tighter than the caps on some of my syrup flavor bottles.

"So, what's this woman's name?"

"Oh." I laughed. I hadn't mentioned that. "Moira Duluth."

"I'm going to talk to my dad," Luke interjected. "See if he knows Rich and what he can tell us about him. We tried to find a connection online between Rich and Walter Shuman, but there wasn't anything that we saw. Dad might have some insights."

"Just warn him not to say anything to Rich, if he knows him. I don't want to tip him off before I've had a chance to speak to him."

"No worries there. He'll keep it quiet."

"So, what *did* you learn today?" I tipped my head, staring at the phone with a slight smile.

Ozzie chuckled. "You're as bad as Claire. There really wasn't much. I spent the day trying to track down a jeweler who would recognize the necklace we found with the body. Now that I have a possible identity, though, I'll reach out to her family." He sighed. "I'm really never going to hear the end of it if you truly identified her before I could."

"You'd have figured it out. That necklace is a good lead." And was a tidbit of information he hadn't mentioned before, probably on purpose. I knew the police held back things they didn't want made public, so they could use it to be certain they had the right person.

"I just happened to recognize a name," I continued. "I hope we're on the right track. If it's not Moira in the wall, I don't know who it is. None of the other women seem to have a connection to Parker's Landing."

"We'll find out soon enough. I'll locate her family tomorrow. Hopefully, they're still in the area."

"Do you want me to look? I have a computer in front of me." I raised my hands, ready to type.

"No, it's fine. I'll look in the morning. It's getting late, so we should all get some sleep." The pointed note in his tone told me that while he was grateful for the info, I needed to let him do the rest.

And I would.

Mostly.

I would still do my own quick search. It was all public knowledge, after all.

He didn't need to know that, however. "Okay. Will you at least let us know if you make a positive ID?"

"Of course. The department will release a statement."

I narrowed my eyes at the phone. That wasn't what I meant.

"Get some rest, Mina. I'll talk to you later."

A quick huff puffed past my lips. "Fine." Bidding Ozzie goodnight, I hung up. Not skipping a beat, I typed Moira's name into the web browser.

Luke chuckled. "You're googling her family, aren't you?"

"Yep." I had her parents' names from the articles we found at the library. With a few clicks, I found out they lived in Juneau.

The laptop lid slowly closed. I glanced up from the screen at Luke, who used one finger to shut the lid.

"What are you doing?" I asked.

"You found your answer. Ozzie's also right. It's getting late, and you still need to drive home."

My lips twisted, annoyed at his logic. I wanted to keep digging. It was no longer about getting back to my café renovations. I mean, sure, I still wanted that, but now that I had a face to go with the sightless eyes staring back at me from the void in the wall, I wanted her and her family to have closure.

"Come on." Luke pushed away from the table to stand and took my hands in his. "You can come back tomorrow, and we'll do more digging."

I wanted to answer. To tell him that sounded like a great idea. I wanted to know more about Moira and what happened to her.

But I couldn't.

The feel of his work-roughened fingers against my skin short-circuited my thoughts and sent me on a spiral of need that descended straight to my core. My muscles quivered as all thoughts of Moira and her unsolved death were pushed to the dark recesses of my mind by the zing of desire his touch provoked.

He felt it too.

Those storm-gray eyes turned turbulent and a muscle in his jaw ticked silently as our gazes caught and held.

His hands turned in mine, lacing our fingers together. "You should go. So you can get some sleep."

Should I? Sleep was overrated. This deep-seated desire, though… it needed my attention.

"Yeah, probably." My voice came out breathy, choked by the rising heat stoking in my belly. I raised our hands, drawing our bodies closer.

His head dipped.

This was insane. Was I really about to kiss a man I'd known for a week?

The first touch of his lips on mine scrambled my thoughts.

You're about to do a whole lot more than kiss him, my inner voice said, then whooped.

She was right. I was.

The feel of his mouth on mine was as addictive as any drug. Even as I parted my lips so he could gain entry and deepen the kiss, I wanted more.

More kisses.

More touches.

Just... *more.*

Untangling our fingers, I speared them into his hair.

The little grunt he let out sent a ripple of giddy pleasure through me. A moment later, a different sort of pleasure slid through my body when he wrapped his arms around my waist and hauled me into his chest.

Yes!

Heat from the fire burning deep in my belly suffused my skin. I needed out of my clothes before I burned alive where I stood.

Tearing my mouth away, I stared into his turbulent gray eyes, now the same shade as the summer storm clouds. "This is insanity, but I don't want to stop."

Fingers clenched and unclenched against my waist. He swallowed hard. "I didn't bring you here for this."

"I know." The simple sincerity in his voice and in his eyes was all I needed to understand I wasn't leaving any time soon.

Throwing my misgivings and all the reasons why I shouldn't stay into the wind, I closed the gap to kiss him once again.

There was no grunt of surprise this time. We were on the same page now.

Luke's hands climbed up my back to grip my hair. The pull on my scalp amped up the need swirling in my veins, and I pressed closer.

Tightening his grip, Luke lifted me off my feet as he

backed away from the table. His mouth left mine but stayed close enough to brush my lips as he spoke.

"I plan to carry you upstairs now, unless you want to leave."

For a split second, the sane, pragmatic part of my brain reared her head and said I should consider that.

I told her to shut up, then gave a little hop to raise my legs and wrap them around Luke's waist. "What are you waiting for? I'm not going anywhere."

A predatory hunger blazed in his eyes, sending a delicious ripple through my body.

"Yes, ma'am." Spinning on his heel, hands still on my back and wrapped in my hair, he hightailed it to the stairs.

Anticipation built in my belly as he bounded up the steps, two at a time. Once we reached the second floor, we were turning into his bedroom in four long strides.

The door shut with a bang as he kicked it closed on the way to his bed. Light from the street filtered in through the window, casting silvery shadows through the room.

Though his steps were hurried, he placed me gently on the bed against the pillows.

But I didn't want gentle. I was already wound tighter than a corkscrew. Clutching the sides of his face, I pulled him in for a deep kiss.

Madness, my mind whispered.

Pure and utter madness gripped me. I knew this was fast. That I barely knew him. But I couldn't bring myself to care. Not when his soft, lush mouth plundered mine, and his work-roughened hands tunneled beneath my shirt to skim my sides.

Tugging at the hem of his shirt, I practically begged him to take it off without saying a word, too caught up in his kisses to speak.

He understood the message, though, and sat back long enough to yank the shirt over his head.

The filtered glow from the street shone in ripples on his muscled chest. Dark blond hair glittered silver in the light.

Reaching up, I ghosted my palms over his chest. Hard work had sculpted his body, not a gym, and it showed in the firm, sinewy muscles.

"Your turn."

The low rumble of his words washed over me, sending shivers racing down my limbs. Even my toes tingled. With a moan, I let my hands drop away from his body so I could peel off my shirt.

As soon as the fabric left my hand, Luke's hands curled behind my back to unsnap my bra. Cool air dusted over my chest as the black lace fell away.

"I like this." My bra dangled from Luke's finger as he held it up, sparing it a glance. A crooked, rakish smile spread over his face, making his eyes glitter with mischief and need in the low light. "Though I like it better off of you." With a quick flip of his wrist, the scrap of fabric sailed over the side of the bed to the floor.

A soft giggle slid past my lips. "You ought to like my underwear, then, too." I had a thing for matching bras and panties. No one typically saw them, because I rarely dated, but they made me feel sexy, and I liked the confidence boost that feeling gave me.

The smile on his face froze, then slowly died as his gaze drifted down my torso to my hips. His throat worked as he swallowed. "Oh yeah?"

I nodded, biting back a smile. Feeling emboldened by the heavy smolder in his eyes, I raised my hands to the waistband of my shorts and flicked the button with my fingernail. "Wanna see?"

His low laugh rumbled through the room. "Hell, yeah. But I get to take these off you." He batted my hands out of the way, deftly unsnapping the button and pulling down the zipper.

I raised my hips so he could tug the denim down my legs.

The soft hum he let out, followed by the stroke of one finger over my lace-covered core, was enough to make my eyes roll back and the breath leave my body.

"Gorgeous. But they'll still look better on the floor." Hooking his fingers over the top, he yanked.

They didn't get very far before his fingers took their place. With one touch, he pulled a sharp gasp of pleasure deep from my soul. Leaning close, his mouth brushed mine. Waves of pleasure rippled through me from both points of contact, meeting in my stomach to bounce around and ricochet down my limbs.

Then he added his other hand to the mix, cupping my breasts and teasing the tips. It was too much, and the waves of pleasure broke like a tsunami, crashing over me, inundating me with a flood of bliss.

Holy moly…

Maybe the secret to the best sexual encounter of my life was a younger man.

Almost as soon as I had the thought, I waved it away. It had nothing to do with Luke's age. *He* was the deciding factor.

While I lay basking in the warm glow of my orgasm, I watched through hooded eyes as he climbed off the bed and shucked his jeans and boxer-briefs, then reached into his bedside table for a condom, sheathing the viper he unleashed.

I was more than happy to let it bite me.

Heat warmed in my blood once more as he put a knee on the bed, then crawled toward me.

"Do you need another round to warm you up?"

"Only if you want to kill me." The first one about did me in, and he barely touched me.

"Can't have that. I'm not into necrophilia."

The chuckle that comment drew from me died a swift

death as he angled his way between my thighs and joined our bodies.

A spear of white-hot light pierced my brain, blinding me to everything. All I could do was feel.

And hang on as Luke spiraled us up to the heavens so we could hang with the stars. For long moments, we moved together, rolling over the bed, finding new ways to heighten the need coiling like a tightly wound spring. Any second, I knew the tension would break and I would fly apart, harder than the first time.

I still wasn't expecting it, though. When the spring broke free of its bonds, the immediate, fiery blaze of passion that hit me stole my breath and rendered my body immobile as my muscles tensed, then released on wave after wave of the most intense pleasure I'd ever known. As I sank, boneless, into the mattress, Luke's dark growl against my ear as his own climax engulfed him sent a final surge of bliss through my now pliant body.

Like a cocoon, I wrapped myself in the feeling. It had never felt like this before. Never been this good.

Even as I enjoyed the afterglow, the first misgivings cropped up in my mind.

This was supposed to be just great sex, but it already felt like the start of something much, much more.

Was I ready for that?

Was he?

We probably should have talked about where this would go after we did the deed before we did it. I didn't typically put the cart before the horse, but for whatever reason, Luke short-circuited the rational side of my brain.

But boy, did it feel *good*.

CHAPTER 13

Mina

Being in lust with someone wasn't all it was cracked up to be.

Crossing my legs to ward off the pulse of need as a replay of the other night ran through my mind, I glared at Luke's name in my contacts. I don't know why I was even looking at it. I opened my phone to call a supplier while I ate lunch, which now soured in my stomach.

It had been three days. Three! And he hadn't called yet. Oh, he'd texted, but it was to tell me he'd been slammed with work and as soon as some time opened up in his schedule, he'd call so we could get together again.

I was *not* some floozy who was at his beck and call, ready to jump back into his bed at a moment's notice. While I understood work was busy for him—he was running the company in his father's absence and still playing the role of architect, after all—I wasn't a booty call whenever he wanted it.

You shouldn't have given it up so easily, my inner voice reminded me.

Rolling my eyes, I told her to shut up. It was the same voice who told me to jump his bones.

The phone rang in my hand, and I jumped, letting out a soft squeak. It was Claire.

Heart thumping in my chest, I answered. "Hello?"

"Hey. Do you want to come over for dinner tonight?"

My eyebrows twitched in a slight frown. "It's Friday. Don't you and Ozzie want to go out?"

"No. I think he has info on your case. I just got off the phone with him, and he said he couldn't talk because he was busy chasing a lead. I want to pick his brain at dinner, and I thought it might go better if we both attack him."

I chuckled. "That poor man. Okay, I'm in."

There was a short pause. "You said yes fast. I take it Luke still hasn't called?"

Any amusement I felt fled. "No."

"You should call him. Invite him to dinner with us."

"What? No. That's a terrible idea." I refused to beg for a man's affection.

"Why? Relationships aren't a one-way thing, Mina. And some men are dense and need a push. Call him. Make him aware Tuesday wasn't a fluke."

I huffed, leaning back in my office chair, a creak filling the room. The sound grated on my already tightly strung nerves. "I thought he knew that." We hadn't parted Wednesday morning like a one-night stand. There had been cuddles and pillow talk and a tender goodbye kiss that left me aching for more.

The "more" had turned into crickets.

"Well, either you call and invite him, or I will."

My chair creaked again as I abruptly sat up. "No, you won't. Claire—"

She cut me off. "You need to talk to him, and he needs to get his head out of his ass. My house is neutral-ish territory. Plus, I'll feed you both, and you'll get info about the body in the wall. Unless you plan to cut all ties with him and find a new contractor, you need to work this out. I'm not excusing his lack of communication, but he probably has just been really busy."

"So, I'm being a needy girl, is what you're saying?" A modicum of fight left me as her reasoning started to sink in.

Claire chuckled. "Maybe a little. I'm not excusing his behavior, either. You have a right to expect better communication than he's given you after what happened between you. But yes, I do think you're taking it a little overboard. I get why," she hastened to add. "But I also think you need to rein in your anger a bit."

My mouth flattened, and I stared at the calendar on my wall, not really seeing anything I had written there as I thought about what she said.

Maybe I overreacted. Just a bit. Could he do better? Yes. Was the lack of communication a deal-breaker? Not yet.

Claire was right. He and I needed to hash this out. Not just for the sake of my renovations, but because I genuinely thought we had a chance at building a relationship.

Leaning forward, I propped my forehead in my hand. "Fine. I'll call him."

"Wonderful." I could hear the cheery smile I was sure was on Claire's face. "I'll see you both at six."

Muttering an agreement, we said goodbye, and I hung up.

Once more, I found myself staring at Luke's name in my contacts. Would he even answer if I called? Or was he too busy?

Only one way to find out.

Mouth pursed, I tapped his name and lifted the phone to my ear.

It rang four times, then five. Resigning myself to leaving a voicemail, I quickly mapped out what I wanted to say.

So deep into drafting a script, it took me a moment to realize it wasn't his voicemail that picked up.

"Hello? Mina?"

Spine stiffening as I realized I had the man on the phone, I forced my throat muscles to work so I could speak. "Hi."

"Hey. I'm glad you called. Sorry I've been so absent."

"Oh. Um, yeah. I—"

"Terry! Make sure you get the extra piping for the King-fisher's remodel, or you're not going to be able to do much else today." After his initial shout, his voice sounded further away as he moved the phone to talk to someone.

"Sorry," Luke said, his voice growing louder. "It's crazy around here. Let me get somewhere quiet."

"No, it's okay. I won't keep you. I just wanted to ask you to come to dinner at Claire's tonight. Six o'clock."

"Claire's? Does Ozzie have info on the case?"

"She thinks so. I'd also like to see you."

There. I put it out there that I wanted more than a one-night stand. It was up to him where this went now.

"I'd like that too." His voice grew quiet. "I'm sorry I haven't called. Work... Well, it's no excuse to ignore you. I should have called. I'm not very good at relationships, Mina."

And just like that, most of my ire evaporated. I wanted to hold onto it, but the fact he apologized without any prompting made it nearly impossible.

A soft smile formed, and I leaned back in my creaky chair. "You're forgiven. This time," I added, meaning it. I wouldn't chase a man who didn't want to walk with me in a relationship.

"It won't happen again. I do want to make a go of this. Tuesday was..." His voice trailed off.

I knew how he felt. I couldn't put it into words, either.

"Yeah, I agree," I said.

A shout in the background of the call drew his attention away again.

"I'll let you go," I said. He wasn't the only one who needed to get back to work.

"Okay. I'll see you this evening. Hopefully, I won't be late.

But I *will* be there, and I promise you'll get my undivided attention."

I smiled. "Sounds good."

With a quick goodbye, he hung up.

Staring at the darkened screen for a long moment, I set the device down and sighed. Cautious optimism lit in my chest. I wanted things to work with Luke. Badly. Our one night together had set aside my misgivings about his age.

But I wouldn't unreservedly fall at his feet. Letting him—or anyone—stomp all over my heart wasn't something I'd ever do.

CHAPTER 14

Luke

Goosebumps prickled my skin and a fine tremor went through my hand as I raised it to press the doorbell at Claire's. Trepidation skittered over my nerve endings. Mina's car was already in the driveway. She'd sounded distant and a little angry when we first spoke earlier today. I couldn't blame her. I'd virtually ghosted her.

Not intentionally.

Well, not entirely.

Subconsciously, I think, something had stopped me from calling her or texting her. Not because I didn't want to spend time with her, but because I wasn't really sure how to handle the feelings she provoked. No woman had ever invaded my every waking thought the way she had. Not contacting her was my way of giving myself space, and I'd used my schedule as an excuse.

The door swung inward, revealing Ozzie's stern but welcoming face. "Hey. Come on in." Stepping back, he nodded for me to come inside.

I walked in, letting my eyes track over the living and dining areas beyond the entryway. Mina sat at the table with Claire, sipping from a glass of water.

My heart sped up at the sight of her smiling at her friend over the rim of her glass. When she turned to look at me, a guardedness entered her eyes. My nerves increased. Was she still upset? I needed to do some groveling.

Lifting a hand in greeting, I smiled. "Hey."

A hesitant, shy smile flitted with her pretty lips. Some of the guardedness was chased away by a quick lick of heat in her blue eyes. "Hey."

"No bedroom eyes in my house." Ozzie waved a finger back and forth between us.

Mina's cheeks colored.

I laughed, hoping to keep Mina from feeling embarrassed about our relationship—or lack thereof. "We'll behave."

"Good. Because as much as I would love to talk about something besides the body you two found, that's not it." Grinning, Ozzie crossed to the kitchen.

I glanced over and saw aluminum trays of crab and other sides on the island. Ozzie hefted a tray of crab legs.

Hurrying over, I gestured to the pans. "Here, let me help." In a couple of strides, I was at his side, grabbing the tray full of scalloped potatoes.

"Thanks," Ozzie murmured.

We carried the food to the table. Someone—Claire or Ozzie—had already brought over dishes and silverware.

"Do you want something to drink?" Claire asked me, getting up.

"I can get it," I replied, looking up as I set the last tray down.

"It's fine. I want some water, anyway."

"Oh. All right. Just water, too, please." Offering her a quick smile, I took a seat across from Mina. Ozzie sat next to me.

When Claire returned to the table a few moments later, I smiled at her in thanks as she set a glass of water at my side.

Rounding the table, she sat down. "Dig in," she said,

reaching for a set of tongs to put some crab legs on her plate. "I'm starving."

"You know, when you said you'd feed us, I was thinking a casserole. Not Kellerman's." Mina took the tongs from Claire.

"Yeah, well, we both had long days and didn't feel like cooking." Claire nodded toward Ozzie.

"I'm not complaining." I took the tongs when Mina passed them over. "I like crab legs. Thank you for dinner."

"Same," Mina said, directing a smile at Claire. "Thanks."

"Anytime." Claire returned her smile.

"You can invite us over sometime soon for that elk stew you make," Ozzie said to Mina.

"Elk stew?" I raised an eyebrow.

"You need to make her make it for you." Claire waved a fork in the air. "It's amazing." A small crease formed between her brows. "Are you putting it on the new café menu?"

Mina nodded as she cracked open a crab leg. "If I ever get the café off the ground." She sent a pointed look at Ozzie.

He held up his hands. "Next week. I'll release the building to you next week. I think we'll have everything we need out of there by then."

She jabbed her fork at him. "I'm gonna hold you to that."

I made a mental note to go over the schedule for next week. Mina's renovation was already on it, but I wanted to double-check a few things. Like, whether or not I had the right crews lined up for the initial work.

"So, what did you find out today?" Claire asked, changing the subject. "You said there were 'developments,'" she air-quoted, fork in one hand.

Ozzie nodded, ladening his plate with crab and potatoes. "The forensic anthropologist got back to me with a tentative age on the bones. He thinks it's a woman in her early twenties. Using the clothing, that points us to the same time frame as Moira Duluth's disappearance. I took the necklace found with the body to her family this morning." His expression pinched, tightening the lines around his eyes. "Her mother has Alzheimer's. She thought her daughter lost the necklace, and I was returning it."

He cracked open a crab leg and took a bite before continuing.

"Her father died a few years ago, but her sister, Kelly, was there. She's their mother's caretaker. Kelly confirmed the necklace was Moira's. Her parents gave it to her as a graduation gift. Apparently, she never took it off."

"I'd say that's a pretty positive ID." Mina scooped up some potatoes, glancing at Ozzie.

"Circumstantially, yes. I asked Kelly for a DNA sample, which she freely gave. It should confirm our suspicions about the skeleton's identity."

"So, what now?" I asked. "Do you have any leads on who murdered her?"

Ozzie tipped his head side to side. "Not exactly. I have leads, but none of them are a smoking gun. Like Rich Stevenson. I asked Kelly about him. She said he was broken up over Moira's disappearance, but she didn't think he was involved. She thought he was sincere in both his surprise that she was missing and in his actions afterward."

"Like what?" Mina asked.

"He was tireless in his search for her for nearly a year, Kelly said. I guess he went out and searched different areas of the wilderness for her. The working theory back then was that she was either abducted and later killed and dumped in the woods, or she went somewhere wanting to be alone and got lost or crashed. Some of the roads just outside of Juneau are fairly remote."

"Yeah," Claire mused. "And some aren't in the best shape or have any guardrails. She could have driven over the side of a mountain, and no one would ever find her car."

"Exactly." Ozzie tipped a crab claw toward her. "That's

the theory the police were leaning toward, since they couldn't find her vehicle."

"Have you talked to Rich?" I asked.

"Not yet, no. I'm kind of surprised he hasn't found me."

"He's out of town," Mina interjected.

All eyes turned toward her.

"Oh?" Ozzie tipped his head. "You know this how?" His voice dropped with his accusatory tone.

A mischievous smile crossed her face that made my blood heat. She was extra cute when she was up to no good.

"I run a coffeeshop, Oscar. People talk."

He hummed. "Uh-huh. Sure they do. Who did you talk to that told you that?"

"Kent Morrison."

"From Parker Supply?" Ozzie's brows dipped.

She nodded. "He came in yesterday morning, and we got to talking. I asked if he knew Rich. He said he did, that they went back a ways, and he'd just seen him last week. Rich asked him to feed his horses while he went on a fishing trip with some friends."

"Where did he go?" Ozzie asked.

"Kent didn't say."

"Did they know each other back then?" I tipped my head, eyeing Mina. "Before Moira's disappearance, I mean."

"I'm not sure. It's possible. Kent's lived here his entire life. We didn't get that far in our conversation. The coffeeshop was pretty busy."

"I'll talk to him tomorrow." Pulling out his phone, Ozzie made a note. "Is there anyone else any of you can think of who might have known Moira and Rich back then?"

I shook my head. While I was from the area, I'd been a dumb teenager and hadn't bothered to learn who'd lived in Parker's Landing for most of their lives. Then I'd moved to Juneau, and it had become even less relevant to me.

"A lot of the old-timers around town might remember

them. At least Rich, anyway, since he's a local. Moira wasn't, right?" Claire said, lifting her glass of water to take a sip.

"No," Ozzie replied. "She and her family lived in Juneau." He tapped his fingers on the table. Lips pursed, he stared past Claire into the yard visible through the sliding door. The dogs chased each other through the grass, stopping every few moments to sniff a leaf or pounce on a toy instead of each other.

Ozzie's gaze found Mina's. "I don't suppose Kent knew where Walter Shuman went, did he?"

She shrugged. "He didn't say, and I didn't ask."

With a nod, he sat forward and scooped up the last of his scalloped potatoes. "I'll ask him that tomorrow too."

"Do you think, maybe, Walter is one of the friends Rich went fishing with?" Claire swiped at the condensation on her glass.

Ozzie tipped his head, a considering look entering his dark eyes. "It's possible, but I doubt it. Shuman disappeared long before Rich Stevenson left on this fishing trip. All the contracts for the antique store were signed via an online contract platform, weren't they?" He aimed a frown at Mina, then glanced at Claire. "I think that's what you said, right?"

Claire nodded.

"I know the real estate agent was Miranda Benning, so I'm not holding out hope she told you anything useful, but did she happen to mention where he was that he couldn't sign the contracts in person?"

Mouth flat, Claire shook her head. "No."

He made another note in his phone. "I'll talk to her tomorrow too."

Mina's soft, throaty chuckle was like a spear straight to my gut. I wanted to hear it again while we talked in bed, nearing exhaustion from multiple rounds of lovemaking.

I doubted I'd get that tonight, or any night, anytime soon. I royally screwed up by not texting or calling.

"Good luck with that conversation," Mina said to Ozzie. "She guarded him and the sale of that building like a bulldog."

"She does that with most of her properties, though," Claire added. "Almost to the point of sabotage. Like, I don't know what she's thinking sometimes. Some of those clauses and terms she wants to include are just nuts."

A corner of Ozzie's mouth kicked up. "Yes, well, it'll be a little harder for her to stonewall me. I'll remind her she could be charged with obstruction, or even aiding and abetting, if she knows where he is and doesn't tell me."

Claire tipped her glass toward him and smiled. "Good luck."

He grinned, the expression slightly cold and calculating. "Thanks, babe."

I said a silent prayer of thanks I wasn't the one Ozzie was about to interrogate. That look was a little scary.

Dinner conversation turned to more mundane subjects, and the four of us fell into the easy rhythm of friendship. I was still aware of the undercurrents passing between myself and Mina every time our eyes met, but the relaxed atmosphere helped to keep it banked. Before I knew it, two hours had passed, and the evening was winding down.

"You know, I enjoyed this." Ozzie's low voice rumbled as he walked over to sink to his haunches beside me as I crouched in front of the fireplace, rubbing Betty's belly. We'd let the dogs in after dinner, and she had immediately demanded attention. I'd been perfectly happy to provide it since.

"Me too. I've been so busy lately, it was nice to forget about work for a while."

"I hope it can happen more often." Ozzie studied me for a long moment. "I see the way you look at Mina. I can also see there's some tension between you two that isn't all the pleasurable kind. Don't hurt her. I won't hold Claire back when she comes after you if you do." His wry smile softened his words, but the look in his eyes told me he was still serious.

"I have no intention of hurting Mina. I was a bit of a dumbass and didn't call when I should have, but we'll work through that. She's amazing, and I'd like to see what happens."

"Good. Now why don't you see her home and apologize properly for your faux pas?" Ozzie's smile widened.

I snickered. "You just don't want the two of them to talk until midnight." I nodded toward the women. They were parked at the dining table still, chatting away.

"Maybe." Ozzie chuckled.

Giving Betty one last pat, I stood, then held out a hand. "Thanks for the update and for dinner. Next time, you and Claire will have to come to my place in Juneau. We've got great pizza."

Ozzie nodded once, rising next to me. "Sounds good."

I headed over to the table, gaze fixed on Mina. Would she let me follow her home? Even if I didn't stay, would she want to say goodnight? We'd laughed and joked all evening, but Ozzie was right. There was an undercurrent of tension there not brought on by our attraction.

When I approached, the women stopped talking and turned to look at me.

"It's getting late. I'm going to head out. Mina, can I see you home?"

Her brow furrowed, but a spark of heat flashed in her eyes. "Oh. Um…" She checked her watch. "Wow. I didn't realize it was so late." Her gaze met mine again. "Sure." Pushing away from the table, she stood. "Claire, I'll see you later." Looking at Ozzie, who'd come closer and was holding Betty, she pierced him with a look. "You better keep the updates coming and keep your word about my café space. Those renovations need to get rolling."

"I will do my best to clear out as soon as possible, I promise."

With hugs and words of thanks, Mina gathered her purse, and I ushered her out the door.

"You don't have to follow me home. I can make it just fine. It's not far."

"I'm sure you can, but I still want to. You and I need to talk."

She blew out a long breath as we reached her car. "Luke, it's late. I—"

I waved a hand, cutting her off. "I'm not asking to come in or to stay the night. I just want to make sure we clear the air, and we both know where we stand."

She pressed her lips together, glancing away for a quick moment, then nodded. "Okay." Rattling off her address, she unlocked her car. "I'll see you there."

I hurried to my truck as she climbed into her car and started the engine. She'd given me her address, so I didn't think she would change her mind, but I didn't want to give her the chance. Going home without some sort of understanding about things wasn't happening.

The drive to Mina's took about ten minutes. Parker's Landing wasn't a large town, but it was long, stretching out over the coastal highway. She lived on the opposite end from Claire and Ozzie. Luckily, it was also the side closer to Juneau. I would be closer to home once we finished our conversation.

Pulling in behind her car, I parked and cut the engine. She was already out and walking up the driveway to the front door of her quaint tan house.

Picking up my pace, I hurried to catch her before she could unlock it. I grabbed her hand.

She turned to look at me. The quiet pressed in around us, broken only by the soft chirp of the crickets and the rustle of wind through the large pine in her front yard.

Her brow puckered. "You keep looking at me like you've got something to say," she said finally, her tone sharper than her eyes, which shimmered with something softer. "So say it, Luke. Don't just sit there staring at me."

I huffed a laugh that wasn't really a laugh. "I love your bluntness. Fine." Inhaling a breath through my nose, I did my best to give voice to the thoughts swirling through my head. "The truth is, I don't know what we're doing or where this is headed. All I know is, I like you. Our business relationship complicates things, and I think you're a little hesitant about my age. Am I right?"

She pressed her lips into a thin line. "Maybe." Quickly, her eyes darted away. "I can't afford for this to be a fling. Not with my business on the line. Not with everything else going on."

I nodded slowly. "I get that. But this isn't a fling to me. I'm sorry if I gave that impression by disappearing for several days, but that wasn't my intention. What we shared..." I trailed off and shook my head. "Well, it scared me. The intensity of it, you know?"

Those gorgeous eyes of hers met mine, shining a silvery blue in the evening sun. "Yeah, I get that." Her gaze darted away again for a quick second, but she didn't pull her hand away, which I found encouraging.

"How do *you* feel about our age gap? I mean, you're six years younger than me. That may not matter to you now, but one day—"

I put a finger over her lips, silencing her words. "No. Six years is nothing. If it were reversed, would you even bat an eye?"

She brought her free hand up and removed my finger but held on to my hand. "I guess I see your point."

"Good," I said, my voice low. "Because I've wanted you since the day I walked into that building with a clipboard and found you ready to stab me with your keys."

That pulled a reluctant smile from her. "You did look suspicious."

I chuckled, holding her gaze. "Age doesn't matter. Titles don't matter. Mina, I want you. That's the problem. I don't just want this job, I want *you*."

Her breath hitched, and a long silence stretched, but it wasn't uncomfortable.

Finally, she shook her head. "You scare me. My feelings scare me."

I untangled one hand from hers to skim my fingers over her cheek. "Ditto." A soft smile lit my face. "Maybe if we're both scared, that means this is real."

Her tremulous smile set a quiver of need through my veins.

"Yeah. Maybe." Her words were nearly a whisper.

I leaned closer, needing to taste her lips. "You should know, I'm not going anywhere. Not unless you tell me to walk away."

For a long beat, she didn't say anything. But then a slow, sexy smile appeared on her lovely face. "Well, don't do anything stupid and maybe I'll let you stick around."

The laugh that bubbled free only just made it past my lips before she cut it off with a fierce kiss.

Groaning, I speared my fingers into her dark hair and clutched her close. I wanted to take her keys from her and let us inside, where I could ravish her before we made it past the entryway.

But I'd meant what I said when we left Claire and Ozzie's.

Ripping my mouth away, I rested my forehead against hers, breathing hard. "I didn't follow you home just to get into your bed."

"I know." She stroked my face with her fingertips, nearly derailing my thoughts.

Swallowing hard, I lifted my head. "If we're going to make this work, it needs to be about more than sex." With a monumental effort, I stepped back. "So, on that note, I'm going home. But"—I tapped her nose—"you and I are going on a date tomorrow."

Her brows dipped. "What if I'm busy?"

I returned her frown, considering that. "Are you?"

She grinned. "No."

I laughed. "Tease." Pecking a quick kiss on her lips, I backed away. "Seven o'clock tomorrow evening. I'll pick you up. Wear something comfortable. Not fancy." While I had no doubt she would look amazing all dressed up, I had a feeling that, like me, she preferred comfort over fashion. A low-key dinner somewhere and hunting for sea glass on the beach felt like a perfect date.

CHAPTER 15

Luke

That same tremulous feeling from our pizza date settled into my gut as I got out of my truck in Mina's driveway the next evening. I swiped my clammy hands over my jeans and tried to tamp down the feeling. This case of the nerves both made sense but didn't. It wasn't our first date. Not really. Maybe our first official one but considering we'd had pizza together and I'd touched and kissed every square inch of her body while we blew each other's minds, tonight should be a cake walk.

But there was a lot riding on this date. Our entire future hinged on tonight.

Reaching her front door, I swiped my hands down my pant legs once more, then knocked on the crisp white wood.

Seconds later, it swung inward, and just like that, Mina stole my breath.

Dressed in khaki shorts and a dusky pink shirt, she had her dark hair pulled back from her face. A bright smile graced her lips. "Hi."

I felt an answering smile spread over my mouth. "Hey. You ready?"

"Yes. Just let me—"

"Mrroww."

The chirp of a cat interrupted her words. We both glanced down at the orange cat that curled around one of her legs.

Mina heaved a soft sigh. "Joe, you can't come."

The cat chirped again and ignored her, twining between her legs.

I leaned down and held out a hand.

"Careful. He'll bite."

Joe, however, did the opposite. He butted my hand with his head and purred.

Smiling, I scratched his chin. "Hey, bud."

"What are you? Some kind of animal whisperer? First Pebbles and Betty, now my demon cat?" Mina shook her head, but a smile toyed with her lips.

I chuckled and straightened. "I just like animals. I guess they sense that."

"Maybe." She lifted a foot and nudged the cat back into the house. "Let me grab my purse, and we can go."

When she stepped back, I stepped into the doorway to make sure the cat didn't escape. "Why did you name him Joe?" It wasn't a name I heard often, especially for a cat.

Mina picked up a gray backpack-style purse. "It's short for cup of joe. I got him about the same time I opened my coffeeshop. I guess I had java on the brain," she said with a quick laugh. "In reality, I should have named him something like Diablo or Ted, after the serial killer Ted Bundy."

That surprised a soft chuckle out of me. "Why?"

"Because he lures mice and bugs to him, then murders them without compunction and plays with their corpses."

I wrinkled my nose. "That's, um, pleasant."

She laughed and motioned toward the door. "It's not, but at least my house is regularly pest-free, even if I do occasionally find a gutted mouse by the back door."

I gave the cat one last assessing glance before I closed the door as we exited the house. I would do my best to stay on the cat's good side, lest he attempt to slice my throat in my sleep some night.

"So, where are we going?" Mina asked as she hopped up into my truck.

Shutting her door, I walked around and got in before answering her. "There's a great seafood place on the water in Juneau. I thought we could go there, then head down to the beach and hunt for sea glass."

Her eyes lit up as she smiled. "That sounds fun."

"Good." I grinned. "I didn't really have a backup plan, but I'm sure I could wing it if truly necessary."

She laughed. "I'm glad I agreed, then, I guess, and that you didn't have to overtax your brain."

"Me too. I do enough of that at work."

"How's that been going? How's your dad?"

Reaching up, I rubbed the back of my neck as I drove out of her neighborhood. "It's going. Busy. Thankfully, not too many fires. Just… busy. And Dad's doing great. We're hopeful he'll get to go home soon."

"Really? That's great."

"Yeah. He's ready. Says the nurses and therapists are pleasant people, but he's ready to be back in his own space."

"I get that. I'm a homebody too," Mina said. "I like vacation as much as the next person, but I'm always ready to go home. I can't imagine how much worse that feeling is when you're somewhere you didn't choose to be because you were ill."

I nodded. "He'll get there. Hopefully, he won't drive us all crazy before that happens, though." My sister and I had been taking turns spelling Mom, just so she could have a break from Dad's orneriness. He wasn't mean about it. Just fidgety and annoyed with it all.

Our conversation turned light as I drove us toward Juneau, and the trip passed quickly.

Turning into the parking lot for the restaurant, I parked, and we made our way inside. With the weather being warm, we opted for a table outside, and the hostess led us to a spot by the railing, overlooking the water.

"I've never been here. This is nice." Mina peered out over the water as I held out her chair for her to sit down. She perched on the chair, and I scooted it in.

"You don't spend a lot of time in Juneau, do you?" I glanced at the water as I rounded the table to my seat. The channel was busy for the hour as people took advantage of the extra summer sunlight and warm weather, staying out on their boats well into the evening.

She turned away from the view to look at me. "No. I'm from Hoonah, like Claire. This place"—she circled a finger in the air—"is too big for me."

"Understandable." Cities weren't for everyone. "What brought you to Parker's Landing? Why didn't you stay in Hoonah?"

"Claire. She came over here because there were better opportunities for her real estate business. When I told her I'd like to open a coffeeshop, she suggested I come here to do it. That Parker's Landing was basically screaming for one, and I could capitalize on the summer tourist season." She lifted one shoulder. "I did some research and realized she was right. She helped me find the perfect location, and I never looked back." A bright smile graced her face. "It's been a lot of fun. I love what I do."

"I can tell. Every time I've seen you at your busiest, you always seem happy."

She grinned. "I get a thrill from the morning rush."

I laughed. "That's good, because I can't imagine that will ever go away."

"No. Not as long as we get all the summer tourists visiting

Mendenhall Glacier. Even in the winter, we get a decent amount of people."

She wasn't wrong. In the summer months, the town's population could triple. In the winter months, it stayed closer to normal, but there were always a few strangers milling around.

"What made you leave Parker's Landing?" she asked. "Your parents still live there."

"I wanted to go to college in Seattle, even though I knew I'd always come back here. When I graduated, having my office in Juneau made more sense than setting up shop in Parker's Landing. So, that's what I did. And it just felt natural to live close to work, so I bought a house in the city as well."

"Do you ever see yourself moving out of Juneau?"

I glanced out over the water, thinking about that. Up until recently, I would have said no. But with Dad's health, moving to be closer sounded quite appealing. "Maybe. I guess it would depend on circumstances and if I could find the right place."

A smile toyed with her lush lips. "You could always design your own and build it."

I laughed. "True."

A young woman, not much older than my sister, sidled up to the table, looking harried. "Sorry about your wait. I'm Trish. Can I get you started with some drinks?" She lifted a pad of paper and a pen from her apron.

I gestured to Mina, indicating she should go first.

"I'll have an iced tea, please."

"Sure." The woman scribbled on her pad. "Lemon?"

"No."

"Okay." Trish looked up. "And for you?"

"Water, please."

"Easy enough." With a nod, she stuffed the pad and pen back into her apron. "I'll be back in just a few minutes."

We thanked her, and she spun on her heel, leaving us alone again.

"So, what do you like to do for fun?" I asked.

She snorted and laughed. "What's that?"

I chuckled, understanding how she felt. "Good point. If you had time, what would you do?"

"I like to read. Spend time with Joe. Claire and I like to hike. I fly back to Hoonah when I can, too, and spend time with my parents on their homestead. They always put me to work, so a lot of my free time is spent repairing chicken coops and fences to make sure the animals don't get out."

"Are you an only child?"

She nodded. "Not for lack of trying. My parents just struggled with infertility. They had me in their early twenties but then were never able to have more kids."

Our server returned with our drinks, then disappeared again when we asked for a few more minutes. Neither of us had even cracked open the menu.

Dinner passed quickly as the conversation flowed easily between us. Once we finished our meal, we got back in the truck and headed further south along the main road. After several minutes, I steered into a pull-off and we got out, heading down to the beach.

"Is this something you do regularly? Look for sea glass?" Mina asked as I helped her over some driftwood.

I didn't let go of her hand once she was on the other side of the log. It felt too good nestled in mine. "I used to. My mom likes to make windchimes and other art out of it. When I was young, she'd take my sister and me to the beach a few times a month in the summer, and we'd spend several hours combing the shoreline for sea glass and bits of driftwood."

"Really? Does she still make things out of all that?"

"Yes. I have some of her art at my house. I'll have to show it to you." I also made a mental note to ask Mom to make a piece for Mina, using anything I found today. Judging by the excitement on Mina's face, she'd love it.

"So, where do I find the best stuff?" Mina glanced at me, then focused on the sand.

"It really depends on where you are. Some beaches get picked faster than others. Around here, we'll probably be more likely to find things close to the waterline, where they've just washed in, or where the waves have recently uncovered them from the sand."

Mina kicked off her shoes, then shook off my hold to peel off her socks, stuffing them down into the toes of her shoes. "Lead the way."

I chuckled, but didn't argue, taking off my own socks and shoes.

We left our footwear on top of a weathered log and headed for the wet sand.

Waves crashed, the cool water lapping over our feet. Time passed as we combed the sand, looking for treasures. It wasn't until the light waned as the sun dipped low in the sky that I realized how late it was. Spending time with her was easy. Effortless.

Pockets heavy with sea glass, a few shells, and some pieces of driftwood, I led her back to our shoes. With our feet still sandy, we elected to walk back to the truck barefoot. Once there, we perched on the tailgate and brushed off our feet before donning our footwear.

Reluctantly, I pointed the truck toward Parker's Landing and her house. I didn't want our evening to end, but I knew it must. We both needed to get some sleep. Tomorrow was Sunday, but we both had to work.

Night was well on its way when I pulled into her driveway half an hour later.

"I had a lovely time tonight. Thank you." Mina put a hand on her door handle as she looked at me.

I put the truck in park, but left it running. "You're

welcome. I had a nice time too." I tipped my chin toward her front porch. "Come on. I'll walk you up." I opened my door.

She met me around front. I ghosted a hand over her shoulder and along her spine as we walked toward the house. I wanted to touch her in so many other ways, but I didn't dare. We needed to slow down the heat building between us and do this right. I didn't want our relationship to be just about sex.

On the porch, she turned to look up at me. "Thank you again for a wonderful evening." A banked fire blazed in the depths of her blue eyes, warming my insides.

I bit back a groan. All I wanted was to sink into the pillowy softness of her body.

I'd have to settle for her lips.

Grasping her chin with my thumb and forefinger, I tilted her face up, then leaned down. "I'm glad we could find the time. I promise to do better about that. Finding time for you, I mean. I want this to work."

That fire in her eyes grew, no longer banked. "Me too."

Unable to resist her any longer, I closed the distance between us and kissed her. Long and deep, hopefully showing her I meant what I said.

Her hands came up to rest on my chest, curling into my shirt. When she moaned and pressed her body to mine, I gentled the kiss and lifted my head.

"Do you want to come in?" Her voice, low and sultry, threatened to destroy any willpower I had left.

Somehow, I held on and shook my head. "Not tonight. I want to do this right. Court you a little first before we take that step again."

She pouted but didn't argue. "Fine," she said with a sigh. Standing on her toes, she whispered another kiss over my lips. "But I hope you dream about me all night and all the wicked things we did together."

A groan ripped from my throat. "You're evil." Already,

images of our night together played on a reel through my mind.

She laughed, low and wicked. "Maybe a little." Taking a step back, she eased toward the door. "Goodnight, Luke."

Swallowing around the lump of need in my throat, I responded. "Goodnight, Mina. Sweet dreams." I knew mine would be.

Very sweet, indeed.

CHAPTER 16

Mina

Words swam before my eyes as I studied the café plans spread out over my kitchen counter. Ozzie had been true to his word, and tomorrow—finally—I could get back into the antique store and Luke could get crews working again to bring my dream alive.

Luke's shoulder bumped mine as he shifted, flipping a pencil between his fingers. "So, once you have the keys, I'll have demo rolling again. The crew is ready, and the dumpster is already scheduled. We'll hit the back rooms first, then the common wall. Hopefully, we won't find any more surprises hiding behind the plaster."

A snort left me. "Yes, please. One skeleton is enough." I tried to keep my focus on the neat grid of lines he'd sketched out on graph paper, attempting to envision what it would look like finished. My brain was just too tired, though. It was only Tuesday, but it had already been a long, busy week.

Reaching up, I rubbed at the knots in my neck.

Luke's hand covered mine, pushing it out of the way. "Geez, Mina. Your shoulders feel like you've been stuffing rocks in your muscles."

I groaned as he hit a particularly sore spot. "Yeah, well, I've been a little stressed." I had an employee quit Monday morning right before her shift, which left me short-handed at one of the busiest times of the year. I didn't know when—or how—I would find the time to replace her.

"I can think of a few ways we can de-stress you." Luke's low voice rumbled in my ear, sending a delicious shiver through me, unraveling a few of the more stubborn knots.

"Mmm, I like that idea." And boy was I ready for it. In the four days since our conversation on my doorstep, we'd been together every evening, and he'd been the perfect gentleman.

I was tired of it.

Spinning in his arms, I locked my hands behind his neck and brought his face down to mine. Our lips brushed.

Ding-dong!

A groan ripped from the depths of my soul, and I turned to glare at the front door. For half a second, I debated ignoring it, but the frantic knocking that followed the bell told me whoever was on the other side wasn't leaving, and it might just be important.

Reluctantly, I released him. "Hold that thought."

Grinning, he swatted my butt as I walked away.

Feeling the delightful sting from that all the way to the door, I drew in a breath, locked my dirty thoughts away, and unlocked the door, swinging it open.

One look at Claire's wide eyes banished the last of my thoughts about what I wanted to do to Luke and told me this wasn't a social call.

"Ozzie's not home yet." She fluttered a hand in the air as she stepped inside. "He caught an assault case earlier today and is wrapped up in that, so I don't want to call him and disturb him, but I had to tell somebody. It's eating me alive!"

Curious, I frowned, casting a quick look at Luke as I closed the door. He wore a similar expression of confusion.

Claire walked toward him, pulling her satchel off her arm to drop it on the counter next to Luke's plans. "Sorry to interrupt. I'd leave, but this is…" One brow quirked, and she shook her head. "It's something." She took out a sheaf of papers.

Luke crossed his arms. "What kind of something?"

"Motive, something."

"Motive?" Even more curious, I sidled closer.

She nodded. "Here. Look." Flipping through the stack of papers, she handed me a page.

Luke moved around her to look at it over my shoulder. "Is that a deed?"

"Yep." Claire nodded an emphatic affirmative.

I traced a finger along the page, stopping as I saw the mark in the top right corner. Beneath a red stamp, marked, "RECEIVED," was the faded scrawl of a signature.

"Whoa." Luke's voice rumbled in my ear.

Whoa was right. It was Moira Duluth's signature. Neat, but firm, she'd signed it just weeks before the timeline Ozzie established for her disappearance. June 1992.

But I was confused. How did her signature on a document constitute motive?

I voiced that to Claire.

She held up a finger. "So, I was pulling historical records for that waterfront listing I told you about last month. The one listed dirt cheap that I was looking at buying as an investment property?"

I nodded, remembering the conversation we had one day as part of a larger conversation about my café. It was Claire's first foray into investment real estate, and she'd been excited. As excited as I was to expand my coffeeshop.

"Well, while digging I found this." She licked a finger and leafed through the papers, pulling out one to slap it down on the counter. "Here's the finalized deed, filed later that same month. Different handwriting, same name—Moira's. The property transferred cleanly."

"Why would there be two copies of the deed signed weeks apart?" Luke asked. "The first one should have been the one processed. Unless there was an error and it had to be amended?"

"Nope. The original is a simple transfer from one person to another. In this case, from a woman named Edna Myers to another woman named Sarah Cole." She pointed at the photocopy of the original I held.

"But in this one"—she tapped the second deed—"it's transferring from Edna Myers to none other than Walter Shuman."

"Holy crap," I breathed. My mind whirled with the implications that brought up, but one question stuck out. "But how is that possible? Wouldn't Edna notice that the property didn't go to Sarah Cole? Wouldn't Sarah?"

Claire's finger popped up again. "Not if Edna died between the time the original and the forgery were signed."

"No way." My eyes widened. "Did she?"

"Yep. And I don't think Sarah made a stink about it, because I don't think she knew. I did more digging into the two women. Edna was Walter's aunt on his mother's side. I also found documentation that Sarah was a home-health aide. I think Edna intended to leave the property to Sarah as a thank you."

"But Walter got greedy and snatched it out from under her." I set the paper down on the counter and crossed my arms, completely disgusted. "I can't say I'm surprised after the way he tried to squeeze every last penny out of me in that sale."

"I'm honestly surprised he sold the store to you," Luke said.

I looked up at him. "Why?"

"Moira Duluth signed off on the original transfer. If she

caught someone altering the deed, that's a damn good motive for murder. With Walter's name on the forgery, it makes sense why she ended up inside the wall in his antique store. My question is why he sold the building and didn't let it languish, unoccupied, until he died. I mean, why risk getting caught? He knew what you wanted to do, right?"

I chewed on the corner of my mouth, my gaze moving from his to Claire's, then back. "Mostly, yeah. That's a good point."

"It's not proof he did it, but it's damn close," Claire said. She rubbed her temple. "Ozzie needs to hurry and wrap up his case for the night so he can come home and look at all this."

A laugh bubbled up, and I couldn't hold back the tiny chuckle that escaped. "He's going to hate you. The man worked all day, finally gets home, probably ready to kick off his shoes and veg for a bit before bed, and you're going to hit him with this stuff."

Claire groaned. "I know. Maybe I should wait until morning."

Luke arched an eyebrow. "Do you think you can play it cool until morning? It's not like you can avoid him. You two live together."

Pursing her lips, Claire shook her head. "No. He'll be able to see something's wrong the moment he steps in the door. I can't lie to the man. Not well."

"Here." I stepped away from the counter to the crock pot by the stove and lifted the lid. "You can hit him with this to soften the blow." Reaching into the cupboard in front of me, I removed a plastic container, then ladled a healthy portion of elk stew into it.

"Oh, bless you. Yes, that'll work."

Luke chuckled. "I'd disagree, but it's definitely some of the best stew I've ever had, so…"

I tossed him a quick grin over my shoulder. "Thank you. I'll send some home with you too."

"Yum. That's my lunch tomorrow."

Filling another container, I put lids on both, then handed one to Claire.

She set it on the counter beside the deeds and the café renovation plans.

For several long moments, we stood in silence, the only sound the soft rustle of paper as I fussed with the deeds.

An image of Moira's pretty face from the picture I'd seen in the newspaper floated through my mind's eye. Her neat handwriting drew my attention. It stared back at me like a beacon, flashing a clue that had never seen the light of day until now. I could almost feel her presence, urging us to keep going—that we were on the right track.

Lifting the papers, I tapped them on the counter to line them up. "If you need backup when you show this stuff to Ozzie, give me a call. I know the timing isn't ideal for him, but this can't wait. Moira deserves justice."

Claire took the papers and slid them into her satchel with a sigh. "Yeah. I just wish I'd discovered it earlier, or even tomorrow, so I don't have to spring it on him so late." An ironic smile twisted her lips. "Or that I was a better liar."

"Nah," Luke said. "I'd rather have a woman who springs important things on me when I'm tired than one who can lie to me to my face. I'm betting Ozzie feels the same."

"True." Flipping the flap over on her bag, Claire picked it up and slung it over her shoulder, then grabbed the stew container. "I'll keep you guys posted."

We followed her to the door, waving goodbye as she hurried down the driveway to her car. Once she was safely ensconced and pulling away, I closed the door and leaned against it.

What just happened? Had Claire really discovered a motive for Moira's death?

"That was a little crazy," Luke commented on his way back to the kitchen.

A quick chuckle escaped me. "Yeah, just a bit." I eyed him, looking for that spark that lit earlier, before Claire arrived, but her revelations had chased away any romantic notions Luke and I had for the evening. It also felt wrong to just shove it all aside for the pleasure that surely awaited us if we continued where we left off.

I pushed away from the door and followed him. He reached for the renovation plans to gather them up.

"I should get going. We'll get an early start tomorrow."

The snort that left me wasn't very ladylike. "If Ozzie gives me the keys now, you will." Even if he didn't need to go through the building again after learning about the deeds, I wouldn't put it past him to hold onto the keys as a "punishment" for meddling in his case again.

"I wouldn't worry about it. There isn't anything new the police can look at, even with the new information. He'll probably be more likely to show up at the coffeeshop in the morning and give you another lecture about sticking your nose where it doesn't belong. I'm sure Claire's going to get the same talk tonight." He grinned.

I chuckled. "Yeah." I hoped he was right. This renovation needed to start. I was so ready.

Papers rolled up and tucked under his arm, Luke walked closer, then leaned down to give me a tender kiss.

My toes curled. So did my fingers as I clutched his shirt.

When he pulled back, the majority of my tension about how tomorrow would play out had melted away.

His soft smile and the sassy look in his eyes told me he knew what he'd been doing.

He kissed me once more, softly, then stepped back. "I'll see you in the morning. Sweet dreams." Heat flared in his eyes, turning them a molten silver.

A soft hum rumbled in my throat as thoughts of what his

kisses promised rolled through my head. He'd wished me that same thing every night since our seafood and beach date. There had been some sweet dreams, indeed.

One day soon, though, I hoped to replace them with the real deal.

Warmth flooded my veins.

That day couldn't come soon enough.

CHAPTER 17

Mina

The morning light glinted against the glass front of the antique store despite the brown paper I'd taped to the inside of the windows before Luke started demolition last week. It was both to keep the interior a surprise for the town and also to protect Luke's equipment against theft.

Dew still clung to the flowers in the planters by the curb as I stood outside, heart hammering harder than I wanted to admit as I waited for Ozzie to show up with the key. He'd texted me at five a.m. to tell me he'd be here at seven-thirty to turn the building over to me. It felt like both a promise and a curse. No doubt I'd get an earful for meddling, even though, technically, it was Claire who stuck her nose in it this time.

Luke's truck rumbled up, followed by two vans. His crew piled out, carrying toolboxes and rolls of plastic sheeting.

"Hey, pretty lady." A brilliant smile lit his face as he hopped down. His gaze scanned the front of the building, then the line of cars parked along the street. "Is Ozzie here yet?"

"No." I glanced at my watch, held on my wrist by a pale pink strap. It was seven thirty-two.

"Did you get any sleep?" Luke set a bucket filled with crowbars and gloves down beside me.

"Some. I ended up drinking some chamomile tea and taking some magnesium. Once my mind shut off, I slept fine. You?"

"Yeah. I took a hot shower, then passed out pretty quickly. I've been working so much, there isn't much that'll keep me awake once I lie down."

That both made me jealous and sad. I knew what it was like to work until you dropped. It wasn't fun. Last night, however, exhaustion would have been a blessing. I tossed and turned for about an hour until the tea finally kicked in.

The low growl of an engine drew my attention down the street. A black truck with a light bar on the top approached. I tipped my chin toward it. "There's Ozzie."

Pulling in crooked against the curb, Ozzie double-parked and got out, leaving the engine running.

My eyes widened as he approached. He looked terrible. Stubble dusted his jaw, and his dark hair was mussed, making him look more dangerous than he did on a normal day. His coal-colored eyes had the hard gleam of someone who hadn't slept much.

He didn't bother with small talk. Just strode up, keys in hand, jaw tight. "Here." His voice short, he held out the key. "The building is all yours again." His eyes slid to Luke. "Please don't find any more bodies in the walls."

Luke huffed a soft snort. "Trust me, I don't want to."

"Ozzie—" I started as I took the key, wanting to thank him for bringing the keys over.

But his sharp look stopped me. "Claire should've brought that paperwork straight to me. Instead, she played detective with you two. I spent half the damn night researching it all to verify it. Could I have left it until this morning? Sure. Would I have slept? Hell no." His voice took on a bit of a frustrated growl. "And it checked out. Which means I should've caught it and didn't." Anger glittered in his eyes, but it was directed at himself and not at me or Luke.

That didn't stop Ozzie from jabbing a finger in our direction, however. "If there's anything else hiding in this place, I want to know immediately. As in, you stop work as soon as you even think something's amiss. Do not pass go. Do not collect two hundred dollars. Understand?" Those angry, dark eyes flitted between me and Luke.

All I could do was nod. Luke did the same.

Ozzie drew in a deep breath, closing his eyes briefly, then blew out the breath through his nose. "Good. I've got meetings. Call me if something turns up. It shouldn't. We went through the building with a fine-toothed comb. But this case is one that likes to surprise me, so…" He lifted one shoulder.

"We'll keep an eye out," Luke said.

"Do that, yes." With a nod and a quick wave, Ozzie spun on his heel and headed back to his truck. In moments, he was gone.

"He's intense, isn't he?" Luke turned his attention away from the street to settle on me.

"He can be, yeah. But I get it. He's under a lot of pressure with this case."

"True." His gaze dropped to my hand. "Let's get this building unlocked and get to work."

Shaking off the nerves from Ozzie's visit, excitement flooded my veins. I strode toward the door and unlocked it.

Morning light filtered into the dimly lit space, dawning inside with a promise of the transformation that was to come.

Luke and his crew filed inside.

"Do you need anything from me?" I asked as we flipped on the lights, chasing away the shadows.

"No. If we do, I know where to find you, though."

"Okay." I backed toward the door, heading next door again to relieve my poor, beleaguered barista crew who were busy with the morning tourist rush.

CHAPTER 18

Luke

Within a half an hour of Mina retreating to the coffeeshop, the steady thud of hammers and the scrape of crowbars echoed off the rapidly disappearing plaster walls. Dust filled the air, and I knew I already had a coat of it in my hair, but I didn't care. After the hard stop to this project last week, it was nice to see progress made.

Currently, I worked in the back room with two of my guys. It was time for the long row of built-in cabinets with their Formica counter to go.

Jamming my demo fork between the cabinet base and the wall, I pushed. Boards creaked and the screws holding it in place screeched, protesting as I forced them from the studs.

The cabinet popped free, and we pulled it away from the wall.

"Should we break this up?" my crewman, Chris, asked.

I eyed the cabinet, gauging whether it would fit in the dumpster whole. Regardless, it would take up a lot of space if we left it like it was. "We should probably smash it."

A devilish grin dashed across Chris's face. He raised a sledgehammer over his head. "On it, boss."

Laughing, I stepped back as the wood splintered.

The three of us made quick work of breaking it down. I leaned my demo fork against the wall and bent to scoop up several long boards.

A glint of gold caught my attention. "What the hell is that?" Brushing pieces of splintered wood away from the object, I plucked it from the dust.

It was an earring. Rather plain in its design, the teardrop curve held a single red stone in the center. I turned it over. The small "M" engraved there made my heart stutter.

Ozzie was going to love this.

I glanced at Chris. "Go get Mina."

Without question, Chris dropped the sledge and took off through the building.

"What did you find?" My crew foreman, Kado, walked over, a curious frown on his dusty face.

I showed him the earring. "I think it might be from the dead woman we found in the wall last week." Flipping it over, I showed him the "M." "Her name was Moira."

Kado muttered a soft curse. "You think we'll have to stop work again?"

My mouth pressed into a tight, firm line. "Not sure. Hopefully not." I looked down at the debris on the floor. "Let's see if there's a match somewhere."

That's how Mina found us a few minutes later.

"Luke?"

Lifting my head, I met her concerned gaze from my crouched position. "Hey. I hate to be the bearer of bad news again, but we need to call Ozzie."

She groaned. "What did you find?"

I rose and opened my hand, showing her the earring clutched in my palm. "It was on the floor after we pulled the cabinet away from the wall. I think it was wedged behind it."

A bit of a frown marred her face. "An earring? Why does that warrant a call to Ozzie?"

I turned it over and pointed at the marking. "Because of this."

Squinting, she leaned in. I knew the moment she realized the significance. Her eyebrows slammed together and she straightened. "Dammit." With a harsh sigh, she pulled her phone from her pocket. Stabbing at the screen, she lifted it to her ear.

She didn't have to put it on speaker for me to hear Ozzie's gruff voice.

"Hey, can you come back?" Mina said. "We found something you need to see."

I heard Ozzie's short response but couldn't make out the words. A moment later, she hung up. "He'll be here in a few minutes."

Turning, I looked at my crew. "Take a break. Tell the others."

The two men nodded and headed for the doorway to the front of the building.

"This better be a coincidence," Mina muttered as they left.

Closing my hand around the earring, I wrapped my arms around her and pulled her close. "Even if it's not, I think it'll be fine. I looked through the debris and only saw the one. It's probably just a one-off."

She tucked her face into my shoulder and nodded. "I hope so."

"Come on." I leaned away. "Let's go wait out front for our angry detective friend."

Chuckling, she took my hand. "Okay."

A few minutes after we emerged out front, Ozzie pulled up again, parking the same haphazard way as before, storm clouds in his eyes.

"We didn't even make it an hour." He slammed the truck door and strode toward the sidewalk.

"I know, but I'm hopeful this is it. There aren't too many

other places for things to hide." I held out my hand and opened my fist, revealing the earring.

Ozzie's sharp gaze took it in. "Why are you calling me about an earring? This was an antique store."

"Look at the back."

Giving me a skeptical look, he took a disposable black glove from his pocket and put it on, then plucked the piece of jewelry from my leather-clad hand, turning it over.

"Oh, hell." The storm clouds multiplied when he saw the engraving. Reaching into another pocket of his cargo pants, he produced a small evidence bag.

"Do you think it was Moira's?" Mina asked.

"Possibly. I'll have to ask her family. It could be nothing." He dropped it into the clear bag, then pierced me with a direct look. "Did you look for a match?"

"Yes. I didn't see one. Do you want to look?" I hooked a thumb toward the store.

He nodded. "Show me where you found it."

The three of us filed inside, past my crew, who were sitting on the floor, sipping coffee while they waited. Their conversation ceased, and they eyed Ozzie as we walked past.

In the back room, I pointed to the rubble on the floor. "It was in all that after we smashed up the cabinet."

Ozzie dropped to his haunches and poked at the splintered wood and dust. "Did you carry anything out to the dumpster?"

"No. We didn't get the chance."

Nodding absently, he turned back to the debris. Finally, after a minute, he rose.

"Was this the last thing to come off the walls before you knock down the wall?" Ozzie pointed to the remnants of the cabinet on the floor.

"Yes," I said.

"Okay. Let me get my evidence kit, and I'll photograph all this, then you can get back to work."

Mina's shoulders visibly slumped. "Seriously? You're not going to shut us down?"

"No." He spread his arms out and looked around the space. "Where else are things going to hide? All that's left are the floors and walls. From what we could tell when we processed the building, she wasn't killed here. There was no evidence of a bloodstain anywhere except in the wall and right in front of it. There's no reason for me to continue to hold you up. Unless"—he raised a finger—"you find another body or the murder weapon. Then, I'll shut you down in a heartbeat."

"Noted." Mina's head bobbed an affirmative. "Go get your stuff." She shooed him toward the door with one hand.

A smile flirted with his face. "I'm going, I'm going."

She grinned. "I don't want to give you a chance to change your mind."

"Trust me," he tossed over his shoulder. "I don't want to be back here any more than you want me here. I've got plenty of other work—on this case and on others—to keep me busy."

We crossed the threshold into the front of the store.

"You guys can work out here until I give you the all-clear," Ozzie tossed over his shoulder.

"Got it, thanks." I gave him a quick thumbs-up.

He walked away, and I shared a look with Mina. "Well, that went better than expected."

She chuckled, the sound relieved. "One hundred percent."

"Are you gonna hang around until he's done?" I tipped my head toward the door where Ozzie disappeared.

"Probably, yeah. Just to make sure he doesn't need anything from me."

A wicked smile spread over my face. I took two steps toward the wall and picked up a spare demo fork. "I'm gonna put you to work."

An answering, sassy smile bloomed, reaching her eyes.

"Yeah?" She took the tool. "Just make sure you point me away from where any more bodies could be hiding."

With a laugh, I pecked a kiss on her cheek. "Sure thing."

CHAPTER 19

Mina

"I'm going to pop next door and check on the crew's progress." Removing my apron, I looked over my shoulder at one of my baristas. She nodded and waved me away.

It was lunchtime, which was usually a bit slow for us, since we didn't have lunch-type food. Soon, though, all that would change.

Excitement lit in my belly as I walked into the kitchen and through the back door. All morning, I'd heard the bangs and thumps and couldn't help but wonder what all they'd gotten done in the few hours since Luke found that earring.

When I stepped into the back room of the antique store, my eyes widened.

The wall was gone.

Well, it was down to the studs, but all the plaster was missing, and I could see through to the front.

As I gaped at the transformation, the front door opened, and Luke walked in, a to-go bag dangling from his fingers.

Smiling, I stepped through the doorway. "Hey. This looks incredible. You guys made a lot of progress."

"We did. And no more bodies."

I chuckled. "That's good." My eyes went to the bag hanging from his hand. "Forget the stew?"

His smile turned sheepish. "It's still sitting in my fridge. I slept well, but I also slept like the dead and turned off my first alarm, then hit snooze on the second, not realizing it was the second. So, I was running late and dashed out the door without it. By the time I remembered, it wasn't worth turning back. I'll eat it this evening or tomorrow."

"So, what did you get?" I hooked a finger over the edge of the sack and peered inside.

"A burger and fries. Did you eat?" He reached for an empty bucket and flipped it over, patting the top, indicating I should sit.

I perched on it and answered as he turned over another and sat beside me.

"I have food next door. I'll grab it when I go back." That probably wouldn't stop me from snatching a few of his fries, though.

Luke took the to-go container from the bag and opened it, lifting the juicy burger from the tray. "Heard some talk at the diner while I waited." He took a bite, then fished for napkins in the sack to wipe burger juice from his mouth.

I raised a brow as I reached for a fry. "Oh? About what?"

"Walter Shuman and Rich Stevenson. A couple of older guys at the counter were talking about the case. One of them mentioned how they were surprised Walter up and sold everything. I guess the antique store wasn't the only property he unloaded recently. Then the guy speculated that Walter and Rich were in it together and killed Moira."

My eyes rounded. "Did he say why he thought that?"

Luke shook his head, chewing another bite and swallowing before he responded. "The other guy cut him off and told him that was dumb. He said he knew Rich back then, and the guy was head over heels in love with Moira. That was all I caught before my order was ready."

"Hmm. That's interesting. Sure makes you think, doesn't it?"

He nodded.

My phone dinged from my pocket, and I took it out to look at the text. It was from Claire.

"Oh, well, that's ironic," I said, reading the message.

"What?" Luke glanced at me with a quick frown.

"Claire said she's been digging deeper, and Walter's name keeps popping up in her searches. She wants me to call her later." I clicked the screen off and looked at Luke, feeling like we might be on to something. "Ozzie's going to hate us, but we should probably all get together with him again soon and share what we've learned."

Luke chuckled. "I think he just needs to accept that nosey busybodies are a way of life up here."

"True," I said with a short laugh. Small-town life meant everyone knew everything, and no one stayed out of anyone else's business. A murder investigation wasn't going to stop that. "So, did you ever meet Rich? I've seen him around town, but I don't really know him well. He rarely comes in for coffee."

"I'm sure I've seen him around, but I don't think I've actually talked to him." Luke stuffed a fry into his mouth. "I asked my dad about him, though."

"Oh yeah?"

He nodded. "He said Rich mostly keeps to himself, but he's friendly."

"Did they ever work together?"

"No. Dad said Rich works odd jobs and never ran with a crew. From the way he talked, I'm betting Rich might once have had ambitions about starting his own construction company, but Moira's disappearance derailed his dreams."

That made sense. Losing someone you loved could alter a lot of things about a person's life. From what I'd learned about Rich Stevenson, I was growing more certain he didn't have anything to do with Moira's death. It sounded like he loved her.

"Yeah." I propped my chin on my fist, thinking about how life would have been different for Rich if Moira hadn't met such a terrible fate.

Luke finished the last of his fries and closed his to-go box. "I better get back to work. This evening, we can talk to Claire. I'm interested to hear about what she found out about Walter."

Sitting up, I nodded. "Me too. And whether any of that information is about other properties he owned and sold."

Pushing to his feet, Luke held out a hand, helping me up. He leaned down and pressed a quick kiss to my cheek.

"Call me later?"

With a bright smile, I brushed a piece of his wavy blond hair away from his forehead. "Yep. Maybe your stew can be tomorrow's lunch, and we can have dinner again?"

A wicked grin spread over his face. "And dessert."

The shiver that went through me at the heated look in his eyes was enough to make my knees shake. "I like that idea. I'll bring the whipped cream."

He leaned in, nuzzling my neck behind my ear. "I like chocolate better."

I had to clutch his t-shirt to stay upright when my knees threatened to buckle. Silently, I cursed him for putting those thoughts into my head. Now I would spend the rest of the day wondering how he would eat that chocolate.

CHAPTER 20

Luke

Whistling softly to myself, I walked up to Mina's front door later that evening and raised a fist to knock. Before my hand could hit the white door, however, the lock clicked and it swung open.

My hungry gaze took in the woman who answered. Since I saw her at lunch, she'd changed out of her jeans and work tee and into a pair of gray capri leggings and an oversized white t-shirt. From the wide neckline, I could see the edge of her pale blue sports bra.

"Hi," she chirped with a sunny smile. Moving to the side, she held the door open. "Come in."

I sniffed the air as I stepped over the threshold. "It smells good in here. What did you make?" When she texted me and told me to come hungry, I had no idea what to expect, except that it probably wouldn't be stew. My nose confirmed that. I smelled bacon. And cinnamon.

"Cinnamon chip waffles, bacon, and O'Brien potatoes." She swung the door shut, then led me toward the kitchen.

"Joe!" Mina hurried forward and shooed the cat off the counter with a huff.

The cat glared, eyeing the bacon for a long second before

he jumped down empty-handed. He didn't wander far, however. I could see in his eyes he was just waiting for her attention to wander again.

Chuckling, I perched a hip on a barstool. "You're going to spoil me. I never eat this many home-cooked meals."

Turning a quick grin on me, she picked up a bowl of batter and scooped some into the waffle maker. "Get used to it. I like to cook. Why do you think I want to open a café?"

"I'm not complaining." Reaching across the counter, I snagged a slice of bacon from the platter. "Did you talk to Claire?"

"No. But she's supposed to call."

As if on cue, Mina's phone trilled from its spot on the counter.

Snatching another piece of bacon, I grinned. "She heard you talking about her."

Mina laughed as she answered the phone. "Probably." Tapping the phone screen, she put the call on speaker. "Hey. Luke and I were just talking about you."

"Good things, I hope." I could hear the smile in Claire's voice.

"Yes," Mina said. "I was telling him you were supposed to call with an update, then you did."

"Oh, well, I won't keep you waiting, then."

I shared a quick look with Mina.

"So, I know Ozzie warned us off the case, but all of this is public record. I didn't do anything shady or anything a realtor wouldn't do when researching property. If anything, he should thank me for saving him some valuable time. It'll be easier for him to verify than to dig it all up in the first place. Anyway, your café isn't the only property Walter Shuman unloaded recently. He's sold two others—both through Miranda Benning—in the last six months."

"Really? That's interesting. And it fits with what I over-heard at the diner today."

"What?" Claire said. "What did you overhear?"

"That Walter unloaded a few properties, not just the building Mina bought."

"Were they commercial or residential?" Mina asked Claire as she opened the waffle maker and removed the now-cooked waffle.

"Commercial. His house has yet to hit the market. I checked."

I frowned. "Why would someone sell all their other properties, but not their house if they were leaving the area?"

A light touch on my leg made me look down. Joe rubbed against my shin. I ate all but the very end bit of my bacon, then let my hand drop to my side, giving the small piece to the cat.

Mina narrowed her eyes but stayed silent. I just smiled innocently. I was still of the camp of keeping the cat on my good side.

"I'm not sure," Claire continued. "He might have plans to sell it. Maybe he needs to find a new place first."

"That makes sense." Mina added more batter to the waffle maker and shut the lid. "What did you find out about the commercial sales? Anything weird?"

"Yep. So, the records' office keeps amended deeds, and after I looked up Walter's real estate holdings, I looked up the addresses for previous sales and such. Two of them went to him through amended filings. In both cases, Moira's real signature is on the original, but the final versions where Walter's listed as the new owner have her forged signature. When I checked the originals, the properties were both supposed to go to Sarah Cole."

With wide eyes, Mina glanced at me. "Just like the antique store," she said.

"Yep," Claire chimed.

The grim look Mina aimed at me matched the dark pit forming in my stomach. Absently, I scratched Joe's head as he stood up on his hind legs, feet pressed to my thigh as he begged for more bacon. Someone back then had been stealing property, it seemed.

"Have you told Ozzie all this yet?" Mina asked.

"No. He's still eyeballs deep in not just Moira's case but that one from yesterday. I want to double-check a few things before I light that fuse." She heaved a sigh, then changed the subject. "I also looked for connections between Walter and Moira's boyfriend, Rich Stevenson."

"Real estate connections?" I asked.

"Yes. I came up with zilch. Legally, they aren't connected, but I don't know about any verbal agreements, like property usage and such. If any of that took place, well, that's a lot harder to trace without talking to people and spreading all this all over town. Even I know better than to do that. I'll leave that up to Ozzie."

Smart woman, I couldn't help but think. He'd be angry enough she didn't let sleeping dogs lie and dug up more property records.

Mina let out a quick laugh. "I can foster some gossip at work. People talk in coffeeshops, you know."

"Oh, I'm sure." Claire chuckled. "But let me deal with Ozzie first."

Mouth cocked to the side and amusement lighting her eyes, Mina let out an aggrieved sigh. "Fine."

Claire laughed. "Thank you. I'm going to go dig a little more before Ozzie gets home. I'll text you after I talk to him and let you know what he says."

"Sounds good." Mina's hand hovered over the phone. "Talk to you later."

"Yep. Bye." The line clicked off.

Mina cleared the call, then sagged into the counter, her eyes meeting mine. "Walter's looking more guilty all the time."

"Yeah." Grabbing yet another piece of bacon, I stared past her as I munched, thinking. "Maybe."

"Why maybe?"

I met her eyes. "I still don't understand why he would sell the antique store if he murdered Moira and put her in the wall. It's risky, you know? He had to know you'd want to renovate the space."

She shrugged and opened the waffle maker. "Maybe he didn't care anymore. It could be he decided it was time for warmer pastures. Ozzie still hasn't been able to locate him. If he fled to a non-extraditable country, it might not matter even if he does."

I shook my head, honestly a little in awe of Walter. It was practically the perfect plan. Some of those countries without extradition treaties were fairly cheap to live in. With the proceeds from his three commercial deals and whatever retirement savings he had, he could live more than comfortably for the rest of his life and never have to worry about being arrested.

"We can't do anything more about it tonight, though, so I vote we table it all until tomorrow." Mina loaded waffles and potatoes onto a plate, then slid it over to me. "Don't give any of that to Joe. He's bad enough about scrounging on my counters for food."

I chuckled, even as my mouth watered at the deliciousness wafting into my nose. "Deal." Reaching for the syrup, I paused right before dousing my waffles in it. "Did you remember the chocolate?"

A pretty pink blush dusted her cheeks, even as a coy smile slipped over her face. "Eat your waffles and find out."

I flicked open the syrup cap with my thumb. "Yes, ma'am."

CHAPTER 21

Mina

"Is it extra busy in here this morning, or is it just me?"

I glanced over my shoulder at the sound of Claire's voice, then turned back to the cup in my hands and finished filling it before responding. "It's a little crazy, yeah." I snapped a lid on the cup, then slid a sleeve on before handing it to the customer.

"I'm not sure what's going on." I tore the next ticket off the stream that dangled from the order printer.

Claire edged to the side as a family squeezed past her on their way out the door. "I'm glad I ordered ahead today."

"It was a good idea, yeah. Did you talk to Ozzie?"

Nose wrinkling, she nodded. "He wasn't too happy with me." A smug smile slipped over her face. "Well, not a first, anyway. I persuaded him later not to be angry."

I chuckled. "I just bet you did."

She laughed and smoothed her hair.

"So, what did he say?"

"Well, he wasn't thrilled, obviously, but he listened and took all the information I gathered to verify it. He also wants to stop by later to talk to Luke about what he overheard at the diner, just a heads-up."

"I'll tell him, so he's not blindsided. Any other news to impart?"

"Nope. I think I've dug up about all I can for now. At least until Ozzie lets something slip I can look into." She grinned over the rim of her cup, making me laugh.

"It's a good thing he loves you."

"Oh, totally." Backing away from the counter, Claire waved. "I'll talk to you later."

"Bye." My hands full, I gave her a sunny smile, and then she was gone.

I eyed the line. Hopefully, Ozzie would wait to talk to Luke until I could pop next door and let him know.

Forty-two minutes later, I finally made my escape.

A saw whined from the front of the building as I stepped through the back door. One of the crew nodded at me in greeting as I passed. Through the stripped-down walls, I saw Luke swinging a hammer as he nailed a two-by-four into place.

Watching him work was its own kind of distraction, and I let myself enjoy the sight for a moment. A white hard hat covered his dark blond hair, and muscles rippled below the sleeves of his gray t-shirt as he pounded in another nail.

Memories of those sinewy arms holding his weight above me last night as he licked chocolate off the tips of my breasts sent a bolt of liquid fire through me. I would never look at an ice cream sundae the same way again.

The clang of a tool hitting the wood floor brought me out of my lust haze, and I jumped. Inhaling a steadying breath through my nose, I wandered through the doorway from the back room and called his name.

He turned, a happy smile spreading over his face. "Hey, babe. Taking a break?"

"Sort of," I said, returning his smile.

Tipping his head, he pecked my cheek.

"Claire stopped—" The loud whine of a circular saw rose over my voice.

Luke jerked his head toward the front of the store. "Let's go outside," he yelled over the sound.

With a nod, I followed him out.

"That's better," he said, coming to a halt in front of the papered-over windows. "What were you saying?"

"Claire stopped in a little while ago. She told Ozzie about her finds. She also told him about your encounter at the diner. I guess he's going to stop by and talk to you sometime today."

"Oh. Okay. There's not much I can tell him, but sure. Whatever he needs."

"Hopefully, you won't get the third degree. Claire's the one who—"

Once more, I got cut off, but not by power tools this time. A female voice drowned me out.

"Luke? Oh my god, it *is* you!"

My head whipped around to see a young woman—probably not more than twenty-two or twenty-three—heading across the street toward us on four-inch heels. Her long legs, visible beneath her short white skirt, were toned and sleek. Long, glossy black hair hung around her shoulders, dusting the tops of perky boobs, which showed above the neckline of her tight lavender sleeveless top. Tucked under one arm, she held a white blazer and a small black purse.

Luke froze for half a second before a polite, but welcoming, smile came over his face. "Taylor."

"I was driving through, on my way up to the family cabin, when I saw you step out of the building. What are you doing swinging a hammer?" She gestured to the tool still gripped in his hand. "I thought you hung up your hard hat for a T-square."

I narrowed my eyes. Who was this woman, and how did she know so much about Luke?

"I did, but Dad's had some health issues. I'm filling in."

The woman's perfect eyebrows drew together. "Oh? I hope he's okay."

"He's fine. Just recuperating yet."

"Good. I always liked your dad."

Still eyeing the woman, I shifted slightly.

Luke glanced at me, a slight deer-in-headlights look on his face. "Taylor, this is Mina, my—" his brows tweaked, and a beat of silence passed before he continued. "She owns this building, and the coffeeshop next door."

What had he been about to say before he so abruptly changed it? That I was his what? Lover? Girlfriend? Cougar toy?

I fought an eye roll. While we'd certainly enjoyed our playtime last night, I wasn't old enough yet to truly be considered a cougar, even if I was older than Luke.

"Mina, this is Taylor Bray. I did some work for her family. Well, Dad's company did. I was on the crew."

With a bright, toothy smile, Taylor held out a hand. "It's nice to meet you."

My smile was tighter, but still polite as I shook her hand. "You too."

Letting go of my hand, she tuned me out and focused on Luke once more. "You should come by the cabin sometime. We've made a few upgrades since you were there last." A heated look entered her eyes. "Like a hot tub. I'll be there all weekend."

"Oh." Luke reached a hand up and rubbed the back of his neck. "Um, thanks, but I"—he cast a quick look at me—"I'm busy."

For the first time, Taylor truly noticed me. Her eyes narrowed, then roved over me from head to toe before she smirked. "I see you still have a thing for jobsite romances."

My eyes widened. Before I could unstick my tongue from the roof of my mouth and hit her with some tart comeback, she was waggling her fingers and turning to cross the street.

"My invitation still stands, Luke." Spinning on her pointy heel, she looked both ways, then crossed the street to a shiny silver BMW SUV.

One of my eyebrows winged upward at the extra sashay she put in her hips. An inelegant snort left me. This time I didn't hold back the eye roll. "I need to get back to work."

I was sure my abrupt spin didn't look nearly as elegant as Taylor's, thanks to my slip-on canvas shoes, but I did my best to keep my spine straight and make as smooth of a turn as possible.

"Mina." Luke grabbed my arm, halting my retreat.

I froze, then turned slowly to stare at the strong, tanned fingers encircling my arm.

"She was just a fling. Years ago," he said, gentling his touch, but not letting go. "We went out a few times, but it was nothing serious."

When I raised my gaze to his, an apology shone back from the depths of his gray eyes.

It didn't stop the edge from entering my voice, though. "I didn't ask." I didn't want details. Thinking about him with another woman—especially one who looked like *that*—wasn't something I was keen to do.

Luke studied me. "You don't need to be jealous, Mina. I've never cheated on a woman, and I don't plan to start now. Taylor's my past, and she can stay there."

While my heart skipped in delight that he didn't want to go running back to that brunette bombshell, I couldn't help but compare myself to her.

"I'm not jealous," I denied, hoping I put enough conviction in my voice to make him believe me, because it certainly wasn't the truth.

One sandy eyebrow quirked.

"I'm not." The words were firm, but I couldn't hold his

gaze. Instead, I glanced back at the coffeeshop. "I need to get back to work." Twisting my arm, gently, I backed out of his grasp. My heart wanted to believe him, but my mind couldn't help but wonder what a man like him, who could have a woman like Taylor Bray, would want with someone like me. I was no slouch in the looks department, but I was a far cry from the young, highly polished woman who just drove away.

"Mina." He reached for me again, but I was already too far away. The call of his name from within the café building stopped him from moving forward. He glanced toward the door.

"You better go see what they need." I nodded toward the windows. "I'll see you later." Not waiting for a reply, I spun around and hurried away.

CHAPTER 22
Mina

I did not, in fact, see him later.

No sooner did I return to the café than two busloads of tourists disembarked in town and inundated the coffeeshop. By the time things settled down and I had a chance to think about what happened earlier, it was closing time.

Wiping down the final prep table in the kitchen, I tossed the dirty rag in the hamper, then headed for my office to get my purse and keys. I wasn't quite sure what was on the agenda for this evening, but I planned for part of my night to include a hot bath. My muscles hurt.

Flipping off the lights and saying goodnight to my employees on the way out the door, I glanced around at the rear parking area.

A wrinkle formed between my brows as I realized something was amiss. It took several seconds for me to figure out that the "something" was Luke's truck. It was gone.

My mouth twisted. I wasn't sure how I felt about that. Part of me was glad. I wasn't ready to unpack my feelings about Taylor and her familiarity with Luke, or about how I felt I came up short in several ways next to her. I knew I shouldn't compare myself to her, but seeing the kind of woman Luke dated in the past made me feel not only my age, but my lack of sophistication. I was just a small-town girl who liked her blue jeans and fuzzy winter boots. Claire was the one who liked the high heels and the silk scarves.

Blowing out a breath that ruffled the tendrils of hair around my face, I shook my head and headed for my car, annoyance creeping in. It wasn't all directed at myself. He'd left without saying goodbye.

The car beeped as I unlocked it. Yanking on the handle, I got in, removing my phone from my back pocket to stick it in the cupholder for the drive home. When the screen lit up, I saw the banner for a text and lifted it to read the preview. It was from Luke.

Maybe he didn't leave without saying goodbye, after all.

Tapping the screen, I read the message. Concern replaced my annoyance. He'd left because his dad had a setback on his road to recovery.

My fingers flew over the keyboard as I responded, asking him to keep me apprised of things and to let me know if he needed help.

With the message sent, I cranked the engine. For a brief moment, I considered heading into Juneau to be with Luke while he waited for news on his dad but then dismissed the notion. If he wanted me there, he'd have asked. I also didn't feel like we were at that stage yet where we were involved with each other's families.

Leaving the parking lot, I turned for home. My mind wandered as I drove, passing the marina on my way through town. Boats—both pleasure craft and commercial fishing vessels—dotted the water, making me smile. I loved summer here. People took full advantage of the warm weather and came out in droves. Not just the locals, either. Tourists flocked to the area. Some people around here didn't care for the tourists, but I didn't mind them—and not just because it brought business to my coffeeshop. I loved meeting all the people who came through and hearing their stories.

I turned away from the water. Ahead, the sign for the grocery store caught my eye. I should probably stop. The contents of my fridge and cupboards were lacking. I could order out for dinner, but even that seemed like too much effort.

Making the turn into the parking lot, I found a space near the door and got out, heading inside.

The doors swished closed behind me, and I scooped up a basket before heading into the produce section. Tonight called for girl dinner.

After picking a ripe pear from the pile, I headed down the pasta aisle. Mac and cheese sounded wonderful. Tossing a box of it in my basket, I moved on to dessert. Ice cream.

As I stepped back from the cooler, a quart of chocolate ice cream in hand, I paused, a small frown wrinkling my forehead, when I caught sight of a man at the end of the aisle.

If I wasn't mistaken, that was Rich Stevenson.

He looked up, and I swiftly averted my eyes.

Should I go talk to him? Introduce myself and ask him about his relationship with Moira? Did he even know Moira had been found? Did Ozzie know Rich was back in town?

"Excuse me."

I jumped, stifling a shriek of surprise. I'd been so engrossed in my thoughts, I didn't hear him approach.

"Sorry. Didn't mean to scare you."

The man had a quiet, kind voice, which did wonders to slow my racing heart.

I swallowed and pasted a polite smile on my face. "It's fine. I was lost in thought. Am I in your way?" My gaze darted to the closed cooler door.

"No." A pinched frown appeared on his weathered face.

"You're the lady who owns the coffeeshop, right? Next to the old antique store?"

"Yes."

He studied me for several seconds, his brown eyes sad. "Do you know who I am?" he asked, finally, his voice even quieter than before.

I could only nod.

He studied me for another moment, searching my face. Looking for what, I couldn't say. "I heard you bought that place." His sad expression took on a hint of something more in the depths of his eyes. Something darker and angry. "And that you found—" He broke off, jaw clenched tight. Swallowing, he looked away. When his eyes met mine again, the sadness was gone, completely replaced by a simmering anger.

"Is it true?" he asked, his voice low.

"Yes." The single word came out as a whisper.

His expression turned stony, but the anger still burned deep in his eyes. "I didn't want to believe the rumors. I always held out hope she just ran away."

It was my turn to frown. "Why would she run away? Was something going on?"

Guilt entered the mix in his brown-eyed stare.

Suspicion and a little dread mixed in my gut. Was I wrong about who murdered Moira?

I dashed that notion away. Why would he say he hoped she'd run away all those years ago if he murdered her?

"Not in the way you're probably thinking," Rich answered. "She wasn't afraid of anyone." His cheeks colored. "She was pregnant."

I couldn't hold back the gasp. "Oh my! Yours?"

He nodded, then offered me a sheepish smile. "I planned to ask her to marry me. I just needed a couple more jobs to save up enough money for a ring."

"Did anyone else know you two were having a baby? Like a jealous ex or something?"

"No. We didn't tell anyone. Not even our families. Her parents would have locked her away so I could never see her again. It wouldn't have mattered that I loved her and wanted to marry her."

That was interesting.

It was also motive. "Do you think they would have hurt her?"

Rich's mouth tightened. "I'm not sure. Her dad would have been plenty angry, but murder?" He shook his head. "I can't really see it. If he did kill her, though, how did she end up buried at the store?"

He had a point. I bit my lip, thinking. "If not them, then who?"

"I don't know. She was tense a few days before she disappeared, but I didn't think much of it. All she told me was there was an issue at work. I told the police this when she disappeared."

"You did?" Ozzie hadn't said anything about that. I couldn't help but wonder if he knew. Maybe it didn't make it into the detective's notes back then.

He nodded.

"Have you talked to the detective on the case now?" I didn't know how long he'd been back in town.

"No. But I will. I just got back from a trip." Moisture gathered in his eyes. "Do you—" He stopped and swallowed hard, then tried again. "Do you know if she suffered?"

My heart lurched. I could not imagine what it was like to mourn your girlfriend all over again after thirty years. "They're not sure. She… um, well, there wasn't really much left for them to be able to tell how she died." I was not about to tell him about the holes in Moira's clothing. Ozzie could break that news.

"Oh. I suppose that's true." He pulled a breath in through his nose. "Thank you for speaking to me. I appreciate the information."

"Of course. I'm sorry for your loss, Mr. Stevenson."

With a tight smile and a short nod, he muttered a thank you, then walked away.

I watched him go, my heart aching for the man. If he murdered Moira, I'd sell my business and live in a dirt hut for the rest of my life.

CHAPTER 23

Luke

"Time doesn't go any faster just because you keep looking at your watch, son."

I glanced up at my dad, guilt gnawing at me that I'd been distracted enough during our visit that he noticed. "Sorry." The truth was, I'd been thinking about Mina and whether to call her. It had been a couple of days since I'd seen her. We'd talked, but I'd been too busy to make it back to Parker's Landing. Kado had been overseeing the job in my absence.

"Don't be. Tell me what's got you anxious to leave."

Leaning forward with my elbows propped on my knees, I rubbed my hands together and stared out the window for a long moment. "It's not so much that I'm anxious to leave. I'm just…" I shrugged and looked at him. "I met someone."

Eyes widening, Dad stared at me. Then, a slow smile spread over his face. "Really?"

"Really." An answering smile kicked up one side of my mouth. "You know her too. Mina Kensington."

Just as quickly, Dad's smile disappeared. "A client? Son—"

I held up a hand. "I know what you're going to say. Don't mix business with pleasure and all that. It wasn't like I was looking to start something with her. It just sort of happened. She's amazing."

"I agree, but..." Dad's voice trailed off and he shook his head. "How's it working out? That reno hasn't been the easiest. Now you add a relationship into the mix?"

I sat back, crossing my arms. "It's definitely complicated. The renovation side of things is going fine."

"Uh-oh. That sounds like the relationship is in trouble."

"It's not that it's in trouble, it's just"—again, I shrugged—"complicated."

"What's complicated about it? You either like the woman and want to be with her or you don't."

"I do like her, but I'm not the one complicating things."

"Mina's being unreasonable?" Dad frowned.

"No. I think it's more that she's seeing things that aren't there."

"Such as?"

"Do you remember Taylor Bray?"

"Henry Bray's daughter? The one you dated after we did their cabin remodel?"

I nodded. "Yeah. She stumbled through Parker's Landing the other day, and it just happened to be when I was with Mina. Now, I think Mina feels like she doesn't measure up. That she's not pretty enough or young enough." I blew out a breath, getting more perturbed about the situation as I talked. "I don't understand it. She's beautiful, and I don't care that she's older than me."

"Have you told her that?"

"I tried, but I got called away before I could, and now I haven't seen her in a few days, and we haven't had more than a couple of phone chats and some text messages."

Dad groaned and pinched the bridge of his nose. "Why didn't you go talk to her the moment you had a second?"

I snorted. "Because I haven't had a second. This happened

the day you had to have that second stent placed. I've either been here or working since."

"I didn't ask you to be here." Dad held out a hand and motioned to his room at the rehab center, where he currently lived until the doctors were happy for him to go home.

"I know you didn't, but it doesn't change the fact that I want to be. You're my dad." Why was he upset I wanted to visit him?

"I get that, but I also know your life is busier than busy with me out of commission. Some days, a phone call will suffice, Luke. If you want a relationship with Mina to work, you need to put some of your time toward her. You can't put in minimal effort for days on end and expect everything to stay hunky-dory."

Jaw working, I looked out the window. I knew he was right, but that didn't mean I liked being called out on my hesitation.

"Why haven't you stopped to talk to her?" He lifted a hand to point a finger at me. "I want a real answer, not some BS line about being busy."

"I guess—" I stopped, shrugged, then tried again, turning to look at him. "I guess I'm just worried she'll push me away. If I don't go see her, everything stays status quo, right?" An ironic tilt drew up one side of my mouth. "I know by continuing to avoid contact, the distance is growing between us, but in my mind, it feels like we're just stuck on the spot we left off, you know? Like we pushed pause."

"Ah. No, I understand that. But eventually, even on pause, things shut down. If you don't want to have to start over with her, you need to press play, son."

Turning away again, I worried the corner of my cheek with my teeth. "I know." And I did, but that didn't make it any easier to get past the fear.

"Why are you still sitting there?"

My gaze snapped to his. "You think I should go now?" I glanced at my watch. It was already after eight.

"Yes." Dad narrowed his eyes. "I already told you I don't need you to babysit me."

"I'm not babysitting you."

"Sure, sure." He waved a hand and rolled his eyes. "If you're not here, it's your mother or your sister. I never get to be alone. But that's a different discussion. Go woo your lady friend. I like Mina, Aalot more than that Bray girl, and I don't want you to screw this up."

I barked a short laugh. "How about this? I'll leave you be, so you can get some alone time. Tomorrow, I promise I will go see Mina."

Dad's mouth opened, and I could see the protest forming on his face.

I held up a hand. "She has to get up early for work and will probably go to bed in the next hour. I don't want this to be a rushed discussion."

"Fine." He wagged a finger at me. "But you better do it. I expect an update tomorrow—with a phone call."

Smiling, I stood. "Yes, sir." Snatching my keys off the table by the chair I just vacated, I turned for the door.

"Luke?"

I paused and looked at him in question.

"I'm not sure I've said it, but thank you for taking over the way you have. I know it's a lot, but you're doing great, and I'm proud of you."

The lump of emotion that formed in my throat temporarily choked off my words. I swallowed it down. "Thank you. And you're welcome, Dad. Even knowing how much work it is now, I'd do it again in a second." Walking over to the bed, I put a hand on his shoulder and squeezed lightly. "I'll see you later. Get some rest, yeah?"

He reached up and patted my hand. "Yeah. Now get out of here."

My smile returning, I stepped back. "Have a good night." With a quick wave, I left.

In the hall, I glanced at my watch once more. I know I said I wanted to wait until tomorrow, but was it wise? It had already been three days. We'd gone the whole weekend with little contact. It was more than last time life got in the way and I turned chicken, but I knew I was verging on being that guy who ghosted her again. After I left Parker's Landing Thursday, I spent Friday at the hospital with Dad or at the office, so I could be nearby if something happened. Over the weekend, I caught up with other projects and spent time with my family. Other than a few phone calls to keep her updated on Dad, a quick chat on Saturday in between moving from one mound of paperwork to another, and a text yesterday to tell her I missed her, we hadn't had a meaningful conversation about Taylor and Mina's reaction to her. Finishing that conversation wasn't something I wanted to do over the phone.

The doors to the facility swished open, releasing me into the warm evening air. I crossed to my truck and hopped in.

While the engine rumbled to life and settled into a steady idle, I stared down the road, debating what to do.

My gaze landed on the clock.

Eight-seventeen.

Screw it.

I buckled my seatbelt and put the truck in gear.

She could just be tired tomorrow.

Or she might slam the door in your face.

Grimacing, I acknowledged that possibility, but I kept my truck pointed toward Parker's Landing.

Nerves ate at my gut the entire way there, until when I finally arrived at Mina's, I was sure if it were visible, it'd look like a moth-eaten piece of cloth.

I didn't let it stop me, though. Parking in her driveway, I walked up to her front door, purpose in every step.

Rapping my knuckles on her door, I waited.

Sweat dampened my palms as the seconds passed. I swiped them on my jeans, and a moment later, the front door swung open.

"Hi."

Her soft, lilting voice sent a wave of yearning through me. I wanted to reach out and fold her into my arms, but I didn't dare. Not until we cleared the air.

"Hey. Can I come in?"

Without a word, she stepped back so I could move past her.

The door snicked closed behind me, and I turned to face her.

"How's your dad?" she asked.

"He's good." Guilt sucker-punched me. For days, I'd kept my distance, used my dad and work as excuses, and here she was, asking me how he was doing. I should have come by sooner.

The first hint of a smile crossed her lips. "I'm glad."

"Me too." Reaching up, I rubbed the back of my neck. "Mina, I—"

Her phone rang from the living room. I bit back a groan as she held up a finger and turned away to answer it.

Following behind, I was close enough to see the frown cross her face as she picked up her cell. Before I could ask what was wrong, she swiped her finger over the screen and answered.

"Hello?"

I hung back and waited, getting increasingly more concerned as her frown deepened. When she gasped and her gaze met mine, worry in her eyes, my senses went on alert.

"Okay. I'm on my way. Thank you." Quickly, she hung up.

"Wheat?" I moved a step closer. "What's wrong?"

"That was the alarm company. The alarm at the coffeeshop is going off. I need to go."

"Put your shoes on." I pointed to her bare feet. "I'll drive."

CHAPTER 24

Mina

The coffeeshop was a hive of activity when we arrived. Blue and red lights attached to two police cars bounced off the windows of the downtown shops as they blocked off the road out front. Luke parked several feet away, and we got out.

"Mina!"

At the sound of Claire's voice, I tore my gaze away from my business and saw her jogging toward us, waving a hand.

"What happened?" I asked once she was close enough. "Did someone actually break in?"

"We only just got here, but the door was wide open." She looked up at Luke. "I'm glad you're here. They hit the café building too. Ozzie's going to want you to walk through and check that none of your tools are missing."

Luke's face pinched. "Yeah, okay."

"Can we go in?" My gaze darted toward the door and the cop standing just this side of the entryway.

"Not yet. Ozzie and the others need to clear the building and take some photographs for evidence. I tagged along to keep you company."

"And to hold me back?" One corner of my mouth crooked as I sent Claire a side-eyed look.

She chuckled. "Maybe."

"I'll behave." Crossing my arms, I huddled into myself and stared at the building façade. I might pace a little and get a bit antsy, but I'd stay put.

Luckily, Ozzie and his team didn't take too long. Within twenty minutes, they were coming outside, and he was walking over to our little group.

I pounced as soon as he was within earshot. "Well? Is my coffeeshop destroyed?"

"No. Someone's definitely been in there, but it doesn't look like they did any real damage." He motioned toward the building with a quick tip of his head. "Come take a look."

He didn't have to tell me twice. Immediately, I was on his heels, following him through the front door.

A gasp of dismay left me as soon as we stepped inside. Many of the chairs were on their sides and so were some of the tables.

"It's nothing we can't put to rights." Claire laid a quick hand on my shoulder.

Taking it all in again, I nodded. "Yeah," I breathed. She was right. Nothing was broken. Just turned over.

Ozzie led us behind the driftwood counter—my pride and joy—and paused.

"This is where things are weird," he said.

I frowned. "How so?" A quick glance around the area showed nothing much out of place. The cabinet doors were open, and things pulled out, but like out front, I didn't see any damage.

"The register is intact." He pointed to the tablet screen and register drawer on the counter.

I felt Luke stiffen behind me and glanced back to see a hard glint in his eyes. My brows puckered as I tried to puzzle out why that would make him angry. Before I could figure it out, though, Ozzie answered the question.

"Your office is the same. They didn't mess with your safe. I think whoever broke in was looking for something other than money."

That only deepened my frown. "Like what? I don't have anything of value here except cash and the machines." I held out a hand toward my several-thousand-dollar espresso machines.

"Information." Luke's quiet voice floated over my head.

I turned to look at him with a quizzical frown. "Informa— oh." That made sense. "About Moira."

"Yes," Ozzie said. "I think they hit the café site next door, then came over here when they didn't find what they were looking for over there."

"What else would be over there, though?" I asked. "You took everything."

"That we know of, yes. But the killer doesn't know that."

"You'd think they would assume you had it, though," Claire said. "The police department has been all over that building. Everyone knows Luke and Mina found a body in the wall during renovations. Most of the town watched you carry box after box of stuff out of the store."

"Right, but we didn't take everything. We went through a lot of it inside, so we didn't have to move it all. They might not know that part. Maybe they were hoping we left something behind." Ozzie took a step toward the kitchen door. "Come check your office, Mina. And then let's look at your surveillance footage."

My nose wrinkled. "You probably won't get much. I just have a camera pointed at the till."

"I still want to look."

The four of us filed through the kitchen, which had a similar disordered look as the dining area. While I was glad nothing was broken, I was still peeved at the mess. I'd wanted to be in bed by nine. It was past that now, plus it would take me a couple of hours to clean everything up.

"This is the only place where there's any sort of real destruction." Ozzie skimmed a finger over the doorjamb of my office door. "They forced the door open."

"But they still didn't take anything?" I asked.

"Not that I can tell." He swept an arm toward the open doorway. "You check, though."

I wandered in and gave the small room a once-over. Nothing seemed like it was missing, but I wouldn't know for sure until I put it all back to rights. The important things, like my computer and checkbook, were still there, and the safe was closed.

Moving over to the latter, I spun the dial and opened it. The cash I put there earlier was still in the same neat pile I left it in.

Closing the door, I locked the safe, then turned to Ozzie. "They didn't get in the safe."

"Good. Do you notice anything missing? I know it's a mess, but first impression. Is anything not here?"

"Nothing of note, I would say." I lifted a shoulder. "I'll be able to tell you for sure once I clean up the mess." Holding my hands out, I gestured to the heap of papers, pens, and other random office supplies littering the floor and desktop.

"Okay. Can you pull up your security footage now?"

"Yes." Reaching into my pocket, I took out my phone. "It's easier to get it off the app." Unlocking my phone, I pulled up my security system app and the stored surveillance footage for my single camera. "Here." I handed it to him, then leaned in so I could see.

Luke and Claire crowded around us, and we all watched the video play. At one point, a dark-clothed figure with a hood up moved into view for a couple of seconds, then disappeared. They never moved back into frame.

Ozzie let out a deep breath as he handed me my phone.

"I'll check with the neighboring businesses and see if any of them have cameras that face this way. Maybe one of them caught something more than a hooded figure slinking around."

"Sorry mine wasn't more help. I've never needed more than just the camera pointing at the register."

He waved a hand. "Don't worry about it. I get it. We're not exactly a hotbed of crime up here."

Not normally, no. I hoped that wasn't changing, though, after what happened with Marie Hammond and now Moira Duluth.

"Can I clean up, or do you still need to process the scene more?"

"I took pictures already and dusted several surfaces for prints. That surveillance footage told me one pertinent thing: your intruder wore gloves. So, yes, I'm done. Let's head next door for a moment. You two can check it for missing items, then Claire and I will help you clean up in here." His gaze encompassed me and Luke.

"You don't have to stay," I argued. "I'll be fine."

Claire rolled her eyes. "Hush. We're helping. End of story."

"Same." Luke's low voice rumbled through me like a warm hug.

Tears pressed against the backs of my eyes. "Thank you," I managed to push around the lump in my throat. It was nice to have good friends who cared, and I was so grateful.

Luke's broad palm smoothed small circles over my upper back. I let his touch seep into me for several long moments before following Ozzie and Claire out the back door of the coffeeshop. We walked the twenty-odd feet to the back door of the antique store and went inside.

"This is all you." I held up my hands and looked at Luke. "Nothing here is mine except the building itself."

Standing back, I watched Luke wander around for several

minutes. Much like the coffeeshop, though, nothing was missing.

"Well, I'm glad they didn't take anything, but it also bothers me they didn't," Ozzie said once we were back in the coffeeshop a few minutes later. "Mina, make sure you lock your doors at home. Maybe keep a weapon close by while you sleep. They might try to break into your house to find whatever it is they didn't find here."

A sliver of unease trickled down my spine. "You're such a ray of sunshine, Oz, thank you."

He had the good grace to look chagrinned. "Sorry. I know I'm blunt, but I want you to be safe."

Leaning down, I shot him a smile as I picked up a chair to right it. "I know, and I appreciate your concern. I'll be careful." And I would too. I owned several weapons and knew how to use them well. I'd load one and leave it near my bed. For a second, I debated asking Claire if I could borrow Pebbles. That dog would set off the alarm if so much as a leaf twitched. My cat would hate her, though. I'd just dig out the jingle bells from my Christmas stuff and attach them to the doors. Hopefully, that would be enough to wake me.

CHAPTER 25

Luke

My blood boiled all the way back to Mina's house after we cleaned up the coffeeshop.

It ticked me off that someone thought they had the right to ransack her business, hoping to find evidence they left behind thirty years ago before we did.

I highly doubted whatever they were looking for was still there, even if Ozzie didn't find it last week. Decades had passed since Moira went into the wall. What else could be left after all this time?

That earring survived, my subconscious mind reminded me.

Gritting my teeth, I tightened my hand on the steering wheel and stared straight ahead.

That earring could be nothing. Just because it had an "M" on it didn't mean it was from Moira. It was in an antique store. I was sure Walter probably processed inventory on that counter. More than likely, it fell back there while he did that, and it had nothing to do with Moira Duluth.

But there was still a chance it was connected to her. And that the killer thought there was more evidence somewhere. Evidence they desperately wanted to keep away from the police.

My headlights swept over Mina's house as I turned into her driveway. The sun had set while we picked up the coffeeshop mess.

The soft snick of me setting the gearshift to park filled the truck cab.

"Thank you for driving." Mina grasped the door handle, and light flooded the interior as she let herself out.

I shut off the truck and exited.

She frowned as I followed her to the door but didn't say anything. I was glad. I wanted to get a foot in the door—literally—before she asked why I didn't stay in the truck.

Giving me another quizzical look, she unlocked her front door. "Well…" She glanced up at me over her shoulder as she stepped inside.

I motioned her forward so I could come in.

"Luke—"

Grasping her by the waist, I maneuvered her into the house with a gentle touch. Once I cleared the doorway, I shut the door and flipped the lock.

"What are you doing?"

"Staying."

"Excuse me?" Her dark eyebrows rose up her forehead. "What do you mean you're staying?"

"Exactly what I said." She'd have to put up a pretty convincing argument to make me go home. Even if she got me out of the house, I would probably camp out in the driveway in my truck all night.

Joe trotted up and wound through my legs, meowing. I looked down at the cat. "See? Even Joe agrees."

"He doesn't count." She ticked a finger at me. "No. We've barely spoken in three days. You knew when we parted ways the other day that I was upset over your stupid-pretty ex-girl-friend, and we've yet to talk about any of that. What makes you think you can just waltz right back into my bed?"

"I didn't say I was staying in your bed. I know I could

have handled the last several days differently. I came here tonight to talk about that, actually. But it's late, and I think that conversation is better suited for when we've both had some rest." Not to mention, my emotions were already in a powder keg thanks to the break-in and the implications for Mina's safety. I didn't want to say something I would regret.

When she opened her mouth to reply, I cut her off. "I just want you to be safe, Mina. I know you're armed and can probably shoot better than a lot of people, but I still don't like the idea of you being alone. All I want from you tonight is a pillow and a blanket. I will sleep on the damn couch."

She drew in a long breath through her nose, and she studied me for several seconds. "You're too tall for my sofa."

"I'll sleep on the floor." My back would not thank me tomorrow, but I would still sleep better there than at home.

I watched a war wage in her eyes as she held my gaze for several beats. Finally, she let out a soft huff of exasperation and a slight smile graced her face. "It's kind of cute you'd go to such lengths."

"So, does that mean you won't fight me, and I can stay?"

Her mouth flattened, and she looked away momentarily. "Fine. You can stay. I'll even let you sleep in my bed, so you don't throw out your back." Her finger came up to shake in my face. "But no monkey business. I just want to sleep."

That was more than I'd hoped for. I held up my hands. "Promise." I would build a pillow barrier between us if it made her happy. Though I hoped it wouldn't come to that. I liked the idea of having her within touching range.

She studied me for several beats. "You can use the guest bath to get ready. There are towels in there if you want to shower and extra toothbrushes in the cupboard."

"A toothbrush is fine. I showered after work earlier." I didn't want to traipse dust and heaven only knew what else through Dad's rehab room, so I cleaned up first.

"Okay." She turned, heading for the stairs, but paused at the edge of the banister. "I, um, guess I'll see you up there."

Before I could reply, she took off.

Once she was out of earshot, I groaned softly and scrubbed my hands over my face. I really screwed up. It was like we were back at square one.

Well, almost square one. I got to sleep next to her.

"Mrroww?" Joe rubbed against my legs.

I looked down at the same time he looked up. A low chirp rumbled through him and his expression seemed to say, "She might be mad, but so long as you pet me, I'm not."

Huffing a soft chuckle, I scratched the top of Joe's head. "You're not luring me to my doom, are you, by being nice? Your mama said you like to lure your prey to their death. Is this you buttering me up so I won't suspect anything when you walk across my chest in the middle of the night a split second before you go for my jugular?"

Joe just pressed his head into my hand.

Sighing, I gave him one last good scratch, then straightened.

Making my way into the bathroom, I found the toothbrushes and went through a modified bedtime routine. After leaving my shoes by the door, I went upstairs. Mina had yet to emerge from the master bathroom.

I turned out the light, then shucked my jeans and shirt, before climbing into bed. Hugging the edge of the queen-size mattress, I made sure to stay on my side.

This was probably a terrible idea. I knew I could keep my hands to myself—I was an adult, after all—but that didn't mean sleep would come willingly with her so close. Maybe I should take my pillow and go downstairs anyway. There were a couple of blankets on the couch. I could make do, even if it was too short for me to stretch out on.

Still hem-hawing over what to do, the decision was made for me when Mina stepped out of the bathroom.

A sliver of light silhouetted her figure for a brief moment before she turned the light out. My body tightened, and I had to remind it I would not be peeling that t-shirt and shorts off her tonight.

She padded softly across the floor to the other side of the bed. The mattress shifted only slightly as she got in beside me. Covers rustled as she got comfortable.

When the room fell silent, I turned slightly. "Goodnight."

"Goodnight." Her soft voice was barely above a whisper.

I pulled the comforter up, tucking it near my chin, and closed my eyes, wishing for sleep to come quickly. Heat radiated from her body under the blanket, reminding me I wasn't alone. The sooner my mind fell asleep, and I was no longer aware of her nearness, the better.

The stillness lasted only a few minutes. She rolled over, tugging on the blankets.

Then she flipped her pillow.

A minute later, she flopped onto her back.

When she rolled again, I turned to face her. Every other night we'd slept in the same bed, she'd barely budged once she settled in.

"You okay?"

"I'm fine."

I hummed. "Sure. That's why you're flip-flopping like a fish."

"So, I'm a little stressed. Sue me." Annoyance colored her voice.

I sighed. Why was she so combative? "Do you want to talk about it?"

"No."

The word was out almost before I finished my sentence.

Again, I hummed.

"Would you stop doing that? Just say what's on your mind."

I sat up. She wanted me to speak my mind? Fine.

"You obviously have something on your mind. For whatever reason, you don't want to talk about it. I don't know if it's just me you don't want to talk to or not at all, but I think you need to let it out if either of us wants to get any sleep tonight."

She sat up next to me and snapped on the bedside lamp. Her eyes flashed with fire in the light's warm glow. "I didn't ask you to stay, Luke. You can go home. I won't be there to disturb your sleep."

I scoffed. "Not physically, no, but metaphorically, you'll be there. Knowing you're here by yourself will be enough to keep me awake." I would probably sleep even less at home than with her rolling around just feet away.

"I can take care of myself."

"I know. Doesn't change anything."

Her jaw worked, and she looked away briefly. "Why me, Luke?"

A frown bit into my forehead. "What do you mean?"

"Why choose me when you can have someone like Taylor Bray?"

Oh, hell. I sucked in a sharp breath. Apparently, we were having this conversation now, whether I was rested enough or not.

"Because I don't want Taylor. I want you."

"Why? You never answered that. I mean, I look at you"— she lifted a hand gesturing to my face and my naked chest above the covers—"and, well..." She trailed off, glancing down at herself and shrugged. "Then I look at her and can't help but think how perfect a match she is for you. She's beautiful."

"So are you." My frown took on a more curious note, but a low anger simmered in my belly. How did she not see how gorgeous she was? "Taylor is no less beautiful than you are, Mina. It's just a different kind of beauty. Hers is flashy and on display. Yours is more subtle. You don't need all the trappings of makeup and clothes to show the world how beautiful you are." I shifted closer and lifted a hand to trace the line of her cheek. "You have the most amazing eyes. Clear. Bright. They're like looking at the sea. And don't get me started on what you do for a pair of jeans. One of my favorite things is to fill my hands with the curve of your hips."

Her pupils dilated ever so slightly, and I knew I was on the right track. I inched closer, brushing her dark hair back from her face and sliding my hand around the side of her head. "I don't want flashy beauty. Honestly, Taylor's a little shallow, and that's not what I want. I want a woman with substance. You have that in spades."

"Oh," she breathed.

I took a chance and moved close enough our thighs touched. "Yeah. Oh. If I didn't want to be here, I wouldn't be. If I didn't think you wanted me here, I wouldn't be, either." My brows twitched with a small frown. I hadn't asked her opinion on the matter. "Do you want me here?"

Those bright blue eyes searched mine. Her hand came up to run over the stubble dusting my face. "Yes."

In an instant, that single word set my heart alight.

Raising my other hand, I skimmed her shoulder, feeling the warmth of her skin through her shirt. "Don't ever doubt I'm with you because I want to be. Taylor's the past. Hell, she was barely even that." I moved my hand over the top of her shoulder, caressing her collarbone and cupping the side of her neck. Those delicious blue eyes of hers fluttered, and a tinge of pink colored her skin.

That same magnetic pull that caused us to throw caution to the wind almost two weeks ago and hop into bed together reared its head again. The world receded as I leaned in toward her lush mouth. Her hands came up, fingertips skimmed my chest. Dipping my head, I brushed a soft kiss over her lips. Memories of our previous bedroom endeavors played through my head.

One thought in particular edged front and center. Pulling back slightly, a slow, sexy, teasing smile tugged at one corner of my mouth. "I think we should try some strawberry sauce."

The little frown that creased her forehead was adorable and sent a shaft of lust straight to my groin. I bit back a groan, only to have her tease it free when she tipped her hips into mine.

She nipped my chin. "Only if I get to lick you like a lollipop."

Oh, yes, please.

"You're on, witch." I sealed my mouth over hers in a hard kiss.

CHAPTER 26

Mina

"Steve!" I called out the name on the extra-tall cup of house brew and set the cup on the pickup counter. Without waiting for the man to come claim his drink, and eager to get through the Monday morning rush, I spun around to make the next order.

And looked straight into Ozzie's scowling face. He stood between the order line and the pick-up station.

"Hi." I offered him a curious frown and a half smile, unsure why he felt the need to give me a dark look. I also couldn't help but wonder why he was here so early. Claire had been in not long ago and bought coffee for him and for herself.

"Hi. You and I need to talk."

My half smile died, but my frown stayed in place, deepening. "Can it wait until the rush dies down a bit?" I tipped my chin to the line behind him.

"No." Not waiting for an answer, he stepped around the counter and headed for the kitchen.

This was not what I needed.

Groaning, I turned to my closest barista, Kayla. "I'll be right back."

At her nod, I hurried after Ozzie, who was already standing in front of the door to my office.

Fishing out my keys, I unlocked the newly repaired door and let us inside.

"What's so important it couldn't wait? Did you see my line out there?" I gestured past him through the open door.

"I did. I promise not to take long. Claire brought me coffee. She mentioned you told her you spoke to Rich Stevenson the other day." He crossed his arms. "Care to tell me what was said? And"—he held up a finger—"why you didn't tell me about it sooner?"

I let out a soft groan and scrubbed my hands over my face. It had totally slipped my mind. "With everything that's happened lately, I forgot to tell you. It was last Thursday. I stopped at the grocery after work to get some things, and he was there. He recognized me and stopped to talk. Did you know Moira was pregnant?"

Ozzie's gaze sharpened. "What? No. Was it Stevenson's?"

I nodded. "He said they were happy about it, and that he planned to ask her to marry him once he saved up enough money for a ring."

"What else did he say? Did he point the finger at anyone?"

I tipped my head side to side. "Not exactly. He asked me if it was true that she was found at the antique store. When I said yes, he said he'd secretly hoped all these years that she just ran away."

Ozzie's brows dipped. "Ran away from what? Him?"

"I don't think so, no. He said no one else knew about the baby, but that if her parents found out, they'd be really upset. He also said she told him she was having some issues at work just before she disappeared."

That sharp look returned to his face. "What issues?"

I shrugged. "He didn't know. I know you're not interested in gut feelings or anything except facts, but I really don't think he killed her."

Rather than immediately agree that he wasn't going off gut feelings, like I thought he would, he paused and studied me for several moments. "Why not?" he finally asked.

I blinked. He really wanted my opinion? "Well, I—" I stopped, brows twitching into a frown as I thought about what to say. "He just seemed really broken up about her death. Like, with the discovery of her body, he's mourning her all over again, you know?" I lifted one shoulder. "He seemed genuinely upset to find out she was dead and not just missing."

"It wasn't guilt manifesting as him being upset?"

Pulling the corner of my bottom lip between my teeth, I thought about my interaction with Rich. Slowly, I shook my head. "No. I think he truly loved her and didn't have anything to do with her death."

Ozzie softly clicked his tongue, glancing away for a moment. "All right. Did he say anything else?"

"He just wanted to know how she died and if she suffered. I told him there wasn't much left of her body to be able to tell him that."

"Did you tell him about anything we found on or with her body?"

"No."

"Okay. Keep it that way if you speak to him again."

My head bobbed. That was fine. I didn't want to do anything to jeopardize the investigation. "I will." I held up my hands. "You can tell him whatever you think you need to."

A crooked smile lifted one side of his mouth. "Yep. He and I are going to have a talk in just a little while. Have you heard anything else about Shuman or Moira around town? I know people like to gossip."

"Not really, no. People talk, but it's all been speculation about what happened." I narrowed my eyes, sensing he knew more than he let on. "Why? Have you?"

Wariness crept into his expression, and I knew my instincts were right.

I quirked an eyebrow and crossed my arms. "You might as well spill. I might be able to point you toward more information. At the very least, I can keep my ears open for someone who might know more."

His mouth pursed. After a couple of seconds, he responded. "Ellis mentioned that a couple of the old-timers down at the docks remembered hearing about a young woman asking questions about some waterfront property way back when. I'm not sure if they're just making stuff up or if Moira was actually going around asking things. He was going to try to get more out of them, but he's the new kid on the block, so they don't open up to him the way they do others."

"Well, if anyone can get them to talk, it's him." Ozzie's brother, Ellis, recently left the Coast Guard to take up the role of commercial fishing boat captain. He was also quite the charmer. "Maybe tell him to talk to the men's wives." I grinned.

Ozzie chuckled. "That's not a bad idea." With a small jerk of his head, he indicated we should exit the office. "Can I get a couple cups of coffee to go?"

I arched an eyebrow as I headed for the door. "Buttering Rich up, are you?"

A full-fledged grin broke out on his face. "Possibly. You catch more flies with honey, you know."

I chuckled. "I've said for a long time that coffee is the nectar of the gods."

"That's the truth. It's a cop's saving grace too."

"For cops and for a lot of other people." I pushed through the swinging door to the main shop. The line was still stretched to the door. Quickly, I filled two coffee cups and snapped lids on them before slipping them into sleeves and sliding them across the counter to him. "Here you go. Now scram so I can get back to work." I smiled, softening my words.

His mouth tipped up as he passed me a ten-dollar bill. "Keep the change. And keep your ears open."

Nodding, I put the money in the tip jar, which would get divvied up amongst my employees at the end of the day. It wasn't worth making the change for the coffee. And heaven knew Ozzie and Claire already spent enough of their money in my coffeeshop.

Lifting a hand in farewell, Ozzie left.

The moment he disappeared, I dove back into filling orders, helping Kayla and the others deal with the rush. It took another thirty-five minutes until only one customer remained in line.

Ready for a break and a drink of water, I pasted what I hoped was a sunny smile on my face and stared up at the imposing man at the register. "Toren, right?"

Surprise lit in his dark eyes for a moment, then he nodded. "Yes. You have a good memory."

"You're a hard man to forget." My cheeks colored as I realized how that sounded. "Sorry. I just meant you're, well…" I trailed off, gesturing to his size.

An amused smile lifted his full lips, turning him from handsome to gorgeous. If I weren't already half in love with Luke, I'd probably flirt my heart out.

"I get that a lot," he said.

I chuckled. "I bet you do. So, what can I get you? Black coffee is what you ordered last time, right?"

"Yes. But I think this time I'd like to try your cappuccino. A large, please."

I nodded once. "Coming right up." I tapped the register screen and read off his total. He tapped his card on the reader. Once the sale was complete, I turned away and grabbed a cup, then started the espresso.

"So, you're the lady who found the body in the wall next door, aren't you?"

My heart sank. Was he just another gossiper, looking for the latest juicy details? "I am," I said, my voice curt.

"Who's handling the case? Is it just the local PD? I'm new to the area, so I don't really know anyone."

Brows knitting together, I glanced back. Why would he ask that? "We have a detective on the force. He's in charge. Why?"

Toren pulled the corner of his mouth between his teeth and glanced out the window for a long moment before turning back to me. "I'm a hunting guide. I was out scouting locations this past week and came across a camp. Some old man was there, and—" He stopped, glancing away again before shaking his head and continuing. "I don't know. He— something just seemed off. I don't spend a lot of time here in town, but I've heard the rumors about what happened next door. I know the cops are looking for the old guy who owned the place. It could be nothing, but I figured I'd still bring it to their attention." His expression darkened and his black brows drew down over his eyes. "If that were someone I loved in the wall, I'd want people to do everything possible to find her killer."

The anger that simmered in his voice spoke of something deeper than just a desire for justice. I'd bet my favorite coffee mug someone he loved had died a violent death.

Picking up the little pots of espresso, I dumped them in the paper cup. "Go to the police station and ask for Detective Quartermaine. I'm not sure he's there right now, but you can leave a message for him or get his direct number and call." Opening the little fridge below the counter, I grabbed the milk carton and poured some into the steamer pitcher.

"I'll do that, thank you."

"You're welcome." Tossing him a quick smile, I finished his drink and handed it over.

"Thanks." With a quick tap of his fingers to his temple in salutation, he left.

I watched him go, my thoughts a jumble as I silently kicked myself for not asking more questions. People camped in the wilderness all the time, especially this time of year. It was probably nothing. But I would like to know what the man looked like and where the camp was.

Not that I would venture out there.

That was dumb and a good way to end up dead. Even if it wasn't Walter, the man could still be dangerous.

I let out a soft huff.

Dang it. Now I had more questions.

CHAPTER 27

Luke

The shaft of sunlight that streamed through the front door as it opened temporarily blinded me as I framed out what would eventually be the pass-through for the kitchen. Blinking several times, then squinting against the bright light, I set my nail gun down when I saw Mina enter.

"Hey." I smiled and crossed to her.

"Hey, yourself." She grinned up at me, then stood on her toes to peck a quick kiss on my lips.

That familiar swirl of desire stirred in my blood. I was very happy we'd made up last night. I'd missed her touch. Missed *her*. "What brings you by?" I kept a loose grip on her hips as she settled back onto her feet. "It's not lunchtime." I frowned, bringing up my watch to look at it. "Is it?" The watch face read ten-forty-one.

"No. We had a lull, so I thought I'd come update you on a couple conversations I had this morning."

"Oh?" I quirked an eyebrow.

"Ozzie stopped in. I forgot to tell him about talking with Rich Stevenson." She wrinkled her nose. "When Claire came in for coffee early this morning, I mentioned it to her. She told him, and he stormed in an hour or so later on the war path.

Anyway, he's aware now, but the interesting part of that conversation is he mentioned his brother, Ellis, heard some fishermen talking about a young woman coming down to the docks back around the time Moira disappeared, asking questions about some of the property along the waterfront."

"Really?" I clucked my tongue. "That's interesting."

"I thought so too. Ozzie's following up on it, as well as talking to Rich. That's not the only interesting conversation I had, though. Do you know a man named Toren? He says he's new around here. A hunting guide. Super tall. Dark hair."

Slowly, I shook my head. "No. Doesn't ring any bells. Why?"

"He's been in a couple of times. Today, though, he asked if I was the person who found the woman in the wall."

My muscles tensed. "Are people bugging you about that?"

"Some." She waved a hand. "But that's not why this is important. He wasn't curious about what we found. He wanted to know who was in charge of the case, because he found something interesting in the woods."

"What did he find?"

"An old man at a campsite."

My eyebrows winged upward. "That's not exactly unusual for Alaska. People—young and old—camp here all the time."

"I know, but he said the guy was squirrely and that the interaction felt off."

"Was it Shuman?"

"I don't know. I didn't think to ask what the man looked like until after he left. I also didn't ask where it was. He just said he was out scouting and came across the camp. I told him to go talk to Ozzie."

"Probably a good move." I looked over her shoulder, not really seeing my crew hard at work as I thought about what she said. The encounter this stranger had could have been nothing. Or it could be the break needed to find Walter Shuman and finally get some answers.

"Yeah. I just wish I'd asked more questions." She sighed, sounding wistful.

I smiled down at her. "Hindsight is twenty-twenty, babe."

She chuckled. "I know. But I still want to know more about Toren's mystery encounter. I might take a quick walk around town and see if he's still here."

"Let Ozzie take care of it, please? Someone already thinks you know too much." As much as I also wanted to know more about the man in the woods, I didn't want her to draw more attention to herself.

Her mouth thinned. "Fine. I'll go back to work."

I pecked a quick kiss on the end of her nose. "Good girl."

She shot me a heated look. "You wanna call me that later? I can stop at the grocery for that strawberry syrup."

My blood heated. I pulled her in close. "You're on."

CHAPTER 28

Luke

Sawdust flew, raining over my hair in a fine golden confetti shower as I cut the last of the boards to frame out the storage closet Mina wanted in the kitchen area. As the scream of the saw died, I heard my name.

Turning, I saw Kado walking toward me. "What's up?"

He held up a box. "We have any more of these screws?"

I took it from him, reading the label. "I'm not sure. The van's empty?" In addition to the personal vehicles some of the crew drove to get here, we had a company van with tools and supplies that Kado drove.

"Yep. I checked all the drawers."

"Let me check my truck." Flipping off the power to the saw, I headed out back to where I parked and unlocked the bed box. I kept an array of miscellaneous items with me, so it wasn't out of the realm of possibilities that I would have some of the screws Kado needed.

But a quick rummage through the box's contents told me that was not the case today. "I don't have any. If you want to take over finishing the framing for the storage closet, I'll run over to Parker Supply and get some."

Kado nodded once. "Works for me."

"Come on. I'll show you where I'm at." Leading him inside, I quickly showed him where I left off, then left the building. Parker Supply was close, so I decided to walk.

The town crawled with summer tourists, making me happy I didn't need to take my truck and fight for parking space. Skirting around a family with two young kids, I entered the store.

A maze of displays met me as I stepped in. The store carried all the necessities and a decent selection of gifts, but that meant it was stocked to the brim. Always.

Winding through the shelves and racks, I found the hardware section and quickly located the screws Kado needed. I grabbed two boxes and headed for the checkout counter.

"Hey there, Luke." Kent Morrison, the store owner, greeted me as I stepped up.

A genuine smile crossed my face. The rotund, on the downside of sixty, bearded man reminded me of Santa Claus. He was also just as nice. "Hey, Kent." Setting the boxes down, I reached into my pocket for my wallet.

"This all you need?"

"For now, yes. We ran out at the building site."

"You're working on Mina's café, right?"

I fought the urge to roll my eyes. He knew damn well I was working on that project. Everyone in town knew. "Yes."

"Had someone else in here a little while ago asking about it. Well, about where to find Detective Quartermaine, anyway. Said he had information."

My gaze sharpened. "Tall guy? Runs a hunting operation?"

Kent paused in scanning my items. "Why, yes, actually. How did you know?"

"Mina mentioned she talked to him. Do you happen to know where I could find him?" I wanted to know more about the man he saw. While I had no doubt Ozzie would do his due diligence to locate and talk to the man Toren saw, I didn't trust that we'd get the full story about him unless Ozzie needed opinions or information. And that wasn't because he didn't trust us. It was just his nature as a police officer to keep things close to the vest.

Kent read my total off the register. "He lives up off of Otter Bay Road. First turn past the twisted pines on your left."

I tapped my card on the reader, then scooped up the boxes of screws. "Great. Thanks for the info."

"You're welcome. I sure hope this business gets sorted out soon. Rich and that poor girl's family deserve answers."

I agreed. "You were around back then, weren't you?"

"Yep. I've lived here my whole life."

"Did you know Moira?"

"Not personally. I knew Rich and his family because they're locals. She was from Juneau, and I saw her around town with Rich. He was just devastated when she disappeared. He's never really recovered."

I grunted an ascent. "Did you ever hear any rumors about her disappearance?"

Kent stroked his beard, his bushy eyebrows drawing down over the bridge of his long nose. "There were the usual things: Rich killed her. She ran away. Normal stuff, you know?"

I nodded.

"Truthfully, I never thought she ran away or that Rich killed her, but I don't have another explanation for how she ended up dead. Though now that she's been found in Walter's wall, well…" He shrugged.

My eyes narrowed. "What? Do you know something about Walter?"

"Walter is…" Kent trailed off and looked away in thought. "He's calculating. Always looking for more ways to make the almighty dollar. It wouldn't surprise me if someone paid him to let them tear a hole in his wall and look the other way.

Now, did he know what was in the wall?" Again, Kent shrugged. "Can't say." He wagged a finger. "But I can tell you he would absolutely take a bribe."

A woman with a school-age child in tow walked up behind me to get in line, cutting off any opportunity I had to ask more questions.

Kent held out my receipt. "Watch yourself, Luke. This is dangerous business, and you might be better off just letting Oscar handle things."

I knew that, but it didn't mean I would heed his warning. One quick conversation with Kent had yielded new insights into Walter Shuman's character. Insights I doubted Ozzie had, because he was focused on leads and not on the rumor mill.

"I'll keep my head on a swivel." Taking my receipt, I gave a quick wave and left.

Back at the soon-to-be café, I gave Kado his screws and got back to work, hoping the rest of the day went quickly. There were only a couple of hours left. I wanted to go talk to Toren.

CHAPTER 29

Mina

At one minute past five, I flipped the "Open" sign over and locked the door. While I would miss closing early once the café opened, I relished the thought of a quiet evening now. Ultimately, my plan was to appoint one of my baristas—probably Gwen—as the evening café manager, but until it was up and running smoothly, I'd be pulling some long days.

That was for this fall, though. Right now, I planned to head to the grocery store for some strawberry syrup, then head home for dinner and my highly anticipated dessert.

Flipping off the lights in the main dining area, I entered the back room.

"See you in the morning," Kayla called on her way out the back door.

"Have a good night." I waved as I walked to my office to collect my purse and keys. We'd been slow for the last hour of the day, so there was little to do except lock up. I tallied the day's receipts half an hour ago.

With my stuff in hand, I exited through the back door and pulled it shut, making sure it was locked, then headed next door.

When I stepped into the café, the sound of construction had already ceased. The crew was busy packing up.

Waving to several of them, I waded deeper into the building until I found Luke, stowing tools in the pile they'd made under the skeleton of the stairs.

"Hey."

He glanced back, then smiled. "Hey. I'm just about done."

"No rush."

Locking the toolbox, he stood. "I'm glad you say that, because I was wondering if you want to make a pitstop?"

A sultry smile ghosted over my lips. "For strawberry syrup?"

Heat licked in his eyes, but to my surprise, he shook his head. "We can, but I had another place in mind first."

With a quizzical frown, I tipped my head in question. "Where?"

"Toren's house."

"Toren's—" My frown deepened. "You told me to let Ozzie talk to him and to stay out of it. Why the change of heart?"

"I have questions."

"I did, too, so what changed?"

"I talked to Kent Morrison and got new information. Did you know Walter Shuman is all about the money?"

I snorted. "Yeah. He hired Miranda Benning to sell his property. That alone tells me he doesn't have much interest in anything else."

He chuckled. "Well, even if Ozzie talked to Toren, my conversation with Kent taught me that sometimes it pays to just shoot the breeze with someone. I wouldn't have learned the detail about Walter's money-grubbing ways if Kent and I weren't just chatting."

"And you want to have a similar conversation with Toren?"

"Yep."

That was fine by me. "I'm game. Let's go. You ready?"

"Yes, ma'am." Taking my hand, he led me through the building to the back door. "Can we swing past your house, so I can drop my truck off? It's on the way."

"Sure." I took a step to the side. "I'll see you there."

He nodded and unlocked his truck.

The drive to my house didn't take long, but it was enough for me to think about what I wanted to ask Toren. In addition to the obvious—where he saw the camp and a physical description of the man—I also wanted to get his impression of the person. What was it about their encounter that set off his internal radar?

I pulled up to the curb past my house and waited while Luke parked directly in front. When we returned later, he would likely pull into the drive behind my garage.

The passenger door opened, and he slid into the seat.

"Where am I going?" I glanced at him.

"Kent said Otter Bay Road. Past the twisted pines on the left."

I nodded once and put the car in drive. I knew exactly where that was. "Got it."

Watching my speed, I headed for the edge of town. The streets were still crowded, even though a lot of the stores were closed for the evening. The few restaurants we had were still open, and the day hikers were coming down out of the mountains for supper.

On our way out of town and up the mountain, we quizzed each other about our day, keeping the topic light. It passed the time, and soon we came upon the twisted pines.

I slowed, looking for the turn-off and quickly spotted it.

Dust bloomed behind us as my car's tires bit into the dirt road. A quarter mile down, a small clearing appeared. Within it, nestled against the trees, was a small cabin and a barn. A small, fenced pasture came off the side of the latter, and several chickens pecked at the ground. In front of the cabin sat a black truck.

I parked next to it and cut the engine. As we emerged from the vehicle, the cabin's front door swung open and Toren stepped out, a hunting rifle in his hands. When he saw me, the fierce, dark frown on his face softened to a perplexed scowl, and he propped the gun against the wall of the house.

"Hi." I smiled and waved.

His scowl remained, and he tipped his head, studying us. "Hi. What are you doing here?"

"We had questions." Luke stepped forward, hand outstretched. "I'm Mina's boyfriend, Luke Decker."

Toren shook his hand. "Toren McCrae."

My heart stuttered to a halt at Luke's description of himself. We hadn't put any labels on our relationship, so to hear him state it so plainly was like a bucket of ice water to the face. I wasn't mad about it, but it gave me pause.

Gathering my wits about me, I focused on the conversation. There would be time later to dissect Luke's comment and how I felt about what we were to one another. "Have you talked to Ozzie yet?"

"You mean Detective Quartermaine?" A hint of confusion colored the man's deep voice.

"Yes, sorry. He's a friend."

"No. He was out when I went to the police department. I left a message with the front desk for him, but he hasn't called. Why?"

"After you left the coffeeshop this morning, I realized I should have asked you a couple of pertinent questions."

"Such as?" Toren crossed his massive arms. Muscles bulged in his forearms and chest.

My eyes widened slightly. He was not a man I would want to cross. He could probably snap me like a twig with those big hands of his. I swallowed around the sudden lump in my throat. "Um, well, for one, what did the man you encountered look like?" I knew Walter Shuman. If Toren saw a heavy-set man or one with dark hair, it wasn't him. Walter was old and slim.

"Older. Probably seventy or so. White hair and a bushy mustache. Skinny."

I shared a look with Luke. That sounded like Walter.

"Did he say anything to you?" Luke asked.

"Only to tell me to move on when I inquired if anyone was home and that he was fine. He had a rifle, and I wasn't looking for trouble, so I told him to have a nice day and left."

"Where was this?" Luke continued.

"Off the Lace River. One of its tributaries. Between here and Skagway."

I let out a little snort. "That's a lot of ground to cover, Toren."

"I have the coordinates written down." He hooked a thumb toward the door. "I plan to give them to your cop friend."

"That's good. Ozzie will appreciate that," I said. "Could you share them with us as well?"

"Why?" Toren shot back. "You're not cops."

"No, but—"

My argument was cut short by the sound of an engine and the crunch of gravel under tires. I shot an alarmed look at Luke and stepped closer. Toren picked up his rifle again, not helping the nerves suddenly cascading down my spine. Who else would come here? Were we followed? By whom?

Luke grasped my wrist and tucked me behind him, using the corner of my car to shield his body.

A moment later, Ozzie's police truck broke through the trees.

I groaned.

"Hell," Luke muttered.

"We're so screwed," I said.

Toren chuckled from the porch.

Ozzie parked behind my car and got out, slamming his door. The dark, angry scowl on his face spoke volumes.

"Once again, I find you somewhere you shouldn't be." He strode closer, eyes locked on me and Luke. "Why are you here?"

"Asking questions you might not think about," Luke answered.

One dark eyebrow rose on Ozzie's face. "Like?"

"Like what gossip Toren's heard."

"Gossip?" Ozzie's tone was nothing short of incredulous.

"You didn't ask about any gossip," Toren said.

I glanced back to see him leaning against a post, arms crossed. His rifle was back against the wall of the house.

"We haven't had the chance yet," Luke said. He turned those gray eyes on Toren. "Has anyone said anything interesting about Moira, her disappearance, or about any of the people involved?"

"No." The single, succinct word came out clipped and final.

"Well, look at that." Ozzie held his arms wide. "He knows nothing I wouldn't have thought to ask about." Sarcasm dripped off his words.

"Maybe not, but that's not always the case. I spoke to Kent Morrison earlier. He gave me some insight into Walter Shuman's character. I guess Walter's all about the money. Kent said it wouldn't surprise him if someone paid Walter to look the other way."

"You think Shuman willingly let someone close up a body in the wall of his store? For money?" While Ozzie clearly thought Luke was crazy if the tone of his voice was any indication, there was a note of curiosity in his expression.

"If he got paid enough, why not?" Luke shrugged.

"Maybe because it would have smelled terribly?"

"So your argument is he's guilty because it would have smelled? That he wouldn't willingly do that sort of thing because of the stench? People do less for money. It would be a simple thing to claim there was a water leak or something and close for a few weeks while it's repaired. Have you looked into whether that happened?"

"No. But the only thing that would prove is that he was aware of the body in the wall."

Luke snapped his fingers and pointed at Ozzie. "Exactly."

Ozzie sighed. "We're getting way off track here." He circled a hand through the air. "I came to talk to Toren about the info he has on my case." He turned his attention toward the porch. "The message said you had information about Moira Duluth's case. Can you elaborate, please?"

"Sure." Toren gave him a quick rundown of the same things he told Luke and me just minutes earlier.

"Can I have those coordinates?" Ozzie asked when Toren finished.

With a quick nod, Toren pushed away from the post and went inside.

"I should arrest you two for obstruction," Ozzie growled once the door closed.

"We didn't obstruct anything." I raised my hands, giving him a look of wide-eyed innocence. "And don't pretend we haven't been useful."

"What you've been is a pain in my backside."

"Yes, but one that got you an identity on your victim and a lead on why she was killed," I pointed out.

His glower returned. "Go home, Mina."

"Can't. You parked me in."

His jaw worked. If he'd been a cartoon character, I swear smoke would have billowed from his ears.

Holding eye contact momentarily, he slowly turned away, then gave Toren his full attention as the man stepped outside.

"Here you go." Extending one long arm, he handed Ozzie a piece of paper tucked between two fingers.

"Thank you." After a quick glance at it, Ozzie slipped the note into his pocket. "Do you have anything else you'd like to add?"

"Just be careful when you go out there. Whether it's the man you're looking for or not, the guy didn't sound like he was willing to play."

With a singular nod, Ozzie stepped toward his patrol truck. "Noted. Thank you, Mr. McCrae." Giving Luke and me a hard look, he climbed into his vehicle.

I glanced at Luke, and we shared a look of trepidation. It might be a bit before we were out of the doghouse this time.

The engine in Ozzie's truck roared to life. When I looked back, his dark expression was still in place as he backed up and turned around. A moment later, he disappeared down the drive between the pines.

Toren's footfalls on the wooden porch steps drew my attention. He stopped several feet away, regarding us silently. A decision warred in his dark eyes. Eventually, he reached into his pocket and withdrew another slip of paper.

My heart thundered in my ears as I accepted it. I took a quick peek and saw coordinates written in a messy, male scrawl.

"Don't make me regret giving you that." Toren stuffed his hands in his pockets and looked past us at the trees. "I'm sure your friend is a good cop, but I've had enough experience with them to know sometimes they have blinders on and can't see past the ends of their noses." His gaze connected with mine, then Luke's. "Now, if you don't mind, I have things to do."

"Of course." I held up my hands and backed toward my car. "Thank you, Toren. Coffee's on the house the next time you're in town."

The big, burly man nodded once and watched us as we got in the car and pulled away.

"He's an interesting fellow," Luke remarked.

I glanced in the rearview mirror. Toren still stood in the same place, arms crossed as I drove down the drive. "Yeah. Definitely." But he was also helpful. Now I needed a map.

CHAPTER 30
Mina

:

"So, are we welcome here?" Luke asked, standing beside me as I rang the bell at Claire and Ozzie's the next evening.

I chuckled. "He's not home yet, so we're safe." And even if he were, he might glower for a bit and remind us to mind our own business before relaxing.

Although with what we were here for, it might take a bit longer. Claire texted me a little before closing to ask if Luke and I could come by to talk about some things she found. She also promised dinner as part of the deal.

"Is Claire safe?" Luke shot me a quick look of amusement.

I chuckled again. "He's given up trying to rein her in."

The door swung open.

"About time you got here." Claire reached out and grabbed my hand, hauling me inside.

"Geez, Claire." I laughed, dodging an excited Pebbles and Betty as she tugged me into her house.

"Sorry. Ozzie's been 'unavailable'"—she air-quoted—"all day, and I *need* to tell someone about what I found."

"Hey!" Ellis poked his head around the corner from the kitchen. "What am I? Chopped liver?"

"I haven't told you anything yet, and the only reason you're learning any of this is because you randomly showed up." Claire tossed the door closed behind Luke and locked it.

He shrugged. "I brought you food, didn't I?"

I laughed. "It's good to see you, Ellis." It still amazed me that he and Ozzie were brothers. The two men looked alike, but their personalities were vastly different. Where Ozzie was more stoic and serious, Ellis smiled all the time, and his serious side only came out when it was necessary.

"You too." A small frown creased his brow. "Who's the dude?" His expression suddenly cleared. "Wait. Are you the boyfriend? Claire said you were seeing someone."

Luke walked forward, hand outstretched and a friendly smile on his face. "Yes, that's me. Luke Decker."

"Ellis Quartermaine."

"So, what kind of food did you bring?" I stooped to pick up Pebbles. "Claire promised to feed us."

"Fresh fish." He tipped his head toward the kitchen. "I was just cleaning it up. I'm gonna fire up the grill."

"I had spaghetti planned, but Ellis brought enough to feed a small army." Claire shot an aggrieved look at him.

"Fish is fine with me." I glanced at Luke, who nodded.

"Awesome. Come talk over here, so I can finish getting it ready to cook." Ellis stepped back into the kitchen.

Luke and I followed Claire. I set Pebbles on the floor, gave Betty a quick scratch on the ears, then took up residence on a barstool at the island.

"So, what did you find that you couldn't wait to share?" I propped my elbow on the island and turned to look at my friend.

"Interesting things. It's actually good Ellis is here. This might pertain to some things he's heard." Claire reached for a stack of paperwork and slid it closer.

"Oh?" Ellis twirled a knife between his fingers and looked up with a raised eyebrow.

She nodded. "You told Ozzie you overheard a conversation at the docks about a woman who was asking about property, right?"

"Right."

"Well, I *might* have convinced Ozzie to give me the coordinates he got from Toren McCrae, so I could research the area."

He frowned. "What does that have to do with the woman at the docks? She was asking about waterfront property."

Claire held up a finger. "I'm getting there."

Ellis gestured toward her with his knife. "My apologies. Go on."

"Thank you. So, I looked up the coordinates and found the property records for that patch of wilderness. You'll never guess what I found." Claire's gaze bounced between the three of us.

"Walter owns it?" I asked.

"No. Sarah Cole does."

"Who's that?" Ellis asked, pausing as he skinned the first fish.

"She's the woman who was supposed to inherit a waterfront property from the elderly woman she cared for. An elderly woman who was also Walter's aunt. I think that's the property Moira was asking about. And it got me thinking. What if she learned about the other property when she was digging into the waterfront one?" She held up a finger. "Remember, I found other property sales that had amended deeds that switched the property from Sarah to Walter. Maybe Moira discovered Walter's misdeeds and he silenced her for it."

"Whoa. Yeah, that's—that's quite a coincidence." He went back to skinning the fish.

"That's what I thought. Now do you see why I couldn't wait to tell someone?"

"But why would Walter go to the property of someone from whom he stole property?" Luke propped his arms on the counter and leaned forward. "It doesn't make any sense."

"What do we know about Sarah Cole?" Ellis asked.

Claire blinked, then looked between him, Luke, and me. "I don't know. I haven't checked."

"Where's your laptop?" I got up, turning to look at the dining and living areas.

"It's in my bag." She pointed to a chair at the dining table and the large black tote sitting on the seat.

I walked over and fished it out, then handed it to her. She opened it and typed in her password, then got on the internet.

Her hands hesitated over the keyboard. "What do I search for?"

"Maybe just her name?" I suggested. "And put the town in, so we don't get a Sarah Cole from, like, Iowa."

"Hopefully, that'll be enough." Claire typed the information into the search bar.

A list of sites populated. She clicked on the top one. It was a LinkedIn profile.

"I think this is her." Claire leaned closer to the screen, reading. "She's still a home caregiver, but in Anchorage."

"How much property does she own at those coordinates you got from Toren?" Ellis laid a prepped filet on a plate and reached for another fish. "Is it a small plot of land, or many acres?"

A small frown creased my forehead as I wondered why he would ask such a thing. The thought barely crossed my mind when it dawned on me: home caregivers didn't make a lot of money. Why would she own a large chunk of land on that sort of salary?

"Good question." Claire changed tabs and entered a records database. I could tell from her tone she'd had the same thought.

Pebbles, who'd retreated to the rug in the living room, barked, getting up. Betty, not one to be left behind, joined her.

A moment later, the two of them took off toward the front door just as the lock turned and it opened.

"Get back, you little heathens." Ozzie fought his way inside, smiling at the dogs circling his feet. Once he made it in and shut the door, he tossed his keys on the entry table and looked up.

A wariness hovered in his dark eyes. "Hi."

Smiling, I waved.

He held my gaze but didn't return my smile before he glanced past me at Claire. "Do I even want to know why everyone's here?"

"I just brought food." Ellis waved his knife, even though Ozzie couldn't see him from where he stood.

But his brother's words prompted him to walk closer. "Fish?" he asked once he could see everyone.

"Yep." Ellis smiled. "We got back early, and I figured you'd like some fresh-caught cod that neither you nor Claire had to cook."

"Works for me." Ozzie walked up behind Claire to give her a quick kiss. "What are you looking at?" He nodded to her laptop.

"Sarah Cole."

His eyebrows drew down. "Why are you still looking into my case?" His gaze swung to me. "Is that why you're here, Mina? I told you all to mind your own business."

Claire held up a hand. "I asked them to come over. I found something with those coordinates you gave me, and I had to tell someone before it ate me alive. Maybe next time, you should consider answering my calls."

"I was out of cell range for a good part of the day," he grumbled.

She grinned and patted his face. "Sure you were."

"I was," he protested.

With a chuckle, she pointed at her computer screen. "Do you want to know why I'm looking up Sarah Cole?"

He blew out a breath and leaned against the back of her chair. "Sure. Why are you digging into my case again?"

Claire shot him a quick, murderous look. "When I looked up those coordinates earlier, I found out that the property belongs to Sarah Cole."

Ozzie straightened, the slightly annoyed look vanishing from his face. "What? You're sure?"

"Yes. I was about to check the size of the parcel and to see if she owned any other property around the state."

He frowned. "Why?"

"This is why you need us," I interjected. "We don't think like you do."

He ran a hand through his hair. "Just tell me."

"How does a woman who works as a home health aide own"—Claire paused to scroll down the screen—"five hundred and ten acres of Alaskan forest?"

"What?" Ozzie nudged her hands away from the keyboard so he could look at the record. "Is that all the property you found?"

"I haven't dug that deeply yet."

He stepped back and gestured to the laptop. "Dig."

"Oh, now you want me to get involved?"

"Woman…" Exasperation colored his voice, thicker than before, and he rubbed his hands over his face.

She laughed. "You make it too easy." Her hands returned to the keyboard.

"It's been a long day. I spent most of it up in a plane, surveying the area. The forest is too dense to see much. We're probably going to need to go in on foot."

"If he hasn't already spooked and left," Ellis said.

"Yeah." Ozzie snorted softly in agreement.

"So, it looks like Ms. Cole has a house in Anchorage… hmm…" The laptop screen moved as Claire scrolled.

"What?" Luke leaned around me, trying to see.

"She also has property near Haines. And more south of

Juneau." She straightened, looking to the side at Ozzie. "They're not small, either. Haines is fifty acres. South of Juneau, she owns three-hundred-thirty."

"Is any of it developed?" Ozzie asked.

Claire reached for a pen and flipped over a sheet of paper.

"What are you writing?" I asked.

"The coordinates for the properties listed on the survey reports, so I can look them up on a map." Once she had them all down, she opened the map app on her laptop and input the first set.

The map zoomed in on an uninhabited stretch of forest.

"Well, that one's a no on the development front," I said.

"Yeah." Claire's hands moved over the keyboard again. "Let's look at the next one." In seconds, a new section of the state appeared. It, too, was forested, but there was a small building visible.

"Hunting cabin?" Ozzie leaned in for a closer look.

"Possibly," Claire said.

"That's the one south of Juneau, right?"

She nodded.

He picked up her pen and circled the numbers on the paper, then closed the laptop with one finger. "And now we're done googling things about Moira Duluth's case."

Claire sputtered, but he laid a finger over her lips. "I have other news." His gaze shifted to his brother, then Luke and me.

I could tell he didn't like having an audience from the pinch around his eyes, but he forged ahead anyway.

"Riggs okayed me taking a couple of days off for the holiday this weekend. I thought we could fly over to Hoonah and see Christine and Tom," he said, mentioning some of their friends. "Maybe do some camping and fishing." He dropped his finger.

A bright smile bloomed on Claire's face. "That sounds great."

"Good." An answering grin turned up the corners of his mouth, but just as quickly, it descended into a mock scowl as he turned to me. "You get to watch our dogs."

"Ozzie! That's a bit presumptuous, don't you think?" Claire said.

I laughed and waved a hand. "It's fine." I glanced at Luke. "Maybe we can take them on a hike?"

"Sure." He glanced down at the dogs, who now sat at Ozzie and Claire's feet, then looked at me with a frown. "Will they make it on a hike?"

"Probably not," I said with a chuckle. "Be prepared to carry one, or both."

"I have a pack you can use that you can put at least one in to carry them. Then your hands are free." Ellis laid the last filet on the plate.

"I'll take you up on that," Luke said.

Ellis nodded once, taking a step back to open the spice cupboard. "I'll bring it by Mina's shop tomorrow." Taking out several bottles, he set them on the counter, then sent a look at his brother from beneath his lashes. "I know you said no more talking about your case, but I have something to add."

Ozzie's mouth thinned. "What is it?"

"I talked to a few of the older fishermen who've been around a long time. Flat out asked what they knew about Walter Shuman. They know who I am and who you are, so it didn't make sense to beat around the bush. Anyway, Bob Dietrich remembered seeing Walter arguing with a dark-haired woman around the time Moira went missing."

"Could he tell you whether it was Moira?" Ozzie asked.

Ellis picked up a container of dill and sprinkled it over the cod. "No. He couldn't even say what they were arguing about. They were up the hill from the dock, near the parking lot, he said. All he saw was a dark-haired woman, some wild gesticulating, then she stormed off. I tried to get him to pin down a better timeline, but he couldn't. He only remembers it was that year because it was the same year the Myers Mansion sold."

"That's the property Walter stole out from under Sarah Cole's nose. It was his aunt's house." Pulling the corner of his mouth between his teeth, Ozzie worried the inside of his cheek. "Why would Bob Dietrich remember that detail? What was important about that house?"

Ellis wagged a finger at Ozzie. "Good question. One I thought of too." He grinned. "See? I could do your job if I wanted."

Ozzie rolled his eyes. "Sure. Go on."

I grinned, enjoying their banter.

Chuckling, Ellis set the dill down and picked up the salt. "Bob said developers were sniffing around, wanting to turn it into a fancy hotel when Edna Myers died."

"Why didn't they?" Claire asked, a small frown on her face.

Shrugging, Ellis reached for a lemon and sliced it in half. "Bob didn't know. All he said was the deal fell through, and since then it's been vacant. Someone pays for upkeep on it. But no one's lived in it since Edna died." He squeezed the lemon, dribbling juice over the fish.

"Okay." Ozzie drummed his fingers on the counter. "I'm not sure how that all relates to Moira's death, but I'll look into it." He rubbed his brow. "I'm still missing an awful lot of pieces to this puzzle. Maybe it'll help me find one or two."

"Yeah, hopefully." Ellis picked up the plate. "Now, let's fire up the grill. I'm hungry."

CHAPTER 31

Luke

S weat dampened my palms, turning them clammy. I swiped them on my jeans before taking Mina's hand as we walked up the sidewalk to the rehab center where my dad currently resided.

Today, Mina would meet my parents.

Well, sort of.

She already knew my dad in a professional capacity; she was a client.

But this was different.

We were walking in as a couple. The playing field was completely different, and I was nervous. Why, I wasn't sure. It wasn't like I thought Mom and Dad would think her unsuitable. Dad liked Mina. He was the reason I showed up in his place that first, fateful day. He'd insisted we not disappoint her by postponing. There were others who weren't so lucky.

And yet, here I was, walking into a cardiac rehab center, thinking they should probably hook me up to a monitor and make sure my ticker was okay. It was about to pound out of my chest.

I could have said no when my mom called to ask if I

wanted to come have an indoor Fourth of July party at the rehab center. I could have told her I already had plans.

Instead, I asked if I could bring a date.

The double doors slid open, and a cool blast of sterilized air hit us as we stepped inside. Thick carpet cushioned our footsteps as we moved through the lobby and down a corridor filled with doors.

I stopped in front of Room 43. It sat cracked open about a foot. Pressing my fingers to the smooth, cream-colored wooden panel, I pushed it open.

A feminine bark of laughter erupted from across the room. I couldn't stop the answering smile as I saw my sister, Lana, laughing from the tan pleather sofa at something my mom said.

Dad chuckled as he turned to look our way, drawn by the door's movement.

The smile on his face widened as he saw Mina at my side.

"I wondered if she was the date you were bringing. Your mother said you asked if it was okay to bring someone." With kindness in his gray eyes, he smiled at Mina. "Welcome."

"Thank you," Mina said. "Luke mentioned barbeque, and I'm not one to turn that down. I also wanted to see for myself that you were okay." Her smile faded as concern took over her features. "How are you feeling?"

"Weak as a damn baby. But"—he held up a finger—"only as weak as a nine-month-old baby. I'm not a newborn anymore, so that's progress."

I chuckled. "That's really specific. Why not a one-year-old?"

"Because a lot of one-year-olds can walk and not fall down. I can barely make it down the hall and back before I'm out of breath. The other day, though, it was the bathroom." He shook a finger. "See? Progress."

Mina laughed. "I like your attitude."

"Me too," my mom said. She sat perched on the edge of

Dad's bed and now ran a couple fingers through his hair, smiling at him with soft pride. "You'll be out of here in no time."

"I hope so. The food is terrible." He spied the food carrier dangling from Mina's fingers. "What did you bring?"

"Cornbread," she answered. "And mini peach pies."

"Oh, my doctor wouldn't like you. That's not on my diet."

A chuckle came from behind Mina and me, and I turned to see a nurse in lavender scrubs enter. About forty, teal-framed glasses perched on her nose and her blonde hair tied up at the back of her head in a messy bun, the woman skirted around us. "I don't think a couple of bites will hurt. Just don't eat the whole thing." She stopped at his bedside and held out the tiny plastic cup in her hand. "And take your meds."

Dad took the cup. Mom handed him his water glass from the table beside her, and he tossed the pills back.

"Thank you." The nurse took the empty pill cup. "Can I get you anything?"

"No. We were just about to eat."

"I'll leave you to it, then. But remember, moderation. Most of your plate should be vegetables."

I couldn't hold back the snicker when Dad's nose wrinkled.

"Yeah, yeah," he said. "I know."

"He'll behave." Mom got up.

"Good. Enjoy your family time." With a wide smile, the nurse left.

"Mina, you can put that there with the other food, if you want." Mom pointed to the dishes lined up on the counter on one wall.

I took the carrier from her, since I was closer, and set the food out.

"Let's eat," Lana said, coming closer. "I'm starving."

"When aren't you starving?" I'd never met someone who could eat the way she could. Lana ate more than some athletes I knew and never put on weight. Her job probably helped. She worked for a catering company and had just started her own event-planning business. It was a rare moment when she sat down.

She elbowed my side, then moved in between me and Mina.

"Hi." Lana held out a hand. "I'm this idiot's sister, Lana."

Mina shook her hand. "Mina. It's nice to meet you."

"You too." Lana handed her a plastic plate.

"Oh, we're introducing ourselves, since this one is lapsing in his duties?" My mom wedged herself into the space beside Lana and grinned as she sent me a teasing look. "I'm Leanne. I know we're not very original with all the 'L' names, but it was easy." Grinning, she held out a hand, which Mina shook.

"I like it," Mina replied. "It shows yours and Les's playful side."

I laughed. "Don't let her fool you. They liked the name Lucas, then didn't want Lana to feel left out."

Mom lifted one shoulder, grinning. "It's true." She lifted the foil covering the pulled pork.

My mouth watered. "That smells amazing."

"Your sister made it." Mom picked up a fork and put a portion of the meat onto a plate.

"I made the slaw too." Lana remarked.

Truthfully, it all looked amazing. "I'm glad we were all able to get together like this. I can't cook the best, but I'm happy to eat the fruits of your labor and pass along my extreme gratitude."

"You helped with the cornbread." Mina poked me in the side.

"I did what you told me to do."

"It's still helping."

I shrugged. "If you say so. I'm just happy we could all get together." And I truly was. Despite my nervousness over Mina meeting my family, I was glad we could spend the holiday together—even if it wasn't technically the holiday yet.

"You got lucky," Lana said. "I somehow didn't get booked the entire weekend. I put in my hours at the caterer this morning to prep for tomorrow and hightailed it out of there before Jeremy could ask me to cover someone's shift."

Lana's schedule was the reason we were celebrating on Friday, the second, and not tomorrow or Sunday. It had the added benefit of freeing me up tomorrow, so Mina and I could go on a hike. Despite the idea of having to tote Ozzie and Claire's dogs around, I was looking forward to it.

"You turned off the ringer on your phone, right?" Mom asked Lana. "So he can't call you in?"

"Yep." Heaping coleslaw on her plate, Lana smiled.

Once we all made our way through the food line and Mom made a plate for Dad, we settled into seats around the room, chatting about things while we ate. Mom, a professional photographer, made a remark about a family she recently photographed, at which point, Dad sat up and waved a hand, pointing toward a corner of the room.

"I almost forgot. Fetch those pictures I had you bring, Leanne."

Mom sent a wicked smile at me, and my stomach sank.

"Pictures?" My gaze tracked her as she got up and went to a large tote sitting on the floor at the end of the long counter where we'd placed all the food. "Please don't tell me you brought my baby book."

She laughed. "No, but I should have." Lifting the bag, she retreated to her chair beside Dad's bed.

"When your mother told me you wanted to bring a date, I had an inkling of who it would be." Dad accepted the first album Mom passed him. "I thought Mina might like to see some old photos of you and hear some memories of your crazier youthful exploits."

I groaned, making Mina laugh. There were a few stories I would rather see die a pauper's death.

With a bit of dramatic flair, Dad flipped open the first album.

Leaning forward, I propped an elbow on my knee and put my forehead in the palm of my hand. *Dear Lord, help me.*

For fifteen minutes, my parents flipped through albums, telling story after story about family trips, sporting events, and disastrous dates. While it was embarrassing to live out some of my life's silliest follies, I enjoyed the relaxed atmosphere. Mina seemed to as well, leaning back into the sofa, posture open and relaxed as she looked at picture albums with my mom.

"Oh, this is an old one." Mom lifted the worn green album from the bag and opened it.

Dad leaned over the side of his bed to peer at it. "Why did you bring that one? That's one of mine from before we got married. There aren't any pictures of the kids in it."

"I just grabbed. I was running late." Mom shrugged and flipped the page.

A frown creased Dad's brow. He reached for the book. "Let me see that."

There was more than idle curiosity in his voice. Something had drawn his attention. "What is it?" I asked.

He quickly glanced up. "An old picture from the summer after high school." He fluttered a hand. "Some party at the beach. I was just looking at who was in it." He pointed to the image. "You'll recognize a few of these faces."

I got up and moved around the other side of his bed to peer over his shoulder.

"There's my buddy, Alex."

My head bobbed as I recognized Dad's best friend, Alex Thibodeaux.

"And that's Tommy Jansen."

Again, I nodded, recognizing another family friend.

But it was a woman in the forefront of the picture, wrapped around Tommy that I didn't recognize. "Who's that?"

"That?" Dad tapped her image. "That's Miranda Corcoran. Her last name is Benning, now, but—"

"You were friends with Miranda Benning?" Mina stood up to come look at the picture.

"Sort of," Dad replied. "We were in the same class, and she dated my friend, Tommy, for a while. I didn't like her much, but she was tolerable, I suppose. Why? Do you know her?"

"In a way. She's a real estate agent now, like my friend, Claire."

"Oh, I know, trust me. She's a pain in my backside at times, demanding this or demanding that, always wanting my firm to cut corners to keep costs down for her sellers." Dad rolled his eyes. "I try hard not to take on jobs from her, if I can help it."

Mina chuckled. "I get that. She's the realtor who represented the seller on the antique store. She tried to sneak some language into the contract that—" Abruptly, she stopped, leaning in to look more closely at the picture.

I frowned, unsure what gave her pause. "What? Is something wrong?"

"I—" she started, then stopped again. A moment later, she lifted her gaze to mine, a concerned wrinkle marring her forehead. "Look at that picture and tell me I'm not crazy."

My frown deepened. "Look at the picture?" Turning my head, I leaned in to get a better view. "What am I—holy crap." I took the album out of Dad's hands. Bringing it closer to my face, I peered at Miranda's image, unable to believe what was right there. In living color.

"What are you two going on about?" Lana asked.

Ignoring her, I looked at Mina. "It's the same, isn't it?"

"It sure looks like it. We need to call Ozzie." Spinning on

her heel, Mina walked over to the couch to get her phone from her purse.

"Who?" Dad asked. "Why do you two look like you've seen a ghost?"

Realizing we owed my family some sort of explanation for our weird behavior, I turned the album around while Mina called. "See these earrings Miranda's wearing?"

Dad squinted at the picture. "So? They're just earrings."

"We found one in the rubble during renovations at the antique store. It was behind the cabinets in the back room."

"He's not answering," Mina said.

I glanced over to see her tap the screen, then lift it to her ear again, probably calling Claire. I turned back to Dad. "Do you know why her earring would be in the back room of the antique store?"

He let out an inelegant snort. "Why would I know how it got there? You said yourself she was the owner's realtor. Maybe that's how it got there."

"If it had just been lying on the floor, I might agree with you, but this was *behind* the countertop, wedged between it and the wall. It fell to the floor when we pulled the cabinet base away. I doubt she was peering into the crack and lost her earring. Did she know Walter Shuman before she listed his property?"

"I don't know. Like I said, I didn't spend much time with her. Just when she was with Tommy, and we were all together. They didn't date long. Just the tail end of our senior year and then that summer. She dumped him when she went off to college."

"Claire didn't answer, either." Mina tossed her phone back into her purse. "They must be out of cell range."

"We can try again later," I said. "Dad, can we take this picture?"

"Sure. Just bring it back. I like that one, despite her being in it."

Balancing the book on my arm, I peeled back the acetate and carefully lifted the photo from the tabs holding it in place. "I'll be careful with it."

"I still don't understand why it's such a big deal to you. That earring could have ended up there any number of ways." Dad took the book back when I held it out to him.

I shared a look with Mina, considering how much to share. Ozzie hadn't forbidden us from talking about the case with others. He hadn't wanted the bit about the earring to get out, but that couldn't be helped in this case. "Miranda is involved in some shady real estate deals from the time Moira died," I said. "This puts her at the scene where Moira's body was. Maybe not at the same time, but it puts her at the location at some point. It's just really coincidental."

"That's... disturbing." Dad's brows twitched into a quick frown. "She was always a little on the type A side and a bit manipulative, but I never got psycho vibes from her."

"Like I said, it could all be coincidence." I passed the picture to Mina, who tucked it into a pocket of her handbag. "We'll let Ozzie sort it out."

I shared another glance with Mina, having no trouble reading her expression. It said Ozzie was going to hate us for interrupting his time off. Although considering the timing, if we didn't reach him until tonight or tomorrow, it would be Monday before he could investigate the lead anyway.

Maybe Ozzie and Claire's weekend wouldn't be a bust after all.

CHAPTER 32

Mina

"Joe!" I lunged, trying to grab the cat as he rocketed past, hot on Betty's heels. The puppy yelped as she dashed through the living room.

My cat eluded my grasp, but thankfully, Luke was there to scoop Betty out of harm's way.

I blew tendrils of hair out of my face and glared at Joe, who now sat perched in the window, tail swishing, as he eyed Luke and the puppy. "You're terrible."

Joe lifted a paw and licked it, then swiped his face, like he hadn't a care in the world.

Luke laughed. "I guess it's a good thing we're taking the dogs hiking."

I sighed. "Yeah." The demon cat was *not* a fan of Claire and Ozzie's dogs. He'd never really liked Pebbles, but he'd tolerated her. With Betty now added to the mix, I think he felt outnumbered, so he'd gone on the offensive to maintain dominance. All he'd really accomplished was to wreak havoc in the house and break a vase.

"Let's get their harnesses on and get going." I turned, looking for Pebbles.

A laugh bubbled free when I saw her peeking out from the

edge of the couch, her gaze fixed on the cat. "Betty's on her own, huh?" Walking over, I picked her up.

Luke and I made quick work of readying the dogs. In minutes, we had them and all our gear and were out the door, heading for the south end of Juneau to hike down Point Bishop Trail.

Thankfully, the drive there was much less eventful than the moments before we left, and we made it there without incident. Pebbles sat on my lap and looked out the window the entire way, while Betty snoozed on the floor at my feet.

The truck dinged for a moment as I opened my door before Luke shut it off. I wrapped my hands in both dogs' leashes and got out. Luke hopped out and came around to take Betty. Once I had a hand free, I opened the back passenger door to get our backpacks.

Pebbles's excited bark broke the silence surrounding us in the forest as Luke and I donned our packs beside his truck. It felt a little crazy to take a Yorkie and a four-month-old black lab on a hike through the wilderness, but here we were. Ellis stayed true to his word and dropped off the pack that would comfortably fit Betty, if she decided she was too tired to walk anymore. Pebbles, one of us could carry without a problem. She weighed next to nothing.

Snapping the final buckle on my backpack, I curled the excess of Pebbles's leash around my hand. Luke shut the truck door and locked the vehicle, then tugged on Betty's leash, getting her moving in the right direction.

"Did you mark the GPS coordinates?" Luke glanced at me as we stepped toward the narrow cut in the trees that denoted the Point Bishop Trailhead. Our plan was to walk to the beach and back, then head home for a late supper of burgers on the grill to celebrate the holiday. At the end of it all, we planned to make some fireworks of our own between the sheets.

I couldn't wait.

It didn't matter that we'd burned up the sheets the last few nights. I was ready to do it again.

"Oh. No. I forgot." Turning around, I pointed back at my pack. "Can you dig it out?" It's in the front pocket." We didn't plan to stray off the path, but on the off chance something happened and we did, having the beginning coordinates marked would help guide us back if we got lost. It might seem silly to some, when we were on a marked trail, but this was Alaska. A predator could alter our direction in an instant. Just feet off the trail and we'd be in dense wilderness.

We also had two rambunctious dogs, one of which had proven a Houdini. I wasn't taking the chance we would get lost.

Device in hand, Luke locked in our starting point, then put it back in my bag. "You ready?"

"Yep. Let's go."

Betty led the way into the woods, black nose to the ground as she clopped along on paws too big for her body. Every few feet, she would stop and chomp at a leaf or pick up a twig, mouthing it until the next one distracted her.

Pebbles followed, less focused on the ground and more focused on the woods around us. Her little head whipped back and forth as she trotted along, tiny toenails tapping on the rocky dirt.

At the rate both dogs were going, I had no doubt we'd be carrying them back to the truck. The question would be whether either of them made it to the place we intended to turn around.

"So, did Claire or Ozzie call you back while I ran to that job site to check the alarm that went off?"

I glanced at Luke, a scowl overtaking my face. "No." When we left the rehab center yesterday evening, we went back to my house, since I had the dogs. Luke stayed the night but had to leave for a little while to check on a job site. Thankfully, it had been a false alarm. He'd also taken the opportunity to run home and grab some hiking gear he forgot. It meant we left a little later than planned, but I was okay with that. It hadn't delayed us that much. Only about forty-five minutes, since he was halfway to Juneau for the job site alarm anyway. One day, maybe, he would move to Parker's Landing and delays like that would be a thing of the past, but for now, we were commuting the half hour to see each other. And while we had the discussion about our relationship the other day, I still felt like we were dangling on the end of the line, the hook not quite set. I knew it was me and my insecurities, but I couldn't shake the feeling, no matter how much I reminded myself he'd chosen me over the dark-haired beauty with long legs and more money than she could count.

"Did you try calling again before I came back?"

Shaking off the disquieting thoughts about our oh-so-new relationship, I focused on the conversation. "Yes. It went straight to voicemail for both of them. Claire left her friend Christine's number in case of an emergency. I called her just to make sure they were all right. She said they were due back this evening and that she'd pass along the message to have them call me back."

"I guess that's all we can do, short of sending someone to retrieve them."

"Yeah. And this is something that can wait. If Miranda is involved, she doesn't know we're on to her, so she's not going anywhere." I shook my head. "I still can't see her as a killer. Sure, she's a sneaky, lying bitch, but a killer?"

Luke shrugged one shoulder, using his other arm to rein Betty back in. "People do crazy things for money."

They did crazy things for a lot of reasons.

That thought sparked another. "What if it wasn't about money?"

He frowned. "What do you mean?"

"What if it was motivated by something else? Like, love."

"You think Miranda was in love with Rich Stevenson?"

"I don't know. Maybe. We never really explored that possibility, did we?"

"No, not really. I guess it could be true. They're the same age and are from the same small town." He looked at me with a smile. "I guess we add it to the list of things to discuss with Ozzie."

I chuckled. "Yeah."

A comfortable silence fell between us, broken only by the shuffle of our feet, the dogs scurrying through the detritus littering the trail, and the birds flitting through the pines. We were far enough from the beach, and the forest was thick enough that only the muffled sound of waves hitting the shoreline reached us.

I cast a side-eyed glance at Luke as we walked. Should I bring up our relationship status? Did I need to? I mean, he introduced me to his family.

Yes, my inner voice whispered. *For your own peace of mind.*

I let out a quick puff of air through my nose. *Fine.*

"So, you know how you've been introducing yourself as my boyfriend?" I tipped my head to the side and looked up to see his face.

His mouth quirked. "I wondered when you would bring that up."

I huffed a short laugh. "So, is that what we are, then? Also, why do I feel like a high schooler asking my homecoming date that question?"

Luke laughed and hooked an arm around my shoulders, pulling me into his taller frame. I gripped his backpack and let out the slack on Pebbles's leash, so I could rest my other hand on the front of his shirt.

"New love has a giddiness to it. I think it makes us feel youthful again." He kissed the top of my head.

I barely felt it. One word reverberated around in my head.

Love.

Is that what this was?

I mulled it over, turning the word and the feeling coursing through me this way and that. But the concept was too new. Too fresh. I couldn't land on an answer just yet.

Instead of dwelling on it and trying to define it here and now, I shelved it for when I was alone and could properly think about it. I feared if I tried now, I might upset him by not having the answer he wanted to hear straight away.

"You're feeling youthful *again*?" I asked, smiling. "How is that possible when you're still a spring chicken?"

"I'm hardly fresh. You're not that much older than me. We've had this conversation." A smirk hovered on his lips and a bit of mischief danced in his eyes.

It was my only warning before he slipped my hold and had me plastered to his front, his mouth hovering millimeters from mine.

"Want me to prove how young we both still are?"

Delight skated along my nerve endings, pricking the skin on my head and neck. Need pulsed deep within me. It was on the tip of my tongue to say yes when Pebbles barked and tugged at her lead.

Chuckling, I backed away. "Later. Once we've worn these two out and they're down for the count all night."

Heat shimmered in his eyes. "We still have strawberry syrup left. And chocolate and whipped cream. I'm about to have the best sundae I've ever had in my life."

A need so intense I felt it to the ends of my hair roared through me. I tugged on Pebbles's leash, picking up the pace.

CHAPTER 33

Luke

I was in the Catch-22 from hell.

On a normal day, I was turned on by Mina, ready to close the door to the bedroom and strip her naked. But today? When we defined our relationship and the word that didn't get bandied around carelessly entered the equation?

I wanted to find the nearest bald pine, pin her against it, and convince her there was no one else for either of us ever again.

Considering the look she gave me before Pebbles barked, I doubted she'd mind.

Which brought me to the catch: the dogs.

Mina was right. The little beasts wouldn't leave us alone unless we wore their butts out or crated them. After the serenade we got last night when we tried that, I didn't really want a repeat.

So, I was stuck on this damn hike until they gave up.

But the moment the second dog flopped, I was scooping her up, and we were heading for the truck.

Ahead, the trail forked, and the trees parted to the right, giving us a glimpse of the water in Gastineau Channel, where the trail met Dupont Beach.

"Do you want to go look at the water?" I glanced at Mina, then at Betty, who veered off into the underbrush.

"Sure. We can let them sniff the beach. Pebbles likes the water. I don't know about Betty, though." Mina tossed me a saucy smile. "I guess we'll find out."

I chuckled. "Here's hoping she doesn't get tumbled by a wave. My clothes and Ellis's pack will smell like wet dog, if so."

"I'm not so sure," Mina said with a light laugh. "She's not getting fatigued yet, and we've walked about two miles."

"Hush. She'll get there." With a wink, I tugged on the dog's leash and headed for the water.

She was right, though. Neither dog was really showing signs of fatigue. We'd stopped a couple of times to offer them water when their tongues lolled out a little too far. The pep in their step had remained.

We broke through the trees and onto the rocky beach. Betty immediately yipped and ran for the water; only the leash clipped to her harness stopped her.

Mina laughed. "I think maybe she likes it."

"Yeah." Chuckling, I walked forward, letting the rambunctious animal reach the wave line. Even though the waves were only a few inches tall, water still crashed over her feet, and she backpedaled, then barked.

"Or maybe not." Laughing, I hooked my fingers into Betty's harness and plucked her off the ground, swinging her just a few feet away. Water still lapped at her feet, but it was more of a creep now than a splash.

Pebbles, however, had no such qualms. She darted to the edge of the water and ran through the tiny waves. Mina held on tight to the dog's leash. While the wave height here was low, they were still half the height of the small dog.

We let them play for several minutes before we walked down the beach, enjoying the sound of the water and the wind. I loved Alaska in the summer. Sunshine glinted off the water, warm and bright. You could even smell it in the air.

I liked winter, too, because it was equally gorgeous. But I also liked my fingers not freezing at work.

After we explored the beach, we headed back to the trail.

"Do you want to go further, or turn back?" I asked.

"Are these two ready to turn back, do you think?" Mina gestured to the dogs. At that exact moment, Betty tackled Pebbles, who sprang to her feet and gave her new sister a solid, snarly bark. It didn't deter the lab puppy at all.

I rolled my eyes. "Not yet, but it's also two miles back to the truck."

"True." But she still didn't look convinced.

"Let's hike another half mile, then turn around. Surely, somewhere in that five miles they'll give in."

She chuckled. "One could hope. Okay."

Turning, we headed south again.

"You know, I think we're close to that property Sarah Cole owns."

I looked around the forest with a new eye. "Really?

She nodded. "I remember it from the map Claire pulled up. It's not too far from here. Most people think this is all state land, but some of it's privately owned." She sent a mischievous smile at me. "You think we should go check it out?"

I laughed. "No. I value my freedom. Ozzie would lock us both up if we did that."

She pouted, but mischief still danced in her eyes. "Party pooper."

Taking her hand, I tugged her forward. "Look at it this way. If we're locked up, they'll separate us, and I do not want to sleep on a thin prison cot when we each have a lush mattress big enough for two."

The mischief in her eyes morphed into something hotter.

"Good point. Let's wear these dogs out."

Chuckling, we picked up the pace and headed down the path.

Several minutes later, a low buzz reached my ears. The dogs heard it, too, and paused, both of them turning toward the shore.

"That sounds like a boat." Mina turned toward the sound. "And it's close." She looked at me with a frown. "Can people come ashore here? Is there much beach?"

"I don't know. I've never walked along the shore this far south." The engine noise grew louder.

"Do you think someone needs help? I mean, we're not that far from Dupont Beach. Wouldn't they try to come ashore there if they were just looking for a place to set in?"

"You'd think, yeah. Let's go check it out."

As we stepped off the trail, Mina picked up Pebbles. I let Betty, who was bigger, trip along until we encountered a series of fallen branches. At that point, it was just easier to pick her up and tuck her under my arm.

In the few minutes it took us to trek through the woods to the shore, the boat engine cut out. Nearing the tree line, I caught a glimpse of the sky and water through the pine boughs. From my left, movement caught my eye.

"There." I pointed.

We changed direction, heading for the boat we could see bobbing on the water.

"Just stop! I told you selling the building was a terrible idea. But would you listen to me? No!"

Mina and I froze, not just at the angry female voice, but at her words.

"Building?" Mina mouthed, eyes wide.

Tipping my head, I motioned her to follow me.

I watched my footing as I crept closer. There was no way to avoid all the dry brush on the forest floor, but I could hopefully not step on some of the bigger twigs and branches that would make a louder snap.

"Get out of the damn boat, Walter, or so help me, I'll let Sarah shoot you when we see her."

"Why are you even helping her? You never did say. You just pointed that damn thing at me and told me to get on the boat. Now you're telling me to get off. She's got nothing good planned for either of us, I can tell you that."

"I'm only involved in this because of you. I tried to do one good thing, and it's come back to bite me in the ass. Well, I learned my lesson. I'm handing you over and heading for Hawaii. Let the crazy bitch find me there."

"Crazy bitch, huh? Can you believe that?"

All the blood froze in my veins at the sound of a second female voice, but it didn't stop my feet from turning.

Ten feet away, an older woman with graying blonde hair caught up in a ponytail held a Remington hunting rifle aimed squarely at Mina's chest.

CHAPTER 34

Mina

I never expected to see the end of a gun pointed at me ever again after Claire and I took down Grace Alonso back in March.

But there was no denying the fathomless black hole in the end of the rifle barrel aimed straight at me. I just wished I knew who held the rifle. Though from her comment when she came up behind us, I had a sneaking suspicion.

"Sarah?"

The woman smiled, the sight scary, because there was no mirth in her eyes. Only cold calculation and a simmering rage.

"That's me, yes." She used the rifle to gesture toward the shore. "Let's go greet our friends, shall we?"

I shared a quick look with Luke. His expression warned me to do what she said. He needn't worry. I had no plans to do anything that would get either of us shot.

Turning around, I headed toward the sound of Miranda and Walter still bickering.

A minute later, we broke through the tree line, and the bickering abruptly stopped. Surprise flickered in their eyes, but not just because Luke and I were there, I noticed. They both eyed Sarah warily. Something told me they were meant to meet elsewhere.

Miranda was the first to break the silence. "Where did you find them?"

"Lurking in the woods. Which one of you let the location of our rendezvous drop?"

Walter held up his hands. "I've been in the backcountry for weeks." He tipped a finger toward Miranda. "Ask her."

Miranda aimed a harsh glare at him. "Shut up, Walter." She looked at Sarah. "I haven't said anything to anyone."

I was not about to enlighten any of them that it was just happenstance.

"Well, let's get going before anyone else joins us." Sarah's gaze flicked toward the forest. "Get your stuff, and let's get out of here."

"What do you plan to do with them?" Walter asked, shuffling forward as he slung a large backpack over his shoulders.

"Not sure yet. But I'm definitely not killing them here where their bodies can be easily found."

My heart skipped.

Well, shit…

Donning her own pack, Miranda walked closer. Pebbles growled.

"Shh…" I put a hand over the dog's head and scratched her face, hoping to keep her calm.

"Wait." Miranda frowned. "Isn't that Claire Holmes's dog?" Alarm widened her eyes, and she glanced toward the trees. "Is she here? Along with that cop boyfriend of hers?"

"Cop?" Sarah's spine stiffened, and she adjusted her grip on her rifle.

"No," I hastened to assure them. "They're out of town. Luke and I are dog-sitting."

A slow, cold smile formed on Sarah's face. "Out of town, huh? That's good. How long?"

"A week," Luke swiftly replied.

I didn't contradict him. They didn't need to know Claire and Ozzie would be home tomorrow. Sooner, maybe, if they got my messages.

Miranda snorted. "Detective Quartermaine was allowed that much time off in the middle of a murder investigation? Give me a break. You're lying."

"No, I swear." Luke held up his hands. "The case has gone a little cold, so Ozzie asked for some time off to let things marinate."

With a hum, Miranda didn't argue.

"Where did they go?" Sarah asked.

"Where did they go?" Mina parroted. "Camping. Off-grid. They took a satellite phone for emergencies and left strict instructions not to be contacted unless it was an emergency." That was sort of true. They had indeed asked not to be bothered unless it was an emergency, but they took a long-range radio, not a satellite phone. When I spoke to Christine Bartles, she said she would try to relay a message to them, but I hadn't heard if she was successful.

Sarah studied us, and I did my level best to keep a straight face and maintain eye contact. She needed to believe my half-truths.

Finally, she looked away at Miranda and Walter. "That should give us a few days to figure out what to do. Even if someone reports them missing tonight or tomorrow, it'll take time for them to get back from the backcountry."

Her gaze slid past them to the water. No boats went past, but this time of year, it wouldn't be long before someone came by on their way into Juneau from a day's excursion. "Let's get off the shore. We still have a bit of a hike, and I want to get there before it gets too late."

She waited while Miranda and Walter moved ahead of her, then motioned for us to follow.

Once more, I glanced at Luke. His normally expressive

face had closed off into a stoic mask. I couldn't tell what he was thinking. Hopefully, it was about a way to get us out of this mess.

Because I had no idea how to do that.

CHAPTER 35

Luke

Of all the dumb luck, why did we have to stumble into the middle of the power struggle between Sarah Cole and her co-conspirators? I kept hoping some distraction would occur, so Mina and I could make a run for it, but no bears popped out from behind a tree, and no moose startled us as it dashed through the undergrowth. There was nothing but the whisper of the wind and an occasional falcon calling overhead.

For two hours, we walked east in what would be an aimless hike if not for the GPS device Sarah kept consulting.

When the cabin finally appeared, I almost thought it was a mirage. One moment, we were surrounded by pine trees and rocks, the next, a small log cabin appeared just yards away.

Marching up the two steps, her hiking shoes making a clomp-clomp as she crossed the worn wooden planks, Sarah kept one eye on us as she unlocked the front door.

Pushing it inward, she stepped back. "Everyone inside."

Sticking close to Mina's side, I followed Miranda and Walter into the dim interior.

Sarah brought up the rear and shut the door, adding to the gloom.

But it was still light enough I could see her face. She speared me with a look, then gestured to the dusty couch. "You two—sit."

Hanging onto Betty with one hand, I took Mina's with my other and led her to the couch. We sat down and set the dogs on the floor, but kept their leads on so they couldn't explore. I didn't trust Sarah not to hurt one or both if they got in the way.

Sarah barked orders at Walter and Miranda, and the three of them roamed the room, gathering candles and dusting off oil lamps, bringing them down off shelves so they could be lit.

"Do we have a plan?" Mina asked, her voice barely a whisper. She stared straight ahead, keeping attention off of us as she spoke.

"Maybe. Does that GPS device transmit coordinates?"

"Yes." The word was little more than a hiss.

I glanced up, holding my next words for a moment as Walter walked past.

"We need to push our—"

"No talking." Sarah stopped in front of us. "I will not hesitate to separate you two if you can't keep your mouths shut. I'm not an idiot." She held out a hand. "Give me your phones."

Deep in my gut, white-hot fury simmered. I held her gaze and tugged open the pocket on the strap of my pack to remove my phone. Never breaking eye contact, I handed it over. She stuffed it into her back pocket.

A glimmer of unease flickered in her eyes as she took the device. I bit back a smile at the knowledge I made her uneasy.

Good.

She needed to be scared of me. Because if she laid a finger on Mina or the dogs, she wouldn't like the man who emerged.

Mina wiggled out of her backpack, setting it on the floor by her feet. She dug into the front pocket and produced her phone, passing it to Sarah, who pocketed it. I took mine off as well, then sat back, watching our three captors move about the room.

Walter seemed pensive, but mostly unbothered, which, honestly, boggled my mind. He either knew something the rest of us didn't, or he genuinely was not scared of either woman. Whether that was because he didn't see them as threats or because he was certain Sarah wouldn't hurt him, I didn't know.

Miranda, though, she held herself with a rigidity born of nervousness. I think she could sense that Sarah had a plan she wasn't sharing. I know I could, and I doubted the plan ended well for anyone except Sarah.

I decided to prod her a little.

"So, what are you going to do with us?"

"Shut up!" she barked.

I raised an eyebrow, unphased by her outburst.

"He asks a valid question, Sarah," Miranda said. "They weren't part of our plan." Her brows twitched in a small frown. "What *is* the plan? You just told me to get Walter and bring him here. You weren't supposed to meet us at the beach." She narrowed her eyes. "Don't you trust us?"

Sarah scoffed. "Of course not. Do you trust me?"

Miranda looked away, not answering.

"That's what I thought." Sarah lit a match and set it to the wick in an oil lamp on the peninsula separating the small kitchen from the living room. She pulled out the rough wooden stool and sat down, facing them. "I asked you to meet me because that detective is getting too close to the truth." She aimed a smile at me and Mina. "It's actually rather convenient that you two happened upon our rendezvous. You can tell us what you know."

"Probably not a lot more than you," Mina said. "Ozzie

plays things close to the vest. We only know what we've uncovered in the building."

"Oh, please," Miranda said, jumping into the conversation. "I know Claire Holmes. She could convince the devil to repent and ascend to heaven. There's no way she hasn't gotten information out of Detective Quartermaine. They live together." She jabbed a finger at Mina. "And if she knows something, you know something, because you two are best friends."

"If Ozzie swears her to secrecy, she doesn't tell me. She wouldn't betray his trust like that."

Miranda hummed a non-answer.

"We know she's told you something, so tell us." Sarah's gaze traveled to the rifle she'd rested against the wall behind her, out of our reach, then back to us. "I don't have to keep you two around."

I held up a hand. "All we know is how she was identified and that she was pregnant at the time of her death."

Walter stilled at that. Miranda blinked in surprise.

Sarah, however, didn't bat an eye.

"Really? That's all you know?" She arched an eyebrow. "Then why is the detective's brother asking questions about the Myers Mansion and other property Edna Myers owned down at the docks?"

Mina quickly jumped in. "The body was found in a building Walter owned." She gestured to him. "It's only natural that the police would look into other property associated with him."

I wanted to smile and high-five her for thinking so fast, but that would only raise suspicion, so I kept my expression neutral and my gaze fixed on Sarah.

The woman narrowed her eyes but didn't disagree with Mina's statement. A moment later, she hopped off her stool. "Walter."

The man's attention snapped to her.

"You need to stay here and watch these two. Miranda and I need to go back to town and make sure Ellis Quartermaine doesn't find out anything he shouldn't. Preferably before his brother returns." She picked up her rifle, then turned to Miranda. "Wait here for a moment."

Before any of us could respond, she walked to the back door and went outside. It slammed shut, then we heard hammering.

"What is she doing?" Mina looked at Miranda.

The other woman shrugged. "Probably keeping you from escaping while we're gone."

Walter frowned, moving toward the window when it went dark. "I'm here too. Who does she think I'm going to run to and tell? I'm in as deep as you two."

"Maybe she's just worried you'll ditch us," Miranda said.

"Does it really matter? We're all on the run. Who cares if we're together?"

He continued to frown as the window on the other side of the small cabin went dark as well.

With each hammer blow cementing the board in place, more trepidation skittered through my system. Unless there was something in here to help us pry off the boards, we could very well be stuck.

Once the windows were boarded up, a few seconds later, the front door swung in. Sarah had her rifle ready but not aimed.

She fixed her gaze on Miranda. "Let's go."

Miranda huffed and didn't budge. "Are we really walking all the way back to Juneau? It's getting late."

Sarah cocked a hip and rolled her eyes. "No. There's an ATV stored in the shed. We're taking that. Let's go."

Giving Walter one last look, Miranda moved toward the door. "We'll be back." She moved out the door past Sarah.

"There's plenty of food in the cupboards. You won't

starve." With that, Sarah yanked the door shut. More banging erupted moments later.

I waited. Until the footsteps on the wooden porch faded and the ATV rumbled to life and sped away, I waited. As soon as I was sure they weren't coming back, I sprang off the couch.

Walter moved toward me, a wary look on his face. "What are you doing?"

"Getting us the hell out of here." I reached the front door and grasped the handle, but the door refused to open.

Dammit. She'd either locked it or nailed it shut.

Spinning around, I marched to the window and unlocked it. The sash lifted easily, giving me access to the board covering the opening. I pushed on it, probing to see how solid it was. The piece of plywood barely moved.

"You can't do that. We need to stay here." Moving from foot to foot, Walter stood a few feet away.

"You can stay, but Mina and I are leaving." I looked at him. "Unless you have some plan to stop us? Sarah didn't leave you a weapon, did she?"

Walter's already pinched expression grew more so. "No. I don't have a phone, either, before you ask. Miranda took my sat phone when she found me."

I grunted and went back to probing the board. "Sounds like they planned to hold you hostage all along." I pushed on the board again, this time putting all my weight into it, but it still didn't move.

"Let me guess," I said, turning to look at him once more. "They were the masterminds behind killing Moira all those years ago, and you were just the patsy who got in over his head."

The old man's grizzled jaw worked, and he glanced away. "I didn't kill her. I never wanted her to die. I just wanted my land back."

CHAPTER 36

Mina

"What do you mean, you just wanted your land back?" I walked up to Luke and Walter, curious about what Walter knew. We might actually get all the answers to this mystery now.

The old man's mouth pursed, and his gaze flicked back and forth between us.

"You've got nothing to lose, Walter." Luke backed away from the window to cross his arms and stare the man down. "In any case, you're going to jail for your part in Moira's death. Make it easy on yourself and cooperate."

Walter's eyes hardened. "You're not a cop and have no way to hold me here any more than I have a way to hold you here. Once we get the window uncovered, I can take off, and you'll never see me again."

"Then it still doesn't matter if you tell us the truth, then, does it?" I argued.

Those dull blue eyes moved back and forth between us again until, finally, he let out a sigh. "Fine." With a quick tip of his head, he motioned us back to the group of seats.

I sat down with Luke on the couch, while Walter perched on the edge of the upholstered chair to our left. He clasped his hands and let them dangle between his knees. "About six months before Sarah killed Moira, Miranda figured out she's my daughter."

A swift gasp left me.

"I'm sorry, what?" Luke leaned forward. "Who's your daughter?"

"Miranda. Her mother, Elsie, and I met at a club twenty-odd years prior. My wife and I were having problems. I thought my marriage was over, and in a moment of weakness, I caved to a beautiful woman. My affair was brief. Guilt ate me alive, so I ended it after only a couple of weeks. But the damage was done. Elsie was pregnant. For years, I funneled money to a secret account for her but only on the stipulation that she never tell anyone I was Miranda's father. My wife and I patched things up and were actually very happy until she died a few years ago." His brows knitted and he looked away.

"When Miranda turned eighteen, her mother and I agreed she no longer needed the support, except for her school funding. I was happy to offer a 'loan'"—he air-quoted with two fingers, never unclasping his hands—"that paid for a portion of her education. Elsie told Miranda she took out a small, low-interest loan through the bank. Miranda was never the wiser. Anyway, when she found out about me, she was out of school. Her mother confessed everything, including how I helped support her all those years. One day, Miranda showed up at the store and demanded I still support her, or she would tell Lucille everything. She wanted to open her own real estate office, and she needed capital."

He grimaced. "I know I should have just come clean with Lucille, but I saw a way out. And her timing was actually great. It was like the stars aligned to make this the perfect plan. My aunt had just died, and I was supposed to inherit her estate. Not just the Myers Mansion, but a few other properties in the area."

I shared a look with Luke. That accounted for the multiple amended deeds Claire found.

"But somehow, Sarah manipulated either my aunt or someone else into putting her name in place of mine on the real estate transfers," Walter continued. "I told Miranda if she could change them back, I would help her start her business."

I looked at Luke. "That's why there were two versions of the same deed, just with different recipients." I turned to Walter. "Why didn't you bring the authorities into it? Were you not in the will now?"

"I don't know if I was or not. I just saw an easy way to fix what Sarah tried to steal. With Miranda involved and her plan to blackmail me, it was just easier to have her fix it than to accuse Sarah of theft and tie everything up in the courts. I was not looking to make waves."

Luke crossed his ankle over his knee. "Okay. So how did Moira get involved, and why did Sarah kill her? How did you get involved in that?"

"Moira discovered the forgery on the deed Miranda fixed. See, my aunt used the firm Miranda worked for. I don't know how well you know Miranda, but she can be… persuasive."

I held back a snort. That was no lie.

"She sweet-talked her co-worker into letting her handle the transaction. I guess the woman just had a baby and was overwhelmed. Miranda promised to turn over most of the profits from the sale commission and only take a small fee for finishing the job. Her co-worker gladly handed it over. From there, Miranda went to a friend she had in the records office—Beth. Beth was supposed to push the new document through the system and shred the old one, but she had a family emergency. The files were on her desk, and Moira just scooped everything up to process it while Beth was out. Since Moira processed the original, she realized what was happening."

Walter let out a little huff. "Moira was too smart and too resourceful for her own good. She got to looking into

Miranda and Sarah Cole. She didn't find anything on Miranda, but she found out that Sarah had been the recipient of another large property from a person she was a caregiver for." He shrugged. "She found it dodgy, I guess."

"How did Miranda and Sarah get involved, then, if Miranda was working for you and not with Sarah?" I asked.

"Beth realized her mistake and called Miranda. As for Sarah, she's got eyes and ears everywhere, and since it was taking so long for the transaction to go through, she got suspicious and called Moira, pretending to be a representative of my aunt's estate. They talked, and Sarah asked to meet so they could look over things in person and sort it out. She also called Miranda, but as herself and threatened to expose her if she didn't cooperate."

He leaned back in his chair and put his arms on the armrests, picking at the worn brown fabric. "Miranda thought Sarah just wanted her to go along with transferring the property to her and not me. What she didn't know is that she was walking into a murder."

My stomach sank. We needed to get out of here and warn Ellis. If Sarah murdered Moira over a contract, she wouldn't hesitate to murder Ellis for asking questions of the old-timers down at the docks.

"I didn't witness the murder, but Miranda did. But after..." He trailed off and shook his head. "After, Miranda brought Sarah to me along with the murder weapon and Moira's body, wrapped in a plastic sheet. She said if she had to keep her mouth shut about the whole deal, then I did too."

"Why did you put the body in the wall rather than dump her in the ocean?" Luke asked.

"The water around here is too cold. It would take too long for her to decompose, and we couldn't risk weights falling off and her floating to the surface. It was easier to just seal her into the wall, then close for a bit and claim the building needed repairs. The knife, though, that went in the ocean a few days later. I probably should have kept it and buried it for insurance, but I didn't. I was too scared someone would find it." He shook a finger. "I didn't tell Sarah I threw it in the water, though. She thought I stashed it somewhere close."

I shared a look with Luke. That explained the break-in at the coffeeshop and café. Sarah was probably looking for the murder weapon.

Walter's jaw worked beneath his white beard stubble. "I wish I'd just come clean with Lucille. Maybe we could have worked things out." A hint of a sad smile ghosted over his lips. "Hindsight is twenty-twenty, you know?"

"Yeah," I murmured. My thoughts swirled as I digested everything Walter said. "Why didn't Sarah demand the property get transferred back to her?"

"It would have brought too much attention. The deeds were final. My aunt was dead. With the increased scrutiny surrounding Moira's disappearance, none of us wanted to bring any new attention to the public records' office, so Sarah just let it go."

That made sense. Sarah was greedy, but she wasn't a fool.

None of this solved our current problem, however.

I looked at Luke. "So, what do we do now? How do we get out of here?"

A slow smile slid over his face. He pointed at my backpack. "Give me your bag."

Frowning, I reached for it. "Why?" I passed it to him, lifting it over the sleeping dogs. They'd conked out not long after we set them down, exhausted from our long trek. Not even Sarah banging the boards into place had made them get up.

Luke took the bag and rummaged in the front pocket. A triumphant smile split his face as he pulled his hand out, clutching the GPS unit.

My eyes widened. "We can send a message!" In addition

to sending coordinates, this particular GPS model could also send short text messages.

"Yep." He tapped a button, waking up the screen. "Do you know Ozzie's number?"

"No, but I know Claire's."

"Give it to me."

Walter's low laugh slowly grew until he held his sides. I stared at him. So did Luke, his fingers poised over the GPS unit as he frowned at the older man.

"Why are you laughing?" I asked, genuinely confused.

Waving a hand, Walter sat up, then swiped at the moisture on his face. "Because—" he hiccupped. "Because Sarah thought she had this all planned out. But her own arrogance will be her downfall. She wrote you two off as bumbling amateurs because you're not the police. She should have searched your bags. I don't even care that I'm going to jail now. It will be worth it to watch that bitch get what she deserves."

"Well, okay, then." Luke offered up a lopsided smile. "What's that number, Mina?"

I recited it, and he quickly typed out a message.

It's Luke. Mina and I are lost in the woods off Point Bishop Trail. Ellis is in danger. Send help.

With a few more clicks, he attached our current coordinates and hit send.

"All right." Stowing the device in my bag again, he moved to the window. "Let's see about busting out of here, shall we?" He glanced at Walter. "Do you know if there's anything in the cabin we could use to pry these boards off?"

Walter got up. "Maybe. She might have some tools stashed somewhere. I've never been here, but it looks pretty well stocked."

It took us fifteen minutes and several different makeshift tools, but we finally made enough space between the wood and the window frame to wedge a piece of firewood in there.

With Walter and Luke pushing against it, they managed to pop the nails free.

Luke stepped back and turned to me. "Okay, babe. You're the smallest, so you get to go first and see if you can get the door unblocked."

I stepped up to the window.

"Lean into me." He moved in behind me.

I did as he asked.

"Lift your legs and I'll help you through the window."

Pulling my legs up, he held my torso while I wiggled and shimmied through the opening. It was definitely a tight fit. Walter might make it through, but Luke's shoulders wouldn't.

Turning as I went through the window, I steadied myself on the window ledge and lowered myself to the ground.

Luke leaned his head through the opening. "Go check if she left the hammer."

After straightening my shirt, I hurried around the front of the cabin and onto the porch.

Right there, next to the stack of firewood, was a carpenter's hammer.

I shook my head as I picked it up. Walter was right. Sarah truly was full of arrogance.

"I found it!" I yelled and attacked the first nail on the boards barricading the front door.

The claw part made quick work of the nails, and in minutes, I had the boards off.

But the moment I reached for the doorknob to let Luke and Walter out of the cabin, I noticed all the nails through the door and into the door jamb.

Sarah had nailed it shut.

"Oh, man." I let out a groan.

"What?" Luke's muffled voice came from the other side.

"The door's nailed shut. I'm going to try to pull the nails, but I'm not sure I can. Some of them are flush with the wood."

"Do your best."

Bending, I peered closer, assessing the nails, then attacked the one sticking up the most. I was able to wedge the claw under it and bend it up, then hook it and pull it out. Two more came out much the same way.

But when I tried the fourth one, there was nothing to get the hammer under. The fifth and sixth ones were the same.

"I can't get the rest," I said. "There are three left."

There was a moment of silence, then the door rattled in its frame.

With a soft squeak of surprise, I stepped back. He was insane. He'd never get it open from the inside.

"Luke, stop! Stop! Stop!" My voice grew louder to carry over the heavy thuds. He finally paused.

"The door swings inward. You'll never bust out. Let me check the back door." Before he could answer, I hurried around to the back of the cabin. This time, I pried up the middle of the board covering the doorway and peered inside.

Metal glinted around the knob. More nails pinned the door to the frame.

"Well, shit," I hissed, letting go of the board and straightening. I turned, looking for something I could use to help me break the door open, but the yard was devoid of debris.

My gaze landed on the shed. Maybe there was something in there.

"Mina?"

"Hang on." I backed away from the cabin. "I'll be right back."

I was halfway to the shed when I heard Luke's voice again.

"What are you doing?"

Glancing back, I saw him with his head poked out the

window. "Checking the shed," I answered, then broke into a jog.

When I reached the shed, I sent up a silent prayer it wasn't locked. There were no windows in it for me to squeeze through here.

But I was in luck. When I grasped the lever-action handle, it moved easily, and the door creaked open.

"Oh, hallelujah." I hurried inside but immediately paused just inside the door to let my eyes adjust.

Once they did, my racing heart sent stars into my vision, threatening to temporarily blind me as I spotted the glint of metal leaning against the wall.

It was an axe!

Blinking furiously and inhaling a breath in an attempt to slow my heart rate, I ran over and grabbed it, then left the shed.

"Holy shit! She really left an axe?" Luke's eyes widened when he saw what I carried.

"Right? The arrogance is astounding."

He thrust an arm out the window. "Give me that."

I paused just out of his reach and frowned. "Why do you get to have all the fun?"

The mixture of confusion and exasperation on his face brought a slow smile to mine. I couldn't stop the chuckle that slid free.

"Woman. Just give me the bloody axe." The smile on his face softened his words.

With an exaggerated sigh, I handed it to him. "Fine."

He took it and disappeared inside.

I made my way back around front. As I reached the porch steps, a mighty bang shook the cabin, sending the dogs into frenzied barking.

Luke had struck the first blow to the door.

I stood back and watched as the door splintered after

several blows. In minutes, he had a hole big enough to put his head and arm through.

"Okay, stay back, Mina." The axe hit the cabin floor with a dull thud. I heard him mutter something, and Betty's name, before there was a short pause. A moment later, his booted foot crashed through the broken door, sending slivers flying.

I took another step to the side.

With a few more well-placed kicks, he made a hole large enough to climb through.

But first, he passed me both dogs and our backpacks, then let Walter come out.

"So, now what?" I asked, shouldering my bag and holding onto Pebbles's leash. "The GPS has that back track function, but it'll take us back down to the shore. Do we need to go that way, or do you think we can head in a general northwesterly direction?"

Luke snapped the chest strap on his bag, a feat in and of itself as Betty, now free to explore the outside world and fresh from her nap, tugged at the leash hooked around his wrist. "I'm not sure how far we hiked in, so it's probably best if we follow the GPS. We didn't bring a map, because we weren't planning to explore off the trail, so without that, I can't plot a course to the parking lot from here." He glanced at Walter. "Do you have one?"

The old man shook his head. "I don't have anything. Miranda wouldn't let me bring anything but some clothes." He gestured to the small bag slung over his thin shoulders.

"All right." I heaved a sigh and turned toward the forest. "Let's get going."

It was going to be a long, long walk back to the car.

CHAPTER 37

Mina

This return hike had officially cured me of ever wanting a dog. Pebbles had decided she was *done* and refused to walk any further. But she didn't want to be carried, either. She simply wanted to lie down on the forest floor and become one with the ground. Every time I picked her up, she growled and barked, wanting down. We even tried putting her into Luke's pack, but the little stinker wiggled her way out. If it hadn't been for Walter's quick reaction, she would have tumbled almost six feet to the ground.

I did not want to explain to Claire why her dog had a head injury or a broken bone.

After the backpack incident, Luke plucked her from my arms and tucked her under one of his, like a football, and handed me Betty's leash.

Betty was more than happy to stay on the ground, but she didn't know how to walk a straight line. After nearly tripping over her for the fourth time in as many minutes, I let out a frustrated screech.

"Do you want me to take her?" Walter asked.

"No." As much as I would like a break, I wasn't about to

hand my best friend's puppy over to a wanted fugitive. Walter was cooperating, but that didn't mean I trusted him.

"Let's all take a break," Luke offered. Through the growing darkness, he gestured to the fallen tree about thirty feet away.

Happy to sit for a few minutes, I guided Betty to the tree and plopped down.

Except she wasn't ready to just hang out for a bit. Her nose had caught wind of something, and she wanted to follow it.

"Betty, no." I tugged on her lead, trying to bring her closer.

The little dog wasn't having any of it, though. She turned, whipped her head as she pulled, and slid her pudgy body free of her harness.

"Crap!" Rocketing to my feet, I lunged, but Betty was on the scent of God only knew what and headed deeper into the forest. I missed getting a hand on her and plummeted to the ground.

Fire, hotter than a thousand suns, raced through my left side, the intensity nearly making me sick.

I'd landed on my chest on a basketball-sized rock.

Grimacing, I wedged a hand under me to lift my face off the ground. My lungs were frozen, refusing to move oxygen, both from the impact and from the shards of pain flowing through my chest.

Male shouts echoed around me, but through the fog of pain in my brain, none of what they said registered. A moment later, feet pounded past me after the dog. Luke's feet.

A second set approached, then pant legs came into view. "You all right?"

With a moan, I rolled, letting the pack still strapped to my back prop me up.

Holy hell. Oh, that hurt. I wanted to nod and reassure

Walter I was okay, but I couldn't. All I could do was bare my teeth and moan.

"Just breathe. Let the pain pass."

That was easier said than done. Eyes closed, I focused on drawing air in and out.

In the distance, I heard Luke yell Betty's name and for her to stop. Gentle pressure on my arm was soon accompanied by something tickling my face. I opened my eyes and looked over to see Pebbles with her feet on my bicep, staring at me. Her ears twitched and her tail wagged when we made eye contact. With a yip, she leaned in and licked my face.

I wanted to laugh at the absurdity, but I didn't dare. It still hurt too much to breathe.

"You just sit there. Let the pain subside while Luke catches that little terror." Walter patted my knee.

"Yeah," I managed. Sagging into my backpack, I let it take my weight and did my best not to tense too much. Something was definitely broken. I hoped I could still hike out of here.

Closing my eyes, I focused on taking slow, steady breaths. The pain faded to a dull roar—so long as I didn't move. Every muscle twitch, every small shift to get more comfortable, sent the fire racing through my side and chest once more.

Several minutes passed before the soft thump of feet and the crunch of pine needles announced Luke's return.

"Mina?"

My eyes snapped open.

His footsteps grew faster, then stopped as he reached my side to crouch beside me. Pebbles barked and stood on his knee. Walter picked her up, so she was out of the way.

"What happened?" Luke brushed my hair back from my face.

"Betty happened. When I dove to catch her, I landed on that rock, there." I nodded toward the rock embedded in the ground at my side. "I think I broke a rib or two."

He drew in a breath, then let it out slowly. "Fantastic.

Okay." He rocked up on his heels. "Um, have you tried to get up yet?"

"No. It was bad enough rolling over to this position."

"Okay, hang on a second. Let me secure Betty." Luke stood, then walked away. It took him several minutes, but he got Betty back into her harness—secured a little tighter than previously—then knelt at my side again.

"This probably will not feel good, but we need to get you up and see if you can walk. But first, we need to take your backpack off. It'll just pull on your ribcage once gravity takes over."

"Yep." Keeping my left arm tucked close to my side, I lifted my right hand and threaded it under the strap over my shoulder.

"Okay, stop there." Luke wedged his left hand under my right side, then took my right hand with his free one. "I'm going to help you up. Let your left arm slide out of the strap as you stand."

I nodded, bending my knees with a wince as I prepared to put my feet under me.

"On the count of three, all right?" Luke adjusted his grip.

"Just do it," I grumbled. It was going to hurt whether he counted or not. I just wanted it over with.

He chuckled. "Okay, then." His grip tightened. "Up we go."

My butt barely left the ground when the searing pain returned. Gritting my teeth, a low moan escaped, but I planted my feet, let my bag fall off my arm, and stood up.

Luke kept an arm tucked tightly around my waist while I let the waves of pain and nausea pass. After thirty seconds or so, I was able to take several normal breaths.

"I'm okay." I patted his chest.

He loosened his grip but didn't let go. "Take a few steps."

Slowly, I walked forward. Sweat popped out on my brow, but my pain level stayed low.

But we were on level ground. What happened when we reached an outcropping or a small gully I had to climb over?

"How does it feel?"

"It's okay, but I'm not going to be able to climb over stuff. Not with any swiftness, anyway."

"What if Luke went on his own?" Walter walked closer, hesitation on his face.

"You mean, leave the two of you here?" Luke frowned.

Walter nodded. "I can keep an eye on her and watch the dogs. You can move faster than either of us on a good day. Ellis's life is in danger. Speed is important."

"He's right, Luke." I took Luke's hand. "My injuries will double the time it takes me to make the trek." As much as I hated the idea of staying out here to await rescue, there was more at play than just returning to town. "Go," I urged.

Luke held my gaze for several seconds. I could see him working through reservations as his expression went from thoughtful to resigned.

He turned to Walter. "How do I know I can trust you not to run off?"

"Because I'm done running. I've carried the burden of what Sarah did for decades. Knowing now Moira was pregnant—" He broke off and shook his head, sadness shining from the depths of his eyes. "I wish I would have owned up to all my mistakes back then. Maybe she'd still be alive and raising that baby and a passel more. It's time for all of us involved in Moira's death to pay." His chest heaved with emotion, and a sheen of tears shimmered in his eyes.

Luke clasped a hand over Walter's shoulder, then gave it a couple of quick pats. "All right. I guess I'll have to take you at your word."

"I won't break it. I mean it, I'm done running." Walter switched both leashes to one hand, then shrugged out of his backpack. "Here. Put some water in this and the GPS. Leave that big pack. It'll just weigh you down and make you more top-heavy."

"That's a good idea." Luke took off his pack.

"Help me sit again," I said. "Then give me the dogs. Then Walter can help you transfer things."

"How about I help you sit, and we tie the dogs up?" Luke slid a hand around my waist and guided me to the fallen log, propping me up against it on the forest floor.

"I guess that works," I muttered through clenched teeth. Right there and then, I vowed not to move again unless my bladder was about to burst or rescue showed up.

While I sat there, staring off into space, trying to get control of the pain again, Luke and Walter switched bags. Pebbles and Betty settled down beside me. I knew it wouldn't last. They'd get a nap in and be ready to cause trouble again soon.

I blinked, bringing the world back into focus when Luke dropped into a crouch directly in front of me.

"For the record," he began, "I don't like leaving you here." He glanced over his shoulder at Walter, who was twenty feet away, bent over Luke's old backpack, stuffing clothing and other items into it. "I don't completely trust him, but I'm going to have a little faith he means what he says, because, frankly, we don't have another option."

My gaze traveled past him to the old man. A small frown formed on my face. "Yeah. Sorry about that."

"It's not your fault. Fate's having a good laugh at us." He raised a finger. "But she won't have the last laugh. Not if I can help it."

His eager confidence brought a smile to my face. I lifted a hand to touch his cheek. "I have no doubt you'll show her who's boss."

He chuckled and covered my hand. A moment later, his expression sobered. Those beautiful pewter eyes held mine hostage. "I know we only touched on the subject, but you should know"—he held up a hand—"just in case something goes wrong and I never get to tell you this—but seeing you lying there, obviously hurt, and knowing the severity of our situation, that emotion we danced around? The one that starts with L and ends in O-V-E?" He raised an eyebrow. "Well, it smacked me hard."

Something warm and gloriously light unfurled in my chest. Recognition of the same emotion spreading through my veins temporarily pushed away the pain pulsing in my ribs.

A slow, happy smile spread over my face. "I love you too. Make sure you remember that and use it to get yourself back to me."

He took my chin in his hand. "I will. Don't trip over any more rocks while I'm gone, yeah?"

I chuckled, then immediately regretted it. Moaning, I grasped my side.

Luke's face contorted into a look of contrition. "Sorry."

"It's fine. I just need to remember I can't laugh."

Leaning in, he kissed my forehead. "I will send help back as fast as possible. Try to get some rest." Rising, he stepped back.

"Walter," he said as he turned.

The old man, who'd finished packing his bag and had moved away to give us some privacy, looked at Luke.

"Take care of her. I'm trusting you."

"I won't let you down. Go save your friend."

Luke looked at me again.

I raised my right hand and made a shooing motion. "Go."

His jaw worked. A moment later, he nodded and backed away. "Watch yourselves."

With a final look, he spun on his heel and loped away.

CHAPTER 38

Luke

Walter's idea to switch bags had been a good one. With the smaller, lighter backpack, I could move much more easily over the rocky ground.

I was thankful it was summer. It meant long days, so even though it was late, the sun hadn't quite set yet. I had enough light to keep up a decent pace. According to the GPS, from where we stopped, I had about four miles to go. A mile-and-a-half through the woods and two-and-a-half miles on the trail. My goal was two hours. Provided I didn't fall or encounter a bear or a moose, that was a more than reasonable amount of time.

But I still felt the pressure to move faster. Mina needed help, and Ellis needed to be warned.

With careful but quick steps, I picked my way over the rocks and deadfall. Three-quarters of a mile into my journey, the sun dipped behind the mountains, and I had to slow down, even with the powerful flashlight I pulled out of my bag.

Darkness continued to gather as I descended toward the trail. A steady prayer that I wouldn't encounter a large predator played in my head like a broken record. When I finally broke through the tree line and onto the trail, it took me several steps before the loop stopped, and I realized where I was.

I let out a quick whoop and turned toward town.

The light bobbed as I ran. My legs already ached from the six miles I'd walked this afternoon and evening, but I pushed it away, keeping Mina's pained face in my thoughts and letting it drive me forward.

Listening to my even breathing, I ran. When lights blinked through the pine boughs as I approached the parking lot for the trailhead, I quickened my pace, sprinting the last quarter mile.

As I broke through the trees, I whipped off Walter's backpack, eyes locked on my truck.

"Luke?"

I skidded to a halt and turned. Across the lot, Ozzie stood next to his cruiser.

"Oh, thank God!" Reversing direction, I jogged over. "We weren't sure if you got any of our messages."

"The last one came through just a little while ago, and I came straight here. Claire and I were on a plane; that's why we didn't answer. What's going on?" He looked past me, up the trail. "Where's Mina?"

Wiping sweat from my face, I frowned. "Your damn puppy slipped her harness. Mina fell onto a rock trying to catch her and broke some ribs. I left her and the dogs in the woods with Walter Shuman."

"Wait. You found Walter?" Ozzie held up his hands. "Back up. Start from the beginning. Your last message was pretty vague. I alerted search and rescue, and they're gearing up, but that's it. I just came down here to scope things out."

Relief punched me square in the gut. Hopefully, soon, Mina would be back in town, getting the medical attention she needed.

I took a deep breath and let it out. "Sorry about that. Character space is limited on the GPS unit. Have you called Ellis?"

"Yes. He's at my house with Claire now."

"Without backup?"

Ozzie's frown deepened, and a touch of confusion entered his dark gaze. "Yeah. Claire has weapons in the house, so they're armed. We figured that was enough until we knew more."

"You need to send a unit over there. I don't know what she's got planned."

A small frown marred Ozzie's forehead. "She? Who are you talking about? Explain."

I huffed and forced myself to start at the beginning. "Mina and I went hiking." I held up my hands. "Just a normal hike. We weren't looking for trouble or poking into anything. Our goal was to wear Pebbles and Betty out, so they'd sleep better tonight."

Letting my hands fall, I continued. "We made it to Dupont Beach, and they still weren't tired, so we decided to go another half mile up the trail. We heard a boat coming into shore, which we thought was strange since the beach was so close. Thinking, maybe, someone needed help, we ventured over in time to hear Walter and Miranda Benning bickering."

"They drove a boat into shore south of Dupont Beach?"

"Yep."

"Why?"

"I don't know why they picked that particular spot, but they chose that area because it's close to Sarah Cole's land." I tipped a finger. "And guess who showed up and ambushed us all?"

Ozzie's eyes widened.

I nodded, confirming his suspicions. "Sarah Cole was the mastermind. Walter was the intended recipient of Edna Myers's estate. Not just her mansion, but all her property. Sarah illegally had it changed. Walter used Miranda to get it changed back, and Sarah killed Moira because Moira was asking too many questions. Oh, and Miranda is Walter's secret daughter. He didn't want that fact to get out, which is why he went along with all of Sarah and Miranda's plans."

This time when Ozzie's eyes widened, they rounded so far, I wondered if they might pop out of his head.

He muttered a curse. "That explains a lot. But how is Ellis involved?"

Before I could answer, recognition dawned on his face. He held up a hand. "Ellis is asking questions. Just like Moira. He's being public about it and stirring up the town's memories from back then."

"Exactly. And Sarah and Miranda have at least an hour head start on me, probably more, because they were on an ATV. They have to be in town by now."

Ozzie backed up and opened his car door, leaning in to grab his phone. Tapping the screen a few times, he brought it to his ear.

A frown formed on his face after several moments. He lowered the device. "He didn't answer." Tapping the screen again, he lifted it once more. "Let's try Claire."

The frown on his face turned fierce when she, too, didn't answer.

Stabbing the red circle on the screen to end the call, Ozzie tipped his head toward the cruiser. "Get in."

I hurried around to the passenger side and hopped in.

Ozzie picked up the radio as we left the parking lot. "PL212 to dispatch, over."

"Dispatch to PL212, go ahead, over."

"I need you to send a unit to my house." He stated the address. "And have all units on the lookout for two females. Miranda Benning and Sarah Cole. Standby." He let go of the mic button and glanced at me. "What were they wearing? And what does Sarah Cole look like?"

"Miranda had on black pants, a burgundy long-sleeved

shirt, and hiking shoes. Sarah was wearing olive green pants and a tan t-shirt. She had a black jacket tied around her waist. And she's about five-five, a hundred and twenty pounds. Graying blonde hair pulled back in a ponytail. I'd say she and Miranda are close to the same age too. Mid-fifties."

Ozzie relayed that information to dispatch, then in the next breath asked for an update on the search and rescue efforts underway. The dispatcher said they were staging and would roll out within the hour.

I breathed a sigh of relief. The weather was warm, and Mina had been stable when I left, but I was glad to know she would soon be out of there. She and Walter were sitting ducks for predators and had no way to defend themselves.

About seven minutes into our drive north to Parker's Landing, dispatch came back over the radio.

"Dispatch to PL212. Officer on scene reports no one home, over."

Ozzie's dark eyes met mine. Worry and anger simmered side-by-side in their depths. Plastic creaked in his hand as he squeezed the radio mic. Bringing it up to his mouth to speak, he rubbed one finger over his top lip, then responded.

"Dispatch, who was the responding officer, over?"

"Chief Riggs, over."

"Thank you. PL212 out." He hung up the mic and picked up his phone. Unlocking it with his face, he handed it to me. "Find the chief's number and call it. Put it on speaker."

I scrolled, quickly finding the contact labeled "Chief Riggs," and dialed.

It rang through the cab of the cruiser, then the chief picked up after a couple of rings.

"Riggs."

"Was Claire's car in the garage?" Ozzie asked without preamble.

"Yes. I knocked on every door. No one answered. What's going on?"

"How about Ellis's truck? He was supposed to be there."

"It was there too. Answer my question, Quartermaine. What's going on?"

"I found Luke. Mina's still in the woods with Walter Shuman. She's hurt. Sarah Cole killed Moira and somehow roped Miranda into it. Luke said they're going after Ellis. Go back to my house and break in. Make sure they're not—" Ozzie's words cut off. He swallowed hard and inhaled a breath before continuing. "Make sure they're not in there bleeding or dead."

Riggs muttered a curse. "Turning around now. I'll call you back."

The line cut. I put the phone down.

"Sonofabitch!" Ozzie smacked the steering wheel.

I could sympathize with how he felt. If it were Mina, I'd feel helpless too.

He flipped on his lights and siren, then pressed the accelerator. "I have a bad feeling about this."

CHAPTER 39

Luke

The next forty-five minutes passed at a snail's pace. Ozzie sped the entire way, but it felt like the world went by at a crawl. Riggs called back about ten minutes after he hung up to report the house was empty. That brought a modicum of relief, but it left us confused.

Why would Sarah take the two of them if she wanted Ellis dead? Why wouldn't she just kill him—and Claire, since she was a witness—then leave?

The other option was that Ellis and Claire ran away on foot, but it had been nearly two hours since Ozzie left Parker's Landing. If they'd escaped, one of them should have called.

We roared into town, making the turn off the highway to go down Main Street to get to Ozzie and Claire's house.

Passing by the shops, we were at the corner on the far side of Mina's coffeeshop when my brain registered something was off.

There were lights on in the café.

"Stop!"

Ozzie hit the brakes, locking our seatbelts. "Jesus, what?"

I hit the button to roll down the window and stuck my

head out to look back. "The construction lights I set up are on at Mina's. In the café side. They shouldn't be."

Checking his mirrors, Ozzie swung the truck around, killing the siren as he pulled to the curb opposite the building. "Give me my phone."

I handed it over. Ozzie unlocked it as he got out. When I met him on the sidewalk behind the vehicle, he had it to his ear.

"Come downtown. The Cozy Cup. Something's up. We drove past, and Luke noticed the lights are on and shouldn't be." He listened for a moment, then bobbed his head. "See you in a few."

Hanging up, he looked at me. "Riggs is on his way."

"Good. He can help you transport." I stepped off the curb. Sarah needed to go to jail for all she'd done, and before she could hurt Claire and Ellis.

Two steps into the street, Ozzie's hand wrapped in my shirt, bringing me to a halt.

"Hold on. We can't charge in without a plan. If they're in there, they probably heard the siren."

Gritting my teeth, I shrugged off his hold. "Fine. What's the plan? And don't say to wait for Riggs."

"We're not going in without him. Not unless they're in mortal danger. Rushing in without backup could make Sarah and Miranda do something rash." Worry etched lines around Ozzie's dark eyes, but the set to his features told me he'd probably handcuff me to the light post if I tried to go in early.

Inhaling a quick breath through my nose, I forced my rational mind to take over. Letting my emotions control things would get people hurt.

"Let's go peek in the windows the best we can. Riggs should be here soon." He let go of my shirt, then backed up a few steps to the truck to reach in and grab a handheld radio.

Closing the door with a soft snick, he tipped his chin toward the café, and we jogged across the street.

Light spilled around the edges of the brown paper we'd tacked to the windows, shining through with a soft glow in places where the paper fibers were thin.

"Are there any tears in this stuff?" Ozzie asked, his voice low.

Mouth flattening into a flat line, I scanned it. We hadn't been super careful about putting it up, but we hadn't been reckless, either. It was meant to, one, keep the interior a surprise to Mina's customers, and two, protect the building from theft. People couldn't see in to tell what materials and tools were inside.

I pointed to a spot on the far side of the front windows, where more light spilled out than anywhere else. "Over there, maybe?"

On quiet feet, we moved. Ozzie crouched in front of a small gap in the paper and looked in. "The angle is wrong," he hissed. "All I see is the far wall. Where the stairs are."

That gave me an idea.

I tapped him on the shoulder. "Let's go around back." Turning away, I headed for the corner.

"Is it any easier to see in back there?"

"No, but we might be able to get inside without being seen." Our dumpster guy had put the roll-off close to the building so we could chuck things into it from the windows and doors. We might be able to climb on top and get in through an upstairs window. They weren't locked.

As we reached the corner, a cruiser rolled up.

We paused as the window went down in the SUV. As the man inside shifted to lean through the opening, the streetlight glinted off the nametag pinned to his chest. This was Chief Riggs.

"Sit rep, Quartermaine."

"We can't see in the front windows, but Luke says he thinks he might know a way in through the back."

"Okay. Put your radio on channel six." He gestured to the radio in Ozzie's hand. "I'll watch the front."

Tossing him a thumbs-up, Ozzie nudged me, and we took off around the corner to go up the alley.

"Shit. Ozzie. Is that smoke?" The light illuminating the rear parking area had a hazy appearance.

"Yeah. I smell it."

A door slammed, and through the shadows, we saw two figures running away.

"Hey! Stop! Police!" Ozzie picked up the pace.

When we reached the back doors to the coffeeshop and café, smoke billowed through cracks around the café's door.

I skidded to a halt. "Go! Catch them. I'll check the building."

"I'll radio it in!"

Turning, I ran to the door and twisted the knob, praying it was unlocked. The steel door would be much harder to break down than the cabin's wooden door.

The knob turned under my hand.

Yes!

Pushing inside, a thick, gray blanket of smoke billowed around me. I couldn't see a damn thing through it except the orange glow of fire from the front of the building. A low roar filled the space.

"Claire! Ellis!" Hooking my shirt over my nose, I ran deeper into the interior.

"Help!" Ellis and Claire's voices penetrated the smoky space.

"Keep yelling so I can find you." Coughing, I held my shirt tighter to my face. Tears streamed down my cheeks now, partially blinding me as my eyes fully protested the acrid smoke.

I followed the sounds of their voices and quickly found them in the back corner of the main room on the floor, back-to-back, their hands tied to the other's behind them, and their feet bound.

"Luke!" Claire's voice held a raspiness that wasn't normally there. "It's Sarah Cole and Miranda Benning." She paused, a hacking cough rattling her body. "They tied us up, set the fire, and left."

"I know. They tried to kill Mina and me too. And Walter. Ozzie's chasing them." Swiping at my face so I could see, I picked at the knots tying their hands together.

"Do our feet," Ellis said. "We can worry about our hands after we get out of here."

Recognizing he made a good point, I moved down to his ankles. These knots were easier to get to and not as well tied. They were meant to keep them immobile, not from escaping, like the hand knots were. Despite my fumbling attempts, I had the rope around Ellis's feet loosened in less than a minute.

While he kicked free, I crawled around to Claire's feet and untied her. Once they were both free, I helped them stand.

"How do we get out of here?" Ellis asked, suppressing a deep cough.

Closing my eyes, I ran through a mental map of the space. We were near the shared wall with the coffeeshop. We could follow it around to the front door.

"This way. I'm going to guide you guys. Claire, you need to walk backward, so just be careful."

"Go fast"—she stopped, coughing—"but not too fast."

Grasping Ellis's shirt, I guided him the few steps toward the wall, then, keeping one hand on the wall and one on Ellis, I walked the perimeter of the room. By the time we reached the door, I couldn't see at all, and we were all continuously coughing. My lungs felt like the flames had reached inside and set them alight.

Fumbling with the old lock, I managed to flip it. With my thumb on the lever, I pushed down, then pulled. The heavy door weighed more than usual, but I got it open far enough to wedge my foot into the opening.

The blare of fire engine sirens split the night as I thrust my leg through, then wedged my shoulder into the space. Using my foot, I kicked it wide and hauled Ellis forward.

It hit him in the shoulder, and he let out a grunt, but didn't fall. The three of us stumbled forward and onto the sidewalk just as the fire engine pulled up.

My vision still obscured by tears, I heard, rather than saw, the truck stop and a series of boots hit the road.

The first firefighter reached us and put a steadying hand on my shoulder as I bent double, hacking.

"Kyle, grab some shears!" he yelled.

I sank to the ground as my adrenaline ebbed. Bending my knees, I rested my forehead on them, inhaling deep breaths in between coughs.

A minute or so later, a firefighter knelt next to me. "I'm going to slip this oxygen mask over your face."

I looked up, my vision blurry, but it was better than a couple minutes ago.

The plastic mask descended over my mouth and nose. Air flowed in, cool and fresh, if not a little chemical-smelling from the plastic.

"Is there anyone else inside?"

I shook my head. "No."

"Okay. You breathe that in and stay put."

I nodded, unable to speak as another cough wracked my body.

When he walked away, I scooted back to lean up against the pillar that was meant to keep cars from driving onto the sidewalk.

Resting against the pole, I rolled my head to the side and saw Claire and Ellis getting similar treatment.

They were okay. We were all okay.

I closed my eyes and just focused on my breathing. Slowly,

the oxygen invading my body reduced my cough to short bursts.

Voices flowed around me, sometimes rising as the fire-fighters hauled gear off their trucks to put out the blaze inside. It wasn't until the energy changed that I opened my eyes and looked around again.

Commotion down the block drew my attention. I rubbed my eyes and sat up, squinting in the strobing lights from the fire engines.

Ozzie and Chief Riggs walked toward us, each of them leading a woman in handcuffs.

I let out a delighted laugh that quickly descended into a cough. As it ebbed, I got up.

"Whoa." My head spun, and I shot a hand out to steady myself on the pillar. There was no way I would sit down, though. I wanted to watch them march past and see their faces—especially Sarah's—when they realized Claire and Ellis were alive.

Once I felt like I could walk and not fall over, I picked up the small oxygen tank and walked over to the others.

Ozzie and the chief stopped in front of us.

Worry etched lines into Ozzie's face. "You guys all right?"

Ellis gave him a thumbs-up.

Claire smiled through her mask. "We're good. Luke"—a wheezy cough overtook her for a moment—"Luke got us out."

Dark eyes found mine. His quick nod was filled with gratitude.

I returned it, not needing any thanks. It's what any decent human would have done.

My gaze traveled to the woman in his grasp. Suppressed anger and defeat warred on her expression, if the hard set to her jaw and the defiance shining in her eyes were anything to go by. Dirt marred her clothing, and the high ponytail she'd been sporting was now knocked askew. Ozzie had worked for this arrest.

I was just thankful he caught her.

"You taking them to the hospital?" the chief asked one of the firefighters.

"Yes, sir. They all need to be under observation for a little bit."

Logically, I knew that, but it didn't make it any more palatable of an idea. I wanted to go to the staging area for Mina and Walter's rescue operation, not hang out in a hospital cubicle with wires hanging off me.

I took comfort in the fact, though, that they'd bring her to the same hospital once they found her. Her ribs would need treatment.

"I'll see you all at the hospital later." Ozzie gave Sarah a nudge forward. "Let's go. You've got a date with our local jail."

CHAPTER 40

Mina

"Hey, Mina. How are you feeling?"

My eyes popped open, my mind ripped out of the delicious daydream brought on by the dose of morphine the nurse gave me just minutes ago.

I blinked, bringing Ozzie's face into focus. "Hey!" What felt like a smile spread over my face. "Morphine is amazing. So is this cloud they've put me on." The pain in my side had faded to a dull roar, and a floaty sensation filled my limbs. Somewhere in the back of my mind, I knew I was on a cot in the ER, but it felt much lighter and softer than that.

He chuckled. "I'm glad you're feeling good. You've got some decent injuries."

"Oh yeah?" Again, somewhere, I knew that, but my brain was a little fuzzy. I remembered my ribs hurting, but that was it.

"Yeah. The staff called your parents since you were too out of it once they gave you morphine to really understand what was going on. The nurse let me speak to them. Your mom said you broke your bottom three ribs, one of them in two places. Luckily, they're not displaced, so no surgery required. You also lacerated your spleen. They're watching that."

"Yikes. That sounds bad."

"Bad enough you're going to be a guest here for a while. The nurse told me they're getting a room ready for you upstairs."

I frowned. "No. I want to sleep in my own bed." With Luke. Because we wore out the dogs.

Wait. Ozzie was back, so he'd take them. Even better.

My frown deepened as my foggy brain tried to make sense of things. Why was Ozzie here and not Luke? Where was he?

"Where's Luke?" I voiced the thought.

Ozzie's amused look faded. "Yeah, about that." His mouth twisted, and he glanced away for a second. "He's down the hall in another cubicle."

"Oh. Okay." My eyelids drooped.

Several beats passed before the implications of that cleared my addled brain.

"Wait, what?" A bit of the fog cleared as concern entered the picture.

"Sarah got to Claire and Ellis and took them to the antique store. She tried to burn it down with them in it. Luke ran in and got them out. They're all here being treated for smoke inhalation."

I kicked at the blankets covering my legs, then put an elbow under me to sit up.

Fire raced through my side, and I fell back to the bed with a moan.

"Easy." Ozzie took my hand and helped me straighten up against the bed. "They're fine. Just hacking. Claire and Ellis might have to stay the night, since they were in the smoke longer, but I imagine once the ER staff cut Luke loose, he'll be up in your room. So, just take it easy. He's okay."

More sober now, thanks to the rush of adrenaline, the throb in my ribs registered. I winced as I shifted. "What happened? Is my building gone?"

"No. It's damaged, but I think it's fixable. It hadn't been burning long, and the fire department was there pretty quickly. Sarah and Miranda set fire to a pile of shop rags and some packing material."

My brows twitched down. At least we wouldn't have to start from scratch, and hopefully, The Cozy Cup could still stay open.

"Did Luke tell you it was Sarah who murdered Moira? That Miranda and Walter just helped hide her body?"

Ozzie nodded. "Both women are in custody. Chief Riggs and I caught them running from the fire. It's over now, Mina. All of it."

I smiled. "That's great news. Moira can finally rest in peace."

"Yeah, and her family gets closure."

That was the best part, knowing her parents could rest easy, and so could Rich.

Ozzie patted my hand. "You get some rest. Claire and I will come see you tomorrow, sometime."

"Okay." Sleep tugged at me again. The pain meds might have backed off a bit, but it wasn't just that making me tired.

With another quick pat, he left.

I drifted off. Not into a terribly deep sleep, but enough that time passed without my knowledge. It was nearly an hour later, when the nurse unlocked the brake on my bed, that I awakened again.

She smiled at me. "Hey there. We're taking you upstairs. You can keep sleeping."

Not about to argue, I let my eyes slide closed once more.

The nurse and a patient care assistant wheeled me through the halls and into an elevator. I barely felt the bump as we arrived on my floor. With a clack of the wheels over the elevator threshold, we were headed down another corridor. Seconds later, they turned into a brightly lit room.

It was impossible to even feign sleep when the ward staff descended on us to take a report.

Fifteen minutes later, my ER escort was gone and the floor nurse left to check on other patients. Blessed quiet enveloped me.

I let out a soft sigh, ready to drop back into dreamland.

The door opened, admitting the chime from someone's IV down the hall.

Frustration bubbled over in the form of a growl. "No, I don't need anything, and you literally took my vitals a few minutes ago. I just want to sleep."

"I can come back."

My eyes popped open. That wasn't the nurse.

It was Luke.

"Don't you dare leave." Lifting a hand, I crooked a finger. "Get over here."

In several long strides, he crossed the room to sit on the edge of my bed. Leaning down, he brushed a kiss over my forehead and took my hand. "How are you doing?"

"Better now that you're here. Ozzie told me about the fire. Are you all right?" His voice held a raspy note that wasn't normally there.

"I'm okay. I'll probably be coughing for a couple days and get winded a little easier for a bit, but I'm fine. Your café isn't, though. I think our timeline for opening is going to have to change."

I wrinkled my nose. "I heard. I still don't understand why she wanted to take them there. Why didn't she just kill them at Claire's?"

"I asked Ozzie that. Sarah's not talking, but I guess Miranda is singing like a canary. She said Sarah wanted the poetic justice of killing them where Moira was laid to rest." He rolled his eyes. "There is something seriously wrong with that woman."

"That's no lie. She's crazy." I let my body relax into the

bed, a sense of rightness taking over me now that Luke was with me and the whole Moira situation had come to a conclusion. "I'm just glad it's over, and that everyone will be okay."

"Me, too, honey." He kissed the side of my head and ran small circles over the back of my hand with his thumb. "I was worried the whole way back to town about how you were. Did you have to walk out?"

"No. The Coast Guard dropped in a rescue team at a clearing not too far away. They debated carrying me in a litter, but it wasn't far, so I said I would walk. They ended up giving me a low-dose painkiller, then just provided some support for the short trek. A helicopter picked us up from the clearing and brought us to town. I took an ambulance ride to the hospital, and Walter took a cop car ride to the police station along with Pebbles and Betty."

He let out a soft grunt. "That sounds better than my run. My legs are stiff. I'm going to feel it tomorrow."

"We all are." I tipped sideways a fraction, so I could lean into him. This sucked. I wished we were back at my place—or his—cuddled up all warm, cozy, and sated in bed.

I also wished I was a little less fuzzy-headed. There had been several huge revelations between us in the last few days, and we needed to figure out what was next for us.

A tear trickled down my face. Turning my head away, I swiped at it.

"Hey, what's this?"

Luke put a gentle finger under my chin, turning me to face him again.

"Why are you crying?" He frowned.

I sniffed—or tried to, anyway. The pain in my side kept me from doing much more than a brief inhale.

He got up and grabbed a tissue from the box on the nightstand, handing it to me.

"Thank you," I murmured, then wiped at my nose.

"You're welcome. Now tell me what's upset you."

"I'm not upset."

One dark blond eyebrow rose over his gray eyes.

"I'm not. I'm just... overwhelmed, I guess."

His forehead wrinkled. "How so?"

"Just all the stuff that's happened. Finding Moira's body. Getting held hostage. Falling on the rock and doing a number on my body." I paused, meeting his gaze. "You."

"Me? What about me?" He sat down again, curiosity lighting his expression.

"You've come barreling into my life. I'm not mad about it, but it's got me wondering where we go from here. Do we continue going on as we have been? You stay with me one night, and I stay with you another? We date when our schedules allow? Or do we try to do more?"

Luke held up a hand. "I vote we do more." He lowered his arm to thread our fingers together. "I meant what I said in the woods, Mina. I love you. Yes, I want to date you, but I'm also willing to turn the dating into something more serious. Your life is in Parker's Landing. Mine can be too. I can draw up architectural plans and make phone calls about projects from anywhere. Dad's company does business all over the region, and I've built a solid reputation since I hung out my architect shingle. I don't need to be headquartered in Juneau anymore."

He leaned closer, earnestness making him look more boyish. "That is, if you want a roommate?"

Maybe it was the pain medication. Maybe it was fatigue. Or even a combination of both. But the happiness that bubbled up inside of me at the thought of seeing his handsome face first thing every morning and last thing every night threatened to float me right off the bed again, like my high down in the ER. A smile so broad, I swear it touched my ears, spread over my face.

I quashed it, though, trying to look serious for a second. "I don't know. Do you snore? That blasted puppy of Ozzie and

Claire's snored, and it about drove me crazy." Which was the truth. Between her whines and her snores, I got very little sleep while she was at my house.

Luke laughed. A deep, down to his soul, belly laugh. "I'll wear the nose strips if I do."

A smirk broke free of my serious mask. "Well, if you're willing to compromise… I guess a roommate sounds okay." I sent him a heated look. "So long as there are benefits to this arrangement."

He bent forward, hovering over me, mere millimeters from my lips. "You can count on that."

Raising my right hand, I skimmed my fingers over his face and smiled. "Good."

Epilogue: Mina

Three months later…

"You still have your eyes closed, right?"

I huffed, gripping Luke's wrists to hold myself steady as he held his hands in front of my face while ushering me through the grass from the parking lot near the marina. "Yes." My foot struck a rock and I stumbled.

"Whoa, there." He quickly removed a hand from my grasp and wrapped it around my waist to steady me.

I chuckled, but kept my eyes closed. He'd been like a little kid in the truck when we got here and he asked me to close my eyes. I didn't want to ruin the surprise. "This is ridiculous. Where are we going?"

"You'll see. But perhaps it would be better if I just carried you."

The next thing I knew, my feet left the ground as he tightened his arm, lifting me into his side.

I let out a little squeal and hugged his neck.

"Hold on. We're almost there."

Clutching tight, I held on through the walk through the grass. I thought soon enough I would hear the thud of his shoes on the dock, but it never happened. When I felt the elevation change, I realized we were walking away from the water.

Where on earth were we going? The marina office? But that didn't make sense, either. To get to it, we had to walk on a concrete path. We'd never left the grass.

A minute later, he set me down.

"Okay. You can open your eyes."

I blinked.

A frown settled over my face as I stared up at the façade of the Myers Mansion. "What are we doing here? And why didn't you just come up the driveway?" My frown deepened as I cast a quick glance toward the empty, circular blacktop drive in front of the house. We were standing on the southeast corner of the building.

"So, I've been a little sneaky. You know those times I had Kado fill in for me at the café?"

I nodded.

"I've been going to see Walter."

"Walter?" My eyebrows descended into a vee. "Why?"

Luke gestured to the house.

Still not understanding, I glanced at the imposing building, then back at him. "What?"

"Lana and I were talking. She mentioned how she had some clients looking for an event space on the water for their wedding. There are a few in Juneau, but they book out over a year in advance. I was driving around town later that day and happened to glance out at the water and just caught a glimpse of this house." Again, he gestured to the building. "It sparked an idea. What if we turned the Myers Mansion into a destination wedding location?"

My frown stayed firmly in place. That sounded all fine and dandy, but how would that work with the owner behind bars? "Walter's in jail. Can something like that happen with him incarcerated? Does he have the funds—funds not frozen by the authorities—to do a project like that? I mean, the grounds look fine, but I'm sure the inside of the house needs some work. If nothing else, it needs updated, right? I mean, it's sat empty for three decades."

"It does, but Walter's not the one doing the work." Luke tapped his chest. "I am."

My eyes narrowed to squints. I still didn't know where he was going with this. "I don't understand. He hired you as a contractor?"

Luke chuckled. "No. I guess I'm not being very clear, am I?"

"No. It's about as clear as mud." One side of my mouth lifted in a smile.

"I bought the house."

My smile died as my mouth dropped open. For several seconds, I just stared at him, agog. "I'm sorry. You did what now?" How was that possible? This place had to be worth millions. I knew Luke wasn't destitute, but not that he had that kind of money.

He put a knuckle under my chin and closed my mouth. "I bought it. Along with Dad and Lana. When I had the idea, the first thing I did, before I talked to anyone, was to go talk to Walter. Just to see if he'd even be interested in selling the place. And, I'll admit, I was curious about why he kept it all these years and maintained it but never lived in it."

My gaze roved over the manicured lawn, turning brown with the descent of fall. The boxwood hedges rimming the center island of the drive around the silent fountain were still green, however. In front of the house, between the windows, small junipers stood sentinel, broken up by more boxwoods. I knew in the spring, daffodils and tulips would spring up, adding pops of color to the monotone landscape.

"What did he say?" I asked.

"After the debacle with Sarah, Miranda, and Moira, he said he couldn't bring himself to live in the house because it was a reminder of what happened. He told his wife Edna left the property to an old lover of hers. When she later asked him why no one had ever done anything with it, he told her the man was elderly and lived out of state, so he just paid someone to do upkeep. Then later, he told her it went into a trust for the man's children, but that they, too, lived out of state. Lucille never questioned it, and the two of them never had children, so there was never anyone to dig into it further."

The wind kicked up, swirling dead leaves around our feet. I crossed my arms, huddling into my jacket as I glanced at the sky. Gray clouds danced overhead, heralding the imminent arrival of our next weather system. Rain was forecast for later today and for the next couple of days. It wouldn't be long and the snow would fly.

"When I asked him if he had any plans for the house now that the case was out in the open, he said he'd probably just sell it. That was the only opening I needed. I asked for a number he'd be willing to sell at. Mina, it was a ridiculously low price. Probably a third of what it's worth. I still couldn't buy it alone, but through the business? I left the jail, called Lana, and asked her to meet me at Mom and Dad's."

"And they agreed with the idea?"

He nodded. "It makes even more sense to turn it into a hotel now than it did when Edna died. Juneau has grown. Tourism to Alaska has grown. It's in a prime location. So, we contacted Claire and had her draw up an offer. Walter accepted it right away. We closed on the deal this morning." He reached into his pocket and withdrew a set of keys, dangling them in front of my nose. "Want to see the inside?"

Once more, I stared at him agog. I couldn't even process his question. My mind was stuck on one fact. "Claire knew about this?"

He laughed. "She did. I swore her to secrecy. She didn't even tell Ozzie."

"Oh, she's so getting a piece of my mind later." I couldn't believe my best friend—or my boyfriend—could keep such a huge secret from me.

Luke took my hand. "Come on. Let's go tour the inside. I want to tell you what I have planned."

Excitement zinged through my veins, replacing the shock, as he led me toward the massive, nine-foot, double front doors. Their rich reddish-brown color blended seamlessly into the orangish-red brick.

I stared up at the three-story façade as Luke unlocked the door. It looked like one of those English houses from one of the old period dramas. Tall and imposing, but also wide. "How many bedrooms does this place have?"

"Ten."

My gaze dropped to his. "Seriously?"

"Yep. There are three sitting rooms, a game room, a formal dining room, a library, a den, two kitchens—a nice one and a prep one—and four rooms near the kitchens that are desig- nated as servants' quarters. I didn't include those in the bedroom total. There's also the guest cottage out back." He turned the handle and pushed the door inward, then swept a hand toward the opening. "After you."

"Why would anyone around here need ten bedrooms?" I stepped inside and immediately forgot my question. A parquet floor stretched beneath my feet, extending in all directions to run into the rooms opening on each side of the giant foyer. Directly in front of me stood a grand staircase, the sweeping first-floor landing taking up over six feet of floor space. Dark walnut balusters swept up to the second floor, leading to a gallery walkway that spanned the twenty-foot space before the hall disappeared beyond the walls.

Luke flipped a switch on the wall, illuminating an enormous crystal chandelier directly overhead, eliciting a quick gasp from me. "Wow. That's gorgeous."

"Right? It's in such good shape. The whole house is, really. It just needs some updates. Especially in the kitchens. They're stuck in the seventies." Taking my hand again, he led me toward the stairs. "Let's go up. We can work our way back down."

Together, we ascended the staircase, then turned left. He led me down the hall to another staircase. This one was smaller and not as grand, but just as beautiful. I ran my hand over the carved newel post as we rounded it and went up to the third floor.

The upper floor boasted six rooms; three on each side of the house. They were all comparable in size, and each one had a color theme.

"Do you plan to keep the themes when you redecorate?" I asked.

"I think, so, yeah. It'll be easy to keep them straight if we do."

I agreed. "You could have a lot of fun with that idea too. Like a lavender room filled with actual lavender and other florals that color. Or a forest green color filled with ferns and natural wood."

The quick look he cast at me from the corner of his eye told me he could tell I was intrigued. "You and Lana will have to sit down and hash out some ideas. I know she had some, but it's a lot of rooms."

Absently, I nodded. My thoughts swirled with possibilities as I wandered through the rooms on this floor and the next. The marketing for this would be so much fun. Each room would have its own personality, and we could lean into that.

"What's your timeline for opening?" I asked as we descended the main staircase to the ground floor.

"Next summer. In time for tourist season. I was kind of

hoping we could open with a bang and have a big wedding in the gardens."

"Oh, that would be pretty," I said, moving into the sitting room to the right of the front door. My gaze locked on the ornate fireplace on the wall to my left. "Did Lana have a couple in mind for that? Those people you mentioned, maybe?" I'd yet to see the rear yard, but I bet it was spectacular.

"No. Actually, I had someone in mind."

Reaching out, I traced the carvings on the wooden mantle. This place was incredible. There was so much detail everywhere I looked. "Oh, yeah? Who?"

"Us."

My fingers froze on the wood.

What?

Slowly, I turned my head. My gaze dropped to where Luke now knelt on the floor on one knee.

With wide eyes, I could only stare. "What are you doing?"

A crooked smile lifted his mouth. He reached into his jacket pocket. "Proposing." His hand emerged, clutching a navy-blue ring box.

Lifting his free hand, he curled a finger, motioning me closer. "Come over here."

Of their own accord, my feet shuffled closer. It was like an out-of-body experience. I was present, but I wasn't.

He took my hand, bringing reality crashing back. Suddenly, I was right in the mix of things again.

The knowledge of what was happening sent adrenaline rushing through my veins. My knees shook like the ground during an earthquake. I sank to them in front of him before I fell.

He let go of my hand to cup the side of my face. "I know this is fast. It's only been a few months. But I don't want anyone else, and I never will. You're it for me, Mina. I love you, and I want to spend the rest of my life making you happy. Will you marry me?" With his thumb, he flicked open the lid on the ring box, revealing an emerald-cut diamond set low in a gold band. On either side, embedded in the gold, were two smaller stones. One was an amethyst, the other a sapphire—our birthstones.

I raised my left hand, covering my mouth. "Oh, that's beautiful," I whispered from behind my fingers.

Luke moved his hand from the side of my head to remove the ring from its velvet bed. Reaching up, he pulled my hand away from my face, then slid the ring over the tip of my ring finger. "So, what do you say, Mina? Will you spend the rest of your life with me?"

A happy laugh bubbled free, along with a few tears of joy. Would I? Only a crazy woman would say no to this man.

I blinked away the water flooding my eyes and nodded. Swallowing the lump in my throat, I managed one whispered word:

"Yes."

~

Thank you for reading *Midnight Witness*! I hope you loved it!

If you'd like to read more about Luke and Mina (and the other characters in this series), join my mailing list to get their bonus scene. But be warned: it's a spicy one! Subscribers also get a bonus chapter or scene after every book and access to exclusive teasers, giveaways, and the occasional book recommendation, as well as sneak peeks into my world as I create my stories. Visit https://ashleyaquinn.com/bonuscontent or scan the QR code below to sign up and get your bonus scene!

About the Author

Ashley started writing in her teens and never stopped. Her first novel, Smoky Mountain Murder, came out in 2016, and she has since published two more series and has plans for more. When not writing, you can find her with her nose stuck in a book or watching some terrible disaster movie on SyFy. An avid baseball fan, she also enjoys crafting and cooking. She lives in South Dakota with her husband, two kids, three cats, and one very wild shepherd mix.

Website: https://ashleyaquinn.com
Facebook Reader Group: facebook.com/groups/
349932159616427

goodreads.com/ashleyaquinn
amazon.com/Ashley-A-Quinn/e/B07HCT4QST
facebook.com/ashleyaquinn.writer
instagram.com/ashleyaquinn.writer

Ford's Fight

Dean's Dilemma

Jordan's Journey

Sam's Salvation

Asher's Assignment

Max's Mission

Parker's Landing

Midnight Secrets

Midnight Witness

Midnight Hunter - coming soon!

www.ingramcontent.com/pod-product-compliance
Lightning Source LLC
Chambersburg PA
CBHW021232310726
48971CB00006B/1783